THE BOSNIAN EXPERIENCE

BOOK 2 OF THE SAUWA CATCHER SERIES

J. E. HIGGINS

MERCENARY PUBLISHING

PROLOGUE

Following her escape from Ireland, the infamous assassin known as Sauwa Catcher disappeared.

Before vanishing, the former operative for the Civil Cooperation Bureau, the Apartheid's international killing machine, had evaded an international manhunt and left a trail of bodies in her wake.

David O'knomo — head of an elite investigative unit for the African National Congress (ANC) charged with bringing in Sauwa Catcher and the rest of her old unit, known as the Dark Chamber, were hard pressed for answers. Had the *Angel of Death* gone home to her roots? Had she linked up with some group previously connected to the Apartheid regime?

With limited time, and the police chasing closely behind, it was unlikely her escape had been well organized. Still, for several months she remained a ghost with the team pursuing leads that were, at best, stabs in the dark.

Then, after months of searching, the British Secret Intelligence Service—known to the world as MI-6—approached South Africa's National Intelligence Service with recent information that Ms. Catcher was possibly in Bosnia.

The incoming mortar round exploding alongside the road felt like a gut punch. It was a good distance from the jeep, but the vehicle's occupants could feel the pounding vibrations. A shower of shrapnel and debris blew into the vehicle as if being poured from a fire hose.

The blast had lifted the wheels of the vehicle into the air. The jeep crashed back onto the road with a resounding thud, painful to the occupants, front and back.

Sauwa could scarcely believe her luck.

Somehow, she had been able to hold onto the roll bar while escaping. It had been, by her loose calculations, the fifth time she had nearly been knocked from the speeding jeep since they had come under attack. She looked down the deep gorge alongside the patch of road they were traveling. It was a long distance straight down with no chance of survival if they swerved into it as they had nearly done a few times already.

Omery, the driver, had proven quite skillful behind the wheel, navigating both the countless bombed-out holes and broken asphalt on the road, while still managing to swerve and miss the mortar shells that hailed down on them. Omery, a Welsh mercenary, claimed to be an ex-member of the elite Special Boat Service, a Special Forces unit of the Royal British Marine Corps, before setting out on a career as a freelance soldier of fortune.

Like all the others who served as private soldiers in the conflict, no one really had means to prove or disprove Omery's identity or resume. One just had to watch and base their conclusions on the person's abilities in combat.

Looking back, Sauwa caught sight of the other jeep following closely behind, swerving with all the same aggressive maneuvers but not quite the same precision demonstrated by Omery. Thankfully, the mortar team firing was not very good, and the mercenaries were able to outpace the rounds. But the mortar shells continued raining down in a terrifying orchestra. They shook the ground while raising thick clouds of dust, smoke, and earthly fragments that seemed to consume everything.

"They're gonna make strawberry jam out of us!" Raker shouted in a tone mixed with both bitter anger and gut-wrenching fear. "If I live through this, I'll kill every fucking Serb that crosses my sight." He snarled to a despondent audience whose attentions were occupied with more pressing issues.

Sauwa detested Raker, whose name she did not fully know or care about. Another mortar shell blasted near them. The tremor shook the jeep and rattled their bones. Again, they owed their lives to Omery's catlike reflexes. He pressed the gas pedal to the floor narrowly avoiding the kill range as they zoomed across the danger area.

Shards of metal flew through the air cutting into their

skin as if they were being stung by a swarm of wasps. Their only comfort was the sight of the bushes and trees a hundred feet or so ahead marking the end of the open road and the end of the ambush area.

Another mortar hit just across the road from them delivering yet another storm of dirt and rocks in their direction. This time, Sauwa inadvertently took in a mouth full of the dusty air. She coughed wildly, striving to clear her throat. She looked back and saw the rest of their squad trying desperately to keep close to their jeep.

"We're almost out of it!" Omery shouted, in a feeble attempt to give everyone some confidence. He swerved wildly trying to anticipate the landing spot of the next mortar.

Gerald, an older American man, was in the front passenger seat. He gritted his teeth as he gripped the side of the front window and clutched the edge of his seat. "This is the fucking Viet Cong all over again!" he screamed as he looked around for some way to fight back against their attackers.

"Augin, that fucking piece of shit kike fuck!" Raker was shouting again. "He's the fucker who led us into this mess. Trusting a French leader, we get what we deserve."

As usual, his comment went ignored. He had been a Skinhead in Germany, recruited by a Nazi group that was building up units of paramilitaries to assist the Croatians fighting the Serbs. Like most types involved in radical politics and sub-cultures promoting violence and beastly behavior as a way of life, he had arrived with a romantic image of himself being a professional mercenary and leaving the country with a truckload of booty. So far, he had proven only to be an obnoxious loudmouth who grossly overestimated his soldering abilities.

The jeep jerked sharply again as it weaved to the side. A mortar shell whistled and screamed as it cut through the air. It flew just past them, the velocity of the displaced air was enough to sting Sauwa's face. Behind them, the second jeep exploded in a fiery blast. The driver had not moved fast enough, and the jeep caught the mortar straight on. It ripped the vehicle virtually in two before dissolving into a ball of flames.

She looked on in horror watching for any sign of survivors, a human body diving from the fiery caldron, or waves or shouts that indicated someone was still alive. She saw nothing. Perhaps it was all for the best. There would have been little she could do to rescue someone under a blanket of exploding ordinance.

With bitter relief, they reached the trees. The lone jeep left the open road and the kill zone. A high wall of hills gave them ample protection. They were now directly below their attackers who could no longer see them or get a good angle to fire.

Safe for the moment, half their team left dead behind them, they drove on, slumped in their seats, eyes forward, the adrenaline rush receding.

THE BASE CAMP was abuzz when the team drove through the security checkpoint. Two pimple-faced young men met the jeep decked out in some cheap movie version of freedom fighter combat apparel, camouflage field jackets over civilian T-shirts depicting the logos of popular western rock bands, black combat boots under cargo pants or jeans. The two young men couldn't have been more than sixteen or seventeen and couldn't speak a word of English. Raker's loose understanding of Croatian allowed him to explain enough to gain entry to the fortified camp.

The camp housed the regional headquarters of the Croatian Defense Council, *Hrvatsko Vijece Obrane* (HVO). It also was the hub for all new recruits, both foreign and local, to come, be placed, and receive orders.

With the same masterful skill demonstrated on the road, Omery navigated the jeep past the disorderly gauntlet of vehicles, people, and piles of what were once homes and buildings. Finally, they came to the half-destroyed structure of what had been an old Catholic church. It now served as the office of Colonel Milvuj Trajic.

Tired, stumbling drunkenly, the team exited the vehicle.

As she hit the ground, Sauwa took a few moments to regain her bearings. The long journey over broken roads, coupled with the continuing roller coaster of being bounced around by exploding mortars, had discombobulated her.

Hearing some childish giggling, she looked over to see a group of teenage boys standing across the way. They were looking back at her with devilish smiles gathered tightly around a young man wearing a pair of sunglasses and a red military beret. He was standing with them smugly acting like he was a famous celebrity. Indeed, he was. He looked back at her smirking as if he had shared an intimate secret with her no one else knew. The young man, who everyone called Smokes, had the uncanny privilege of knowing what the mysterious South African woman looked like under her combat fatigues.

Since arriving at the camp, Sauwa had been the sexual

interest of most of the pubescent boys who saw her athletic body and exotic foreign features as enticing. Annoyed, she had found an elderly woman who earned her money running a makeshift laundry business. The woman allowed Sauwa to use her house facilities to wash in to save her from having to dodge her male comrades in their own shower areas.

It wasn't long before the local teenagers found out about her washroom. Smokes had been the only one brave enough to climb in through a slightly open window and sneak into the bathroom. For a good five minutes, hidden behind a pile of dirty clothes, he watched as she turned washing herself under the rusting shower faucet. Normally, an alert and thorough professional, she was tired and had let her guard down in the sanctuary of the woman's home. And in doing so had failed to notice the young intruder right away.

When she did see him, the response was to grab her Makarov pistol sitting close at hand. She fired several shots in the boy's direction, loud enough for all the boys hanging outside to hear it and confirm to everyone that their young compatriot had indeed completed his mission.

Since then, the few others who had dared to follow their compatriot's act had come away with nothing to show for their troubles but enduring battle scars of the young woman's wrath. This left Smokes the hero, as the only one of the group to successfully see her in the buff. The story never got old. Every time they saw her, the hormonal youngsters would gather around tightly and listen to their friend describe everything underneath her clothing as they looked her up and down with glee.

Retrieving her weapon and Bergen from the back of the

jeep, Sauwa shrugged off her little fan club and followed the rest of her team inside the church.

Sliding her way through the half broken, oak doors, she was met by the overpowering stench of male body odor, recently exploded ordinance of some sort and the charred remains of what had once been people.

"We were attacked recently." A large bear-like man, sitting behind a warped folding table functioning as his desk, explained the recent destruction in the camp as the mercenaries entered. "Obviously."

Colonel Milvuj Trajic, or Rommel as his men affectionately referred to him, looked more the part of a soldier than most of his men. "The Serbs are trying to re-establish themselves in this area." He frowned. His uniform consisted of a dark green and black camouflage like most Eastern European militaries. Unlike his men, his uniform was also complete from the outer garments to the brown T-shirt underneath. It made him look more professional, which made it easier for the foreign professionals that augmented the Croatian forces to take him seriously.

"It looks it," Gerald said. Since the Viet Nam vet was the oldest mercenary, he liked to think of himself as the most seasoned. He tried to play the part when in front of the Croat paymasters, even if the notion was not mutually shared by his mercenary colleagues. Gerald swaggered as he led the remaining members of the squad toward the commander. "Not as bad as when I was in Hue City back in '68 though."

By the look of the grimacing faces in the room, his comment was not well received.

"You prevailed, that's the important thing." A soft French-accented voice emerged from the back of the room and drew attention.

The voice belonged to Maurice Augin, a large muscular man dressed in black military fatigues. He moved behind Rommel studying the four mercenaries carefully, pausing for an uncomfortable beat on Gerald. Always the consummate professional, Augin detested unnecessary drama and theatrics which only wasted time and detracted from the more important business. "Where is the rest of your team?"

"We saw some action out there," Gerald babbled. "We were caught by the enemy, and I had to lead these youngsters out."

The commanders' bored expressions bordered on irritation. They wanted an answer, not self-adulation or a long-winded speech.

Sauwa cut off Gerald off. "We got caught by a Serb mortar team on the open highway, and one of the shells caught the other jeep dead on."

Rommel and Augin nodded; her answer was sufficient. Her eyes shifted to see Gerald's pinched face glaring at her. She gave a slight sniff to show her indifference and returned her focus to Augin and Rommel.

"So we lost Gazzetti, MacMasters, Gilgood, and Dumas." Augin named off the four men who had unfortunately been in the other jeep. "They will be a great loss to us." He was remorseful but a professional as he continued with the debriefing. "You were sent to recce the village."

Omery spoke up. "We recce'd the perimeter and watched the road and river ways for a few days. The Serbs are doing something…"

Gerald interrupted. "We've seen a steady buzz of Serbian forces in the area. They looked more like they were simply wandering about. You know, just doing simple battlefield circulation of sorts, viewing the river, walking through the village and talking to the troops. We've seen a few trucks moving in and out on a regular basis. That's about it. It was an education for the kids here to get soft training in field craft."

"Can you please be more specific?" Rommel asked calmly. He looked sternly at Gerald. Colonel Trajic was an uncommon figure in war. Unlike many of the other military commanders in the makeshift Croatian army, Colonel Trajic had been a commander in the Croatian National Police when the war broke out. That the Yugoslav army had been largely Serbian dominated meant that the Croatians had to virtually build an army in haste and from scratch. This meant making people with little more than a college education into officers with no formal training or previous experience. For a number of foreign professionals, it had proven frustrating having to take orders from inexperienced novices, especially since many of them were not much better than those they were trying to lead.

Gerald was tongue-tied. Omery shifted his eyes but remained silent.

Rommel said nothing. He rubbed his face in a vain attempt to mask his exasperation. Augin turned to look at Sauwa. As if being caught up in some sort of hypnosis, she walked over to the commander and produced a plastic zip lock bag encasing a small notebook. Pulling the notebook from the bag, she placed it on the table. "They're recceing the area as a possible location for a staging point."

Augin picked up the notebook and flipped it open. It contained sketches of the village and surrounding area. There were also lists of what rank insignias had been noticed and how many. "What makes you think it's being looked at as a staging area?"

Sauwa continued. "What we saw weren't local militia or nationalist mercs. They were Serb army by their uniforms and a more professional operational movement. And, they weren't just junior rankers. There were a couple of senior level officers walking about. They weren't doing a battlefield circulation. They were checking water depths and looking at housing accommodations, most likely to see how much equipment and personnel they could hide in the area to avoid detection. They were also carrying out long-range patrols and studying the landscape of the surrounding area to determine threat concerns and defensibility.

"There were a couple of men, definitely foreigners, walking with the Bosnian commanders. They were pointing out various things and seemed to be advising them on some sort of in-depth planning. They wore standard uniforms of the Serbian army, however, their tactical habits and operational knowledge far surpassed the abilities of any Serbian soldier. My guess is Russian, possibly Spetsnaz."

The commanders listened attentively. She pointed out several sketches she had made in her notebook. "They had initially set up defensive positions along the road and now had several observation posts up and down the river. The last time we recced the area a month ago, security was light. It was a garrison force of less than a hundred men with just the basic defense positions in key areas around the village. They had a few heavy machine guns but otherwise light armaments only. This time, the security forces had grown to at least four or five hundred. And they weren't a local village defense force. These guys were vets and battle-hardened. They moved about their posts like they were anticipating an attack. And the weapon systems—we spotted RPG rocket launchers at every defense point guarding the perimeter. The waterways were guarded by fifty caliber machine guns watching either end as well as the main entryway into the village. Truthfully, they're building the place up to defend against a serious attack."

With their interest peeked, Augin and Rommel walked over to the map and studied it intently. "The village is a remote part of the Neretva Valley. It is well hidden and enjoys both access to the Neretva River and close proximity to several key locations. It would be a good place to bring in supplies and personnel from across the river and launch attacks from seemingly unlikely places." Augin compared the dot marking the village on the map to the sketches in Sauwa's notebook.

Rommel scratched his bearded chin. "We have intelligence that the Pakistanis and other Islamic countries have been supporting the Bosnians with arms and advisors in direct defiance of the UN order. The Serbs must be concerned about the possibility of a new front developing against them. Especially now that we have re-established our previous alliance with the Bosnians. This must be in preparation for a front of their own."

Sauwa felt somewhat embarrassed by her display. It had not been her intention to show off in front of everyone.

In the past, she had been content to let others take the lead when briefing or offering professional advice. However, that was when such advice or information had been given by MacMasters, Gilgood or Dumas. They had been the true professional soldiers of the squad with MacMasters and Gilgood both being former British soldiers who had seen considerable time in the fields of Northern Ireland. Dumas was a former French Legionnaire with an extensive record fighting in conflicts all across Africa. She had been rather suspect regarding the others. She had seen a less than stellar performance from them, so far.

She could feel the eyes of Gerald burning into her. Bad enough the self-proclaimed mentor to the squad had been shown up by a young upstart. That the insult was delivered by a female—who he had explained numerous times should be at the base camp tending to meals and the men's more carnal needs—was pure heresy. Omery and Raker were less insulted than intimidated by her continuing ability to outperform them in a field where they had espoused to be seasoned professionals.

"Further action needs to be considered carefully." Augin cautioned. He watched Rommel pacing nervously. "At this moment, we have only hypothetical assumptions about what is going on there. If these reports are correct, this village will be considerably more difficult to contend with."

Rommel stopped pacing and returned to observing the map, Sauwa's notes in hand. With nothing more to be said, Augin dismissed the remaining members of the squad. As tired and shaken up as they were from the recent ordeal, gleaning more precise information would be futile.

The mercenaries exited the church with Raker leading the pack followed by Omery and then Gerald. Sauwa came out last, not sure what reception awaited her once they were away from the command.

WITH A DEEP BREATH, Sauwa walked outside expecting to be berated. Instead, she watched her comrades head for the tent used as the cafeteria. Glad for the reprieve, she set off after them looking forward to her first hot meal in two days.

The ground was muddy from a recent rain shower. She trudged along feeling the soles of her boots sinking into the softened ground. Pulling the flappy curtains aside, she entered to see a nearly deserted room with several long tables surrounded by a strange assortment of old wood chairs, folding chairs, and benches.

Her squad members had collected their food from the makeshift kitchen and taken up residence at separate tables. Comradery and comradeship were not things shared by her squad. The relationship was more of a mild tolerance and utter indifference.

Collecting her food — a menu of brown mashed potatoes, some eggs, and a strange pudding-like substance that was supposed to be ground meat — she grabbed a seat at a nearby table.

She had no sooner taken her first bite when Gerald sat down across from her. He smiled a disingenuous, toothy grin. "You're quite the little soldier enthusiast, aren't you, young lady."

Sauwa said nothing. She didn't raise her head or offer the slightest acknowledgment of his existence.

Gerald continued talking, oblivious. "You know it was an okay brief that you gave in there, but it was still amateurish. In the future, you should run these things by me before you speak up. You know, so I can make sure you know what you're talking about. I've been in this game a long time, and I have some wisdom to impart to youngsters like you who haven't really seen anything of combat."

Gerald knew nothing about Sauwa. He still believed from her accent she was British or maybe Australian. He had never even considered South Africa or Rhodesia. She had never felt the need to correct him as that would have only led to further conversation.

All anyone knew of her was that one day, several months ago, she mysteriously appeared in camp with a Croatian supply convoy coming from the seaport city of Rijeka. No one thought anything of the young foreigner until she was met by the Croatian's chief advisor, Maurice Augin himself, who instantly ushered her off to a secretive meeting in his private office. Afterward, he made the unprecedented move of putting this woman in a combat squad of mercenaries.

At first, the others thought she might have been some sort of international reporter covering the war. When she was immediately given camouflage fatigues, an AK-47 and combat webbing, the journalist theory vanished.

Within her first week of being in camp, with no explanation given, she was in a vehicle with a squad of mercenaries heading out on a mission. Awaiting some sort of briefing or at least an introduction to the mysterious young woman, the men were awash with theories and questions.

The woman said nothing and neither did commander Augin. He only uttered to the girl, "Let me know your assessments," before stepping back into his office.

Commander Augin had gained serious respect as a competent field commander from both the mercenaries and the Croatians. If he thought this young lady was fit to go into harm's way, the career soldiers such as MacMasters and Gilgood felt it was good enough for them. They inquired no further. She was obviously conducting some sort of side mission for the command and that was all they were meant to know.

Out on patrol, she offered nothing in the way of conversation and very few words when responding to questions from others. In the vehicle with MacMasters, Gilgood, and Raker, it did not go unnoticed that she kept her attention focused on the landscape and the tree line. She held her weapon at the tactical ready, aimed outward prepared to engage any sort of threat.

She had been the first to notice strange movement in the bushes ahead only seconds before the lead jeep was hit in an ambush that exploded in a massive hail of gunfire.

MacMasters and Gilgood quickly leaped from the vehicle to the side of the road in the direction of the shooting. Predictably, Raker shot wildly in all directions from the back of the jeep. He whooped and screamed like a cowboy in an American western. His gunfire hit next to nothing. Equally distressing was the sight of Dumas and Gazzetti taking cover behind the jeep laying down some kind of return fire with Omery cowering behind them, and Gerald reduced to a bundle of nerves unable to do anything but scramble around on his hands and knees.

Expecting to see Sauwa curled up in a ball crying her eyes out, MacMasters and Gilgood were surprised when she hunched down next to them, her demeanor cool and calm, looking intense, scoping out the battle scene ahead.

"We haven't entered the danger area," she said. "We can move into the tree line and approach them in a flanking maneuver."

The two men were frozen in bewilderment listening to this young lady speak to them with such tactical knowledge.

With Gilgood in the lead, the three scrambled behind the jeep and into the thickets at the tree line. Quickly, they fanned out getting some dispersion, keeping their bodies low in the bushes.

MacMasters started the move with a rapid push through

the bushes hoping to close the distance between him and the assault team. Stopped by a dirt clod hitting him in the stomach, he looked over to see Sauwa glaring at him and pointing to the ground in front of him. At first, he couldn't see what she was pointing to. He moved up a little closer to see a partially hidden row of wooden stakes protruding from the dirt — a booby trap reminiscent of what the Viet Cong used against the Americans in the sixties.

Grateful, he nodded back.

She motioned to both men to continue slowly, bypassing the rows of dangerous sticks, inching toward the enemy who was only a stone's throw ahead and well within the range of their guns. It wasn't long before they could see outlined camouflaged figures lying prone, delivering gunfire onto the forces on the road.

Raising his rifle, MacMasters belched off a few rounds in the direction of the nearest attackers. His shots tore into the first man's body. The dying man let out a wail that quickly alerted the rest of his squad. The other ambushers turned and looked up just in time to see the gunfire from Sauwa and Gilgood tearing into their positions.

The three kept up a good combination of talking guns, each one firing a short burst followed by the next.

The enemy soldiers found themselves in a crossfire between the trio flanking them and the rest of the team shooting from the road. The Bosnian shouts turned into a chorus of terrified screams. Panic-stricken, the ambushers broke from their positions and made off into the woods in a wild pack leaving behind three of their dead comrades.

Seeing Sauwa's skills and calm reserve in a crisis, Gilgood and MacMasters realized they were dealing with someone different.

Since that time, she had had no trouble being accepted — at least by those who counted — working in the field as a soldier. In a world full of supposed professionals who greatly inflated their skills and resumes, it was easy for the genuine soldiers to spot the real thing.

And, she was it.

2

David O'knomo and his staff — the unit investigating war crimes for the African National Congress (ANC) — along with their new allies in British intelligence were hard pressed for answers.

Following her escape from Ireland, the professional assassin of the Civil Cooperation Bureau known as Sauwa Catcher had disappeared.

Her killing spree across Ireland over a period of two days — which resulted in twelve deaths — left the British, South African and Irish intelligence services humiliated. Despite their best efforts, the notorious agent of the Apartheid killing machine could not be located. The situation was intolerable.

The generally accepted assumption was the notorious *Angel of Death* would have gone home to her roots and attempted to link up with some group previously connected to the Apartheid regime or, at least, sympathetic to the cause. Dr. Eugene Walderhyn, the analyst who had pointed O'knomo and his team in the right direction to find her the first time, had argued that, with limited time and the police chasing closely behind, it was unlikely her escape would have been that well organized.

For several months she remained a ghost. O'knomo's team pursued leads that were, at best, stabs in the dark. Then, three months ago, the British Secret Intelligence Service, known to the world as MI-6, approached South Africa's National Intelligence Service with recent information that Ms. Catcher was possibly in Bosnia.

The intelligence was sketchy. It had been collected from former British soldiers serving as mercenaries and returning from the Balkan war zone. Operatives, posing as former soldiers, informally collecting intelligence over drinks at the pub, heard stories of a female mercenary operating in the country.

This information had somehow come to the attention of one Jeffery Talamadge, the MI-5 agent who had pursued her in Ireland and had since developed his own obsession with her capture.

Following up on the case he, along with officers from MI-6, found some former mercenaries who purported to have seen and met her. The descriptions they provided seemed to match those of his quarry. These mercenaries also described the young lady as someone with top-notch military training, presumably Special Forces level. These men had been former soldiers and marines in her Majesty's service. Talamadge and his colleagues could assume these were professional assessments and not the evaluations of some nitwit journalist who couldn't tell Special Forces training from a military marching band.

What ultimately caught his attention was an additional

piece of information. Although seemingly unrelated, the mercenaries had also discussed rumors of a series of mysterious assassinations of several Bosnian military and civilian officials as well as other acts of sabotage and terrorism. This was all believed to be the work of one phantom individual, whose identity remained unknown.

Of course, the mercenaries presumed this was some tall tale the Croats had put out to create morale issues amongst the enemy: the mythical killer who could walk through walls, sneak past details of armed security and become one with the shadows at will. But Talamadge's interest was piqued. He had forwarded these reports to the South Africans, who reviewed them against their own records.

O'knomo held off discussing the matter with his superiors until he had more conclusive evidence than random accounts from dubious sources. British intelligence expanded their inquiry by reaching out to other intelligence agencies, who also had some of their populace serving privately in Bosnia. They reported a female mercenary matching their own descriptions and accounts.

In the past few months, NATO had begun preparing to go into the war-torn Balkans. As part of the preparation, the Royal Air Force flew regular missions over the conflict area photographing as much terrain and identifying as many military camps as possible.

With a great deal of wrangling and diplomacy, Talamadge had been able to get photos of Croatian military camps, particularly camps located in the central part of the country, north of Mostar, where most of the reports had placed the mysterious female mercenary.

Weeks of scrutinizing blown up pictures of various

camps had finally born fruit when they caught sight of long black hair on a woman dressed in combat fatigues. It was possible she could have been just another Croatian volunteer. But, with the hair and features and more pictures of her rolling out with clearly identified mercenary units, the reports made it all too probable they had found their girl.

Sauwa's attention remained on her meal while the Vietnam vet droned on.

"To be honest, we didn't just lose half our squad. We lost the only other men who were remotely on a par with me as far as experience. I have to step it up now since you all don't have anyone else to mentor you."

Gerald's voice had the twang she had come to associate with the southeastern United States. If that weren't enough, his need to bring up the exploits of his ancestors and their service to the Confederacy would have led her to a similar conclusion.

"In fact, I should probably be giving the briefs from here on out." Did this man ever shut up? "You know, 'cause I'm thorough, and they can glean information to help plan their next mission. With Gilgood dead, I just know they're gonna approach me about taking over this squad. When I was in Nam, I spent a lot of time working in black ops. I know they're gonna remember that and demand that I step up and look out for all you youngsters. They begged me to take the job last time, but I said no. Said I was just a shooting man, a foot soldier for this little vacation. Time to let someone else take the reins." None of what Gerald was saying was true in regard to his circumstances of employment.

It was nothing she or any of the squad had not heard numerous times. Even when Gilgood was alive, Gerald was constantly complaining about how badly Gilgood functioned running the squad, constantly second-guessing all of the plans. He did the same with Augin as well. Every time they left a meeting at headquarters, the Vietnam vet would launch into his diatribe about all the mistakes the Frenchman was making with the counsel he was giving to Rommel and the other Croat commanders. However, rarely did Gerald offer any alternative solutions. And those few times he did, they were poorly thought out, fanciful concepts easily torn apart by more logical minds.

She chewed her meal having tuned him out. The only thing she ascertained was how he was upset or something about how she had briefed. One could fill in the rest. In his subtler way, Gerald was telling her to keep her mouth shut from now on. He was the star of the show, as he saw it, and she was not to embarrass him.

Finishing the last few bites of her meal, she casually eyed her unwanted dinner companion. Gerald hardly looked the part of a soldier, his salt and pepper hair was long and unkempt, he had facial growth from several days of not shaving. His clothing choice for the field resembled more of what she saw from the Croatian youngsters and novices. He frequently sported civilian tank tops and a baseball cap or red greasy bandanna over his head — even when out on a mission.

She met his gaze for a moment. Neither one said

anything. He looked at her with a sly, disingenuous look while she stared back with a blank expression of disinterest. Gathering up her tray and utensils, she rose from her seat. "We should clean up."

Gerald resumed speaking. "When I take control of this squad, you can bet I'll be training you all up good to make sure you actually know what you're doing for a change. You'll be elite fighters yet."

Sauwa discarded her tray and headed out of the tent opening leaving the older mercenary to his lonely table. The message had been all too clear. Gerald didn't like being shown up. She would need to tread carefully from now on.

Outside she started to walk toward another burnt out building that had been haphazardly rebuilt into a living facility. It was the housing quarters for the mercenaries on base. Her mind was filled with thoughts of a warm shower and several hours of needed sleep.

Halfway to the barracks, she was intercepted by Commander Augin waving his hand trying to catch her attention. "Sauwa, may we speak, privately?" His accent was polished, and his English nearly flawless.

"Of course, sir," Sauwa replied following the commander.

Commander Maurice Augin cut a fine image of the consummate professional ready to walk out the gate onto a mission at any time. He was dressed neatly in his uniform of black combat fatigues, every pocket buttoned, the laces of his black boots tucked away. His combat webbing was adjusted, situated, and based on a tactical logic. His hair was neatly trimmed, his face showing only a day's growth. His body was trim and athletic because he worked to stay in shape in his limited free time.

He was indeed a man Sauwa respected. A graduate of the prestigious French military academy in Saint-Cyr, Augin had spent ten years as a commissioned officer with the French Foreign Legion's 2eme REI mechanized infantry regiment. He had cut his teeth in various conflicts throughout North Africa. The story of why he left halfway through his career had never been explained. However, he had proven a most valuable asset as a competent field commander, eventually becoming the trusted advisor to Colonel Milvuj Trajic. Though more cop than soldier, he possessed a keen eye for talent and bullshit. With the help of Augin, the operations launched by the Croat forces improved immensely.

Following closely in silence, Sauwa could only assume this was to be another one of the commander's special missions she occasionally performed. Such missions involved eliminating certain key personnel of the enemy. This was a job she carried out on her own, to the greater ignorance of her squad mates and everyone else.

Arriving at a side door behind the church with two armed men standing guard, she followed Augin into a small office. The office was dark, with all the windows painted or boarded over to prevent anyone from looking inside. Augin pulled on a small dangling chain, and the room became illuminated by a single light bulb hanging from an overhead lamp. The light revealed a large wood desk with maps and paper strewn across it. The walls and tables were lined with books, newspapers and other periodicals. Unbeknownst to anyone beyond Rommel, Augin and a select few of the mercenaries, this was the planning room for special operations. This was the room where the more intricate and secretive plans were made.

Taking a seat in a chair at the edge of the desk, Augin

looked Sauwa over. He seemed to be debating whether to tell her something. "We have a mission we need you to carry out."

"I assumed that, given we're meeting here," Sauwa replied, taking up a seat at the opposite end of the desk.

Augin paused. His eyes darted about, searching for an answer he did not yet possess. "This will be the last job you will do for us. After it is completed, you will no longer be in our service."

Sauwa was puzzled but said nothing.

Augin continued. "In the months you've been here, you have proven your worth time and again. MacMasters, Gilgood, Dumas, and Gazzetti spoke often about your abilities in the field, and how you were a much-needed addition to the squad. That's in addition to the discrete missions you have performed on your own in our service. You've been quite successful in the elimination of certain Serbian military commanders since our truce with them was broken a few months ago. Just as your elimination of certain key Bosnians officials has helped make our re-alliance with them more amenable. For that, we owe you profound gratitude."

"It wasn't something I necessarily enjoyed doing," Sauwa said quietly.

"And it should never be," Augin spoke with the tone of a father. Sometimes it felt like that was the relationship they had with each other. "But now it has to come to an end. When you've completed this job, you'll have to be moving on."

"I don't understand?"

Leaning back in his chair, the Frenchman sighed. "As you know, the United Nations has been trying to bring order to this muddle. NATO is now going to get involved. They are setting up to execute Operation Deliberate Force. This won't be the impotent blue-helmeted peacekeepers of the United Nations. It will be a full military force intent on bringing order to the region by force. When this happens, it will be only a matter of months before the warring factions conclude a peace settlement.

"The UN intends to push immediately for war crime investigations and, through NATO forces, start rounding up suspected war criminals.

"I understand you have committed no such crimes while working for us. You have acted properly keeping your business to enemy combatants. However, you are an internationally wanted criminal currently sought by several countries. When this war comes to an end, most likely abruptly, you will be on that list of individuals wanted by the UN. If you stay too long, you will find yourself in a country entirely without friends.

"The Croatians will hand you over in a second to show they're being cooperative. And, let's not forget, your private actions for us have earned you a fearsome reputation. Killing high ranking commanders and officials and carrying out other various acts of terrorism makes enemies. You've sent chills and fear through the ranks of the enemy. And, they don't even know who you are. The Black Widow has garnered a mythical image of demonic proportions. It also means that when your identity is revealed, both Bosnians and Serbs will demand your head."

It was irritating to think how her actions had been so grossly blown out of proportion. The targets she hit were not nearly as protected as they were believed to be. And as much as she didn't want to admit it, Augin was right. Once the British learned she was in the country, they would use their influence to ensure she was a high priority. If they didn't, allies of the prominent figures she had killed in Bosnia would give her nowhere to go.

For a moment, Sauwa felt defeated. "So then, what's the plan?"

Augin could sympathize with her, but there was still his problem. Reaching into a leather satchel he produced a thin, dark-brown folder and dropped it onto the desk. "This is the target." He opened the folder and turned it in her direction.

She looked down to see a low-grade, black and white photograph depicting a man with a light crop of facial hair and receding hairline. The man looked mild and ordinary, sporting a short-sleeved collared shirt.

Other pictures showed the same man dressed in a similar fashion walking about with men she knew to be officers in the Armija Republike Bosne I Hercegovine (Army of the Republic of Bosnia and Herzegovina or ARBiH). It was the prime military force of the Bosnian Moslems. It was also the only recognized army in Bosnia by most of the outside world. In the various pictures, the ordinary looking man was making gestures and speaking to the Bosnian officers as if advising them.

The pictures were of better quality than she usually received; especially given that the modern conveniences taken for granted by most militaries were not available to Croatian intelligence, who made do with equipment new in the late fifties.

Following the collection of photographs was a series of handwritten notes on a few loose sheets of paper. The notes were an attempt at a dossier. It was a God-send they had someone who could translate the notes, none were written in English. Fuzzy and disorganized as they were, the scribblings explained the target was a Selim Abhajiri, an Iranian national.

"Iranian?" Sauwa asked calmly.

It was an open secret the Bosnians were receiving support from other Islamic countries. Pakistan had been smuggling in caches of weapons from small arms to rocket launchers, and Iran had been sending in military and intelligence advisors in the hundreds, traveling under false diplomatic credentials, to help develop the Moslem forces in the war. Even though the Croatians and the Bosnians had rekindled their previous alliance, factions on both sides continued their hostilities toward each other.

"From what we've ascertained," Augin said in his sophisticated and quiet voice, "Selim Abhajiri is traveling under the diplomatic cover of an agricultural advisor gathering facts about Bosnian food production. Our intelligence sources say he is Iranian military, part of the Al-Quds Special Forces."

"That's nothing new," Sauwa interrupted. "We've known about these advisors for quite some time."

The Frenchman reached over and tapped the photograph at the top of the folder. "You're right, this is nothing out of the ordinary. However, in this case, the situation is different. As you know, in the last few months the Bosnian operations carried out in this region have been profoundly more effective resulting in some seriously disastrous results for our forces. Our intelligence sources argue that this man is the reason. They believe he has been instrumental in planning and directing many of the more debilitating attacks."

Sauwa chuckled. "And, they're basing this off of what? Forgive me sir, but intelligence, even from the best organizations, can be murky. What makes for the Croatian intelligence network around here is a loose-knit band of locals collecting gossip and viewing things from a distance. The quality of their reporting is questionable bordering on back-fence prattle."

"Your concerns are well founded," Augin said. "Yet, you must also have noticed the Bosnian operational execution has improved significantly over the last few months, and it correlates with the arrival of this man. He is, after all, a soldier traveling in disguise."

Sauwa's eyes trailed off toward the blackened windows. "Or that's what a bunch of amateurs think and opportunists want you to believe. Killing a diplomatic figure is bad enough, even when it's an accident. When it's intentional, the repercussions could be fatal if it turns out we were wrong."

Augin sighed. He knew she was not wrong about any of it. What made for Croatian intelligence was often a dysfunctional mess, being operated by people who had little idea what they were doing. And deliberately assassinating a diplomatic figure, especially from a country like Iran that had some significant global pull, was playing a dangerous game.

The Frenchman maintained his silence.

Sauwa continued. "I understand war and understand mistakes happen. I also understand you're taking a big risk based on nothing more than grainy pictures and a few randomly collected notes. Are you sure these are the orders you want to give?"

"Not without carefully looking at those photos and putting the pieces together," Augin finally answered. "Intelligence means working with only the pieces of the puzzle you've got." He tapped the photos again.

She flipped through the packet of photos once more and saw the same theme over and over. A supposed agricultural advisor in the company of uniformed military officials. His movements always posed in a directing manner, with the Bosnians looking on, soaking up every word. "He definitely looks more involved than he should be." She raised her head to look back at her commander. "What's the plan?"

He plopped another folder in front of her. It was thicker than the dossier. From it, he pulled out a folded-up map and spread it across the desk. It was a map of the region, not unlike the one directly underneath it, except this one had pen markings scribbled on it. "The mission is in Jablancia." He pointed to a dot with a red circle drawn around it. "As usual, you will leave base camp as part of a visiting patrol. This will provide you cover against anyone observing our camp movements."

"You will arrange to slip from the patrol, make to the wood lines, and follow the river to a predetermined location." He pointed to an area marked with a small black X several miles north of the base camp. The area looked to be well away from any roadways and was only a short distance from the river. "One caveat: this time you'll be going out with your squad."

"Absolutely not!" To help maintain secrecy, Sauwa had never deployed with organic forces from their own camp. The visiting units knew nothing more than she was traveling with them. Somewhere in transit, she would slip discretely from her vehicle into the tree line. Her transporters would assume she was doing something they weren't meant to know.

She folded her hands across the top of the photos. "After today, all the real soldiers are dead. Raker is a sadistic racist who sees this war as a means to make his fortune by pillaging at every opportunity, jeopardizing the mission in the process. He's entirely indifferent and hateful to the Bosnians and Serbs. The only reason he hasn't committed murder or violence against innocents was that Gilgood and MacMasters kept him in line. Now that they're gone, Raker's a war crime waiting to happen. Omery may be a decent driver, but he and Gerald are fakes who greatly overestimate their abilities. Gerald, in particular, hates me and will probably try to kill me given the chance. I'm not working with the remaining men anymore."

She felt Augin's hand rest on hers. He looked tired and sad. "The mortar that killed Gilgood and McMasters killed the squad. Truthfully, Rommel thinks without them, Gerald, Raker, and Omery will be dead within the week. Another reason it's time for you to move on."

"If that's the case, I prefer to go out with one of the local squads."

Augin removed his hand and leaned back in his chair stone-faced and serious. "You won't be with them alone for very long." She could see his mind was made up.

She rubbed her hand over her face. "Who will be the new squad leader?"

"Gerald will be told he's in charge just to quell him and his ego," Augin replied in his professional soft tone that suggested the decision was not up for discussion. "The Serbs have intensified their campaign limiting our abilities to work with units from other camps or give our local friends the liberty of movement they had enjoyed. So we have to work with what we have."

Sauwa looked coldly at the French officer. "He's no soldier."

35

Augin cracked a smile. "Rommel didn't need me to peg him for a phony regarding his bullshit about Vietnam and his black operations experience. But Gerald and the others did what we needed them to do to augment the rest of you. As I've said, you won't be with them much longer."

Reluctantly, Sauwa nodded.

Augin went on. "We have planned for your squad to go out with a larger force of Croatians. They'll accompany you to the current Serb controlled areas to where we think the Bosnians are operating more heavily. At a certain point, your squad will break from them. They'll go on to their mission, and you and your squad will move out to perform a mission we've set up to give you some cover. It will be to recce a small farmhouse potentially being used by Bosnian guerrillas. It's not likely, but someone should check it out, and it will keep the squad busy. During the recce, you will lose yourself in the bushes and move out on your mission."

He pointed again to the black x on the map. "You'll move to a predetermined location where we have arranged for you to meet with Croatian partisans familiar with the area. From there, they will guide you to your destination and give you support to complete your mission. Because of the limited degree of information we have been able to obtain, you will have to gather your own information and make your own plan. Devise whatever method you can to ensure success. Following the completion of your mission, they have instructions to guide you to another group, who will help you get past the border into Montenegro and, hopefully, put you in contact with someone who will help get you out of the Balkans entirely."

"Hopefully?" The word was not lost on her.

"It's the best we can offer," the Frenchman said apologetically. "Frankly, I was amazed Rommel had the connections to arrange transport for you as far as he did."

"Montenegro?" She questioned. "Why not north to Croatia? Wouldn't you have better connections there?"

"We do," Augin explained. "Rommel and I discussed it as a possibility. The UN security forces have a very strong presence guarding the border. Your chances of getting across are not good. Rommel's connections there are still caught in a war and could possibly be consumed in the upcoming NATO mission. Montenegro is largely outside of it all and offers the best possibility of keeping you out of the roundup."

Sauwa massaged her brow. "The Croats and the Bosnians had a mutual enemy in the Serbs who were out to annihilate both groups through genocide. When the Croats saw a chance to gain more land of their own, they abandoned the Bosnians and threw in with the Serbs. It's all politics, and it's disgusting."

The Frenchman's eyes went soft. "I appreciate you holding your tongue on the matter in public. This war is not easy. Remember though, you're a mercenary who is paid to fight and kill for an employer. Their enemies are your enemies because the paycheck says so. This is the world in which you and I both belong." Despite trying to say his piece in the most tempered way, it still hit deeply. She was a person with a skill-set that offered limited markets for viable employment.

Augin continued with his brief, offering the code words and names she would use. In her usual manner, she took notes in her special coded writing only she could interpret. When he finished with the final points of the plan, he assisted in going through the disjointed notes that passed for

37

a dossier. What little information could be gleaned would still be of immense help in preparing.

The meeting ended with the Frenchman collecting all the documents pertaining to the mission. Because of poor security, it was necessary to burn all sensitive information. When she left the room, the only evidence a plan ever existed would lie in Augin, Rommel, and the minimal notes she was allowed using a code she had developed. After doing a sweep to ensure there was nothing that could compromise the mission, he gave her a nod. Sauwa cracked open the door. Seeing no one but the two guards outside, she edged her way out.

Catching their eye, she pretended to adjust her bra and wipe her mouth. The two guards smiled at one another as they looked on. They might have been part of Rommel's most trusted guards, but they were still soldiers who lived on the base and conversed with others. It was an added degree of security if they believed the activities that went on in the planning room between her and Augin were of a conjugal nature. Better her reputation should suffer than her secrecy. A lowly mercenary soldier having secret meetings with the unit's top leadership in the confidential briefing room would assuredly get around. It would also make people very interested in her and where she went when she wasn't with her squad.

The day was catching up with her. She crossed the open area making her way past the assorted cast of soldiers, refugees, and black-market business types, less alert than usual. In her diminished, lucid state, there was only one concern; the concern she had when she first arrived in Croatia so many months ago. It was the feeling of uncertainty toward her future. The war, for whatever else it was, had protected her from the intelligence agencies of an ever-growing list of countries. It had also been a distraction from having to think about her situation as a fugitive. When NATO forces came, that would end.

The old woman she had come to know as Nona ushered the young woman into her home and led her to the wash-room. After Sauwa handed the woman a few coins for her trouble, the old woman disappeared going back to her washing.

Sauwa discarded her lizard patterned camouflage top and trousers, followed by the black T-shirt, knit watch cap and, finally, her cotton underwear. Before she started, she made a quick check of the room and the neighboring rooms to ensure Smokes or his friends weren't trying for another show. She didn't think they would. The last miscreant was thwarted by the sight of a gun barrel shoved tightly against his cheek. Satisfied she was alone, she stepped into the shower, scrubbed away her camo face paint with a rough washcloth and then lost herself in the one pleasure in this place.

The door to her barracks creaked when she pushed her way inside. The place was dark. Like Augin's planning office, light from a few ancient bulbs hung from the ceiling. Faint beams of sunlight filtered in from small, dirty windows lining the walls creating an eerie environment. The barracks was largely deserted except for a few mercenaries resting. There were a couple of Irishmen, whose history she was unclear on.

There was never any form of assigned sleeping quarters since people came and went — some killed, some deserting — so everyone just took whatever bed was available.

At the far back, on the folding bed she typically used, a

man groaned and rustled about, his hand inside his pants. She was not surprised it was Raker. Deciding it would be less awkward to relocate, she dropped her gear on a relatively clean looking bed across from the Irishmen and sank onto the springy mattress.

The mission, the ambush, and the meeting with Augin had all taken its toll. Her mind was fading. Slipping off her leather combat boots, she placed them next to the rest of her gear and weapons. Down to her T-shirt and trousers, she lay down on the bed and tucked her fatigue top under her head. It was only seconds before the darkness of the bland ceiling became a blur and she was gone.

4

The sun had not risen yet when the squad assembled in their vehicles in preparation to move out. All that existed was a thin reddish-orange crack at the very base of the darkened sky. It was the ideal time to move. They had the cover of darkness on their side and the natural lethargy that begins to consume any enemy who has been out all night or just waking up.

Sauwa woke early as usual to ensure more time for last-minute prep. She sank behind a building and took a lighter to the hardened patches in her camo paint packet. When they were soft enough, she applied the paint, smudging the darker colors over her nose, forehead, and high cheeks and the lighter colors to the side of her face and neck. Preferring to wear gloves she opted not to extend her artistry to her hands.

She was first to the jeep and had just finished checking the rest of her gear making sure it was packed tight — all things gleaming or jingling taped down with dark tape — when the rest of her team began to assemble. She bounced up and down to ensure nothing would fall or rattle at an inopportune time.

"You look the little soldier," Gerald said smugly. "But this ain't no playground. This is the real thing, so stop playing G.I. Joe."

Sauwa said nothing. There was no point. She looked at the older man and could only mask her own judgment. They were going into the woods to conduct a recce, and he was wearing a light camouflage bandana over his head littered with juvenile sketches. The bandana failed to cover his grey hair. He had a solid light green field jacket, brown US army T-shirt, and green tiger-striped camouflage pants. The only facial paint the man had applied was some weird assortment of colored lines drawn sporadically and loosely across his face. It was something out of a cheap action movie clearly meant to make him look fearsome and not logical for a man about to go into the tree line.

Omery and Raker were not far behind and, like their new leader, neither seemed to appreciate the nature of the mission. Raker's choice of a green cutoff shirt showed off his pale white arms and overdone tattoos of the white supremacist message. Omery, at least, made a good attempt with a camouflage field coat that matched the area and less distinctive black knit watch cap. His camo paint covering his face was better than the other two, but was all a mint light green and failed to capture anything else. Neither Raker nor Gerald had bothered to tape their combat webbing and packs.

This came as no surprise to Sauwa since none of their previous missions had involved getting off the road or away from the local towns and villages. The closest had been a quick patrol into the forests. MacMasters, Gilgood, Dumas, and she had handled any deep incursions into the woods leaving the rest with the jeeps.

The Croatian unit they were to ride out with bundled into their convoy which consisted of two small Toyota pickup trucks and a jeep. They did not look remotely like professional soldiers, each wearing a mixture of military fatigues and civilian clothing. Most of the fighters were young men, barely more than twenty. Her old friend Smokes shot her a naughty smile as he mounted the back of one of the Toyotas.

Raker had already assumed his post in the driver's seat with Gerald taking the passenger side leaving Sauwa and Omery to nestle down in the back.

No sooner had she sat down then the jeep roared into action. The German pressed the gas pedal, and the vehicle flew onto the dirt road and sped out the front gate. He had barely missed hitting the two sentries, who had managed to jump out of the way in the nick of time.

Fagots! He yelled to the two angry men as he raced out of the base camp.

Clutching her AK-47 in a tactical grip, Sauwa aimed her rifle at the landscape across from her. Omery seemed lost in his own world. He leaned his rifle haphazardly in the opposite direction and proceeded to let his eyes wander, lost in his own thoughts. Glancing behind her she saw the Croat squad following. Inspired by the audacious behavior of the German, they raced wildly trying to keep up.

"You all just follow my lead when we get there," Gerald shouted to a disinterested audience. "I did this stuff all the time back in Nam. I know what I'm doing so do as I say, and you youngsters will be all right. It's time you learned from a real pro."

43

Sauwa looked across at Omery, who rolled his eyes. She returned her focus to the other side of the road having no illusions about how badly this could all turn out. Out of the corner of her eye, she could see the old Vietnam vet lazily kick his feet up on the dash and rest his rifle on his chest. *God help us if we get hit*, was the one thought going through her mind.

At the intended break, the Croatians waved their good-byes from the back of their trucks and blew past the mercenaries onto another road.

Raker drove a short distance before turning the jeep into a soft patch of tall grass and some bushes. The forestry of Bosnia was more in line with a North American State park than the thick jungle vegetation of some tropical countries. This made bushcraft concealment — finding a good piece of vegetation that could hide a vehicle — a difficult process.

Pulling the jeep deep into the shrubbery, the team disembarked. Sauwa grabbed plants from the surrounding area to throw on top of the vehicle to provide additional concealment. Omery and Gerald, seeing the logic, chipped in to help. Raker stepped off to take a piss.

There might be enemy forces nearby, but looters were a bigger concern. It would be a long, dangerous walk back to base camp should their transportation disappear. It wasn't much. The shrubbery barely broke up the outline. Normally Sauwa would have spent more time on it, but she had no intention of returning, so the matter was pointless.

Retrieving her gear from the back, she untied a rolled up bundle tied to another bundle. Untying the smaller of the two, she unrolled a hat-like article with darkly painted strips of frayed burlap spread over it. The burlap matched the colors and scenery of the surrounding forest. She flipped the smaller article over her head and positioned it on her knit watch cap. She looked like a cross between an animal and a bush.

Gerald snickered, "I'd say you're taking things to the extreme with that little getup."

She didn't bother with a reply. In a war that favored the use of snipers in a terrain that was largely open forests, it should have been self-explanatory why one would want to conceal themselves better. But, for these three, it did not seem to be the case. She adjusted the camouflage field coat — a size too big to break up her outline a little more — and threw her Bergen over her shoulders.

With gear collected, the team was ready to move.

Omery took the point of the formation. Raker and Gerald moved back eight meters on each side of the flanks, leaving Sauwa to fall back another ten meters watching the rear. It was a good diamond patrol formation. With Omery leading, the team ventured into the wood line. Gradually, the surrounding trees towered over them like big, leafy umbrellas consuming the sunlight and leaving the woods in a gloomy patch of shadows. The team took up their weapons in a tactical manner facing outward, eyes focused on the landscape. Sauwa found it somewhat reassuring that her three team members were capable of that much.

Everyone was tense. The location was known to be patrolled by of the *7 Muslim Brigade* of the army of the Republic of Bosnia and Herzegovina forces. They were one of the better trained and equipped units in the Bosnian forces.

On edge, they maneuvered cautiously through a landscape that changed frequently, mindful of every shadow, every noise. They moved at a steady pace through lush grass into piles of decaying leaves and across patches of bare dirt. The trees provided some protection, but the open patches made it easy to be seen from a distance. It was not ideal terrain in which to move about covertly.

Sauwa scanned for any signs they were not alone — broken twigs hanging from trees or ground that had recently been disturbed. This was made more difficult by her position in the back, having to differentiate between traces left by her team and those made by someone else.

So far, she had seen no indication of an enemy patrol but worried about the possibility of a sniper. A few months earlier, she had been out with Dumas on a recce when a gunshot echoed, followed by a rifle bullet screaming by inches from her head appearing as if by magic. And just as easily, the gunman vanished without a trace.

As expected, Gerald's nerves were getting to him. He shook as he looked out into the expanse of the forest. Despite having been in Bosnia for a year and a half — not to mention his extensive experience in the jungles of Nam — the old man hadn't adjusted well to the open forests of Eastern Europe. He claimed his expertise ran more toward cities and urban locations. Sauwa didn't believe him for a second. Raker, by contrast, took in the foliage with an almost sinister delight. His eyes were wild, hungry for action. The times he had killed, he had behaved as if it were some sort of orgasmic experience. Now his face read like a hunter waiting for the chance to strike. For him, it was not if, but when. He clutched his weapon and smiled.

Omery insisted on keeping the compass despite the danger of it distracting him from acting as a lookout. The marine commando was sure he could do both. At about a kilometer out, he lifted his hand to call a halt. The team stopped and held their positions. Then, with another flick of the hand, the Englishman waved everyone to join him.

Sauwa had dropped to a knee and slipped up close to a large bush. When the others started to gather up front, she rose slowly and made her way toward them. Backing up to them, she kept looking at the surrounding area and again took a knee. Gerald and Omery sat comfortably against a tree, while Raker knelt near Sauwa.

"All right, we're only a kilo away from the place," Omery announced in a half-hearted attempt to whisper. "We follow this trail here." He pointed with a chop of his hand.

"All right," Gerald interrupted trying to assert his fictional image as the team leader. "We move up until just in sight. Then Omery and I will move to the right, Raker and the girl will pull to the left." For some reason, he was never able to call Sauwa by her name. "We'll hold positions on opposite sides for about ten minutes then meet back at the breakpoint."

It was a plan, no one bothered to argue.

"Remember, we're on a mission, so you two, stick to the job," Gerald said pointing his finger at Raker and Sauwa. "I don't need you two getting it on while we're out there."

Raker shot a cold look at the old man that made everyone uneasy and Gerald flinched. He knew he had overplayed his hand, said too much and to the wrong man. He gulped nervously and attempted to speak but decided against it.

Raker eyed Sauwa like the thought had just been put into his head. He would be alone with this pretty young thing. As if reading his mind, she glared back at him tapping her rifle, daring him to make a move.

Omery motioned everyone forward. The team rose to their feet and started moving. Again, Omery took the lead with Gerald and Raker following and Sauwa at the rear. A short way down, they saw the roof of the farmhouse.

Sauwa tried to stop the team in the hopes they would break right while far enough away. All three ignored her. They pressed closer. The second story of the house was now in sight. Sauwa was sure that anyone looking through the window of the top floor would notice four armed people coming through the trees.

The team, once again, assembled around Omery as they checked the place out. The house appeared deserted. Gerald and Omery took the right flank. Sauwa and Raker slipped off to the left with the German in the lead. He navigated around keeping within the tree line but not much more than that. To Sauwa's frustration, he failed at every chance to take advantage of the numerous bushes and additional vegetation that would have better concealed them. She tried to mitigate the situation by digging further into the shrubs while still not straying too far from her partner. Nervously she kept viewing the house hoping that Augin's intelligence was accurate, and it was a dead location. The team was just here to confirm it. If not, it was a miracle they had not been seen yet.

Rounding off to the flank, Raker and Sauwa found a location that gave them a good view of the front and side of the house and the shed. Hunkering down behind a large shrub between two umbrella-like trees, the two mercenaries watched in silence. Sauwa assumed Raker's lack of conversation was more to do with his disdain for her than any tactical professionalism.

Fine by her.

She would be away from him and the team soon enough. When the recce was done, she would arrange to get lost on the way back to the rendezvous and start out on her mission.

The house showed no signs of life. Raker was getting bored. He dropped to his side. Resting on his arm and elbow, his rifle leveled over a nearby rock, he drew in the dirt with a twig. Sauwa placed herself in a kneeling position up close to the bush limiting her silhouette as much as possible. She figured they would hold for a few hours and leave. Until then, she would play the part.

Raker devoted his energies to the sketch and became oblivious until the monotony was interrupted by the sound of a woman muttering. A heavyset woman waddled out the side door of the house, a hijab wrapped loosely around her head, and a flowing grey garment draped over the rest of her body. It was easy to guess the woman was a Bosnian Muslim. She didn't appear to be anyone dangerous, just a local working what she could of her farm. Sauwa held steady. There was nothing worth noting. The emphasis was on remaining undetected.

Raker, seeing the woman, rolled over onto his stomach and took up his rifle. He whispered something in German, his eyes taking on the same sinister gaze she had seen at the start of the mission. Sauwa didn't have to speak the language to know he had something bad on his mind, but as long as he kept cool, he was free to think what he wanted.

The old woman fussed about her yard, and it was making Raker agitated. The situation escalated when the sound of another voice resonated from the house. Its voice was female and belonged to someone much younger.

The two mercenaries held steady, neither one exactly sure what to make of the situation.

Soon the second female emerged from the house. They

could tell she was younger by the sound of her voice, and she was more agile. She leaped from the doorway and charged across the distance to meet the older one. She wore a hijab in a similar fashion around her head. However, unlike the older woman, she wore a T-shirt, jacket, and jeans.

The two Bosnian women began jabbering away in their native tongue. Sauwa could only understand bits and pieces of what they were discussing, but by what she could understand, she concluded it had nothing to do with any military operations. It was a girl talking to her grandmother, apparently worried about the old woman's health.

Sauwa took a breath of relief. It didn't seem as if there was cause for concern.

Then she saw Raker. His sinister look became even more unnerving with the sight of the young girl. He was licking his lips, a four-star meal in front of him. "How old do you think the young one is?" He asked in his accented English. "Fourteen-fifteen maybe?"

"What does it matter?" Sauwa asked. "We're here on a recce, nothing more. Whatever you're thinking, forget it."

The German smiled. "We're here looking for enemy forces. There are none, just these two rag head fucks. Nobody will care if I get a little exercise with the young one. Especially if neither are around to talk about it afterward." He spoke as if his strategy made everything about his intentions all right.

"We're not here to make a show of ourselves," Sauwa whispered. "We need to stay hidden."

"From two women!" Raker growled. "No, I need to work up a sweat; the young one will do nicely. And I could enjoy the knife practice with the old bag."

It was clear Raker had made up his mind. He was a

hungry predator eyeing his next prey. In the past, his intentions had been thwarted by the heavy hand of Gilgood who had kept the German in line. Gilgood was gone now, and the predator was now unleashed.

Sauwa looked up at the two women. The grandmother was embracing her granddaughter. In this beastly war, they were making the best they could of it. Raker was about to destroy what little they had left.

Drawing back on her heels, Sauwa shifted behind the German. At the same time, she reached behind her and slid a six-inch double-edged knife from a sheath on her belt. Her colleague was too engrossed watching the two Bosnian women to notice anything else. He was biting his lower lip with his upper teeth when she quietly came up over him.

With one quick motion, she drove the blade fast and deep into the back of the man's head slicing through his brain stem and into the brain. His body immediately went limp as he dropped to a whispered death.

Sauwa looked up, relieved to see the two Bosnians were talking to each other, unaware. Slowly she pulled the knife from its embedded place, feeling the brain and bone matter as she gradually worked it free then wiped it off with the aid of some large leaves.

Sheathing the weapon in her belt, she waited. The two Bosnians finished their chat and disappeared back into the house. Quietly Sauwa grabbed her Bergen, surveyed the area and crept back into the forest.

It would be another thirty minutes before the team was set to meet up. That would give her ample time to get some distance away.

For all their talk, Gerald and Omery weren't the types to stick around and commence a search if the rest of their team missed the rendezvous. Even if they did eventually find Raker's body, they were not likely to go in pursuit of anyone when enemy forces could be in the area. They would assume their teammates got ambushed by some enemy troops which alone might send them running to the jeep.

Omery and Gerald were soldiers, not psycho killers like Raker, so the women, at least for the moment, were safe.

Concealed from the house, hunkered down in a thicket of bushes, she pulled the larger roll from her Bergen and placed it on the ground. Rolling it out, she retrieved a small cape-like article. She threw her Bergen back over her shoulder and the cape over the top. It draped just below her waist and hung about her like wrinkly animal fur. Tying it firmly in place, she made a few adjustments to ensure it gave her adequate cover.

It wasn't the best camouflage field jacket, it didn't cover her entire body. Normally such camouflage would be made of old flight suits or larger size military fatigues, but for what she had to work with, it did the job.

Despite the shadows offered by the trees, she was still very much out in the open. The sun wouldn't set for another three hours which meant she needed to find a place to hold up until then. In the absence of any night vision equipment, she would move mostly in the period between sunset and sunrise when there would be enough light to see where she was going while providing enough darkness to help mask her presence. How far she moved at night would depend on clear skies and moonlight.

With the aid of a map, she got her bearings. Staying close to the trees she kept her movements slow, picked up her feet, and set each step down carefully. Fast movements were the quickest way to attract the attention of enemy patrols or, worse yet, snipers. She remained vigilant on the ground and stayed clear of decaying leaves that would crackle under her feet. In between the trees' shadows, she directed her path through any thickened foliage that presented itself.

It was in these moments that she was thankful for the extensive training she had received formally from the South African Recce Special Forces course at Fort Doppies and the additional lessons taught to her by her uncle and his former comrades from his Selous Scout days.

In the silence of the trees, she tried not to stew over the approaching end of her days in Bosnia. When she completed this mission — when NATO forces arrived and began their hunt for war criminals — she would once again be on her own, another unknown future ahead of her.

These people she was linking up with might help get her to Montenegro, but then what? She wasn't even sure these guerrillas would follow through with the arrangement. They might abandon her, leave her to find her own means of escape. Such thoughts were distracting, and she tried to push them from her mind. But they were genuine concerns that warranted an answer. One she didn't have.

5

D avid O'knomo had warned Gahima at the beginning that it would not be easy bringing the Angel of Death to justice. Cognitively, he understood; however, deep within the back of his mind, he and many others in the higher echelons of political power were sure the capture of one of his country's deadliest assassins would be achieved quickly.

Robbed of a swift victory, Mr. Gahima had been on pins and needles for almost a year waiting to hear news of Sauwa Catcher. Responsibility for the deaths of three policemen and seven members of the Irish Republican Army at the hand of the deadly assassin rested squarely on his shoulders. And her vanishing act had been another black eye for South Africa.

Armed with NATO photos and reports indicating her possible location, O'knomo felt it time to brief his superiors. He gave his presentation, delivering each piece of intelligence in order, laying out his case to ensure it did not look like a desperate collection of random facts supporting a loose theory.

Gahima listened intently to the brief.

When it was completed, the elder statesman began strategizing ways to push for her capture. Through diplomatic channels, they could demand to have her handed over. It was a war zone; the Bosnians would be obliged to comply, or the South Africans could send in a Special Forces team and abduct or assassinate her.

O'knomo pointed out that her whereabouts were desultory at best. How long could distinctive South African Special Forces soldiers remain in the area before being compromised? He recommended they wait and let NATO go in first. When NATO brought order to the chaotic country, let the British lead the charge to find her.

But Gahima didn't want to hear it. He didn't want to wait. He wanted her capture to be a triumph of the new government — not someone else's achievement. Negotiations for her future in a British prison or one in South Africa could be discussed later.

This had been the fight O'knomo and his team had anticipated after months with high officials breathing down their necks. The team had presumed once Sauwa Catcher was located, officials would concoct some insane plan of action, even if that location was in some war zone.

The meeting ended with Gahima in a state of agitation.

Drained and feeling battered, O'knomo wished he could go home early and salvage what was left of the day. His plan ended when he entered his office and saw Jamie Nawati and Dr. Eugene Walderhyn waiting.

He had hoped they had already gone home giving him until tomorrow to explain the results of the briefing. Instead, they had opted to wait.

Coors Ravenhoof sauntered in after a trip to the washroom.

The faces around O'knomo were painted with serious looks — he conceded, his evening plans gone. He made his way to a nearby chair and sank into it. "Well, the old man wouldn't accept the situation. He isn't ready to hear we're at a loss to do anything."

Knocking his fist gently on the table, he looked about as he prepared his words. "While Gahima didn't come out directly and say it, he is not letting this matter drop for the time being, as I had hoped. Instead, we are to continue working closely with the British to develop the intelligence to confirm it is her beyond question. Once NATO moves in and secures order, we are to begin planning courses of action for her retrieval."

O'knomo's team expressed mixed reactions to the news. On one hand, it was a relief to be back in the chase after so many dead ends and failures. On the other hand, a volatile area of the world made for an unpredictable future. Who knew where all this would lead?

He finished outlining the details of the meeting and concluded with, "They're tense. The idea of the British being the ones that might have to take her was not well received."

"Diplomatic action indeed," scoffed Jaimie Nawati irritably. As a man accustomed to the anarchy of war, the very idea of such actions only illustrated sheer stupidity.

O'knomo remained quiet as his team vented their frustrations. For months, they had worked to find the proverbial needle in the haystack. During that time, it had seemed as if they were personally responsible for her escape. Senior figures of the intelligence community never tired in their sideline criticisms of how the operation had gone in Ireland.

Ravenhoof, having been the man on the ground in her pursuit, had been excoriated by the leadership as if he had actually led the operation in Ireland himself. It was only a miracle he had not been forced into retirement. O'knomo had burned a lot of favors protecting his subordinate's job. Something the old Afrikaner had not forgotten.

Dr. Walderhyn remained more reserved yet still irritated. "I'm glad you talked them out of a covert mission. But I still harbor concerns when you say they entertained the notion of a military special operation!" As an academic of foreign policy and politics, he had little patience for such things. Military adventurism had a habit of reaping bigger problems then it solved when not properly thought out considering the bigger picture not taken into consideration. Something the professor felt rarely happened.

Ravenhoof said nothing. The grinding mill he had come home to after Ireland had left him tired and defeated. The cruelty of the allegations regarding his inabilities and incompetence had been hard on a man who had served for so long in the trenches of police and intelligence work. Many of the most scathing attacks were over things he had no control over. He probably would have accepted retirement after it all was said and done, but to leave under such a dark cloud was unthinkable. He was going to see this last mission through to the end when he personally placed the handcuffs on Sauwa Catcher.

6

I t had been an arduous two-day journey of cold nights and unnerving days.

Sauwa had been largely unmolested through the enemy-controlled territory, having had only one near encounter with a patrol of Bosnian soldiers. They had been part of the feared 7 Muslim Brigade and had been moving a short distance from her. She had hidden and felt her heart race as they passed, their green bandanas sporting Islamic holy script in white Farsi lettering. They moved out in a practiced tactical formation with good noise discipline that showed good training.

Sauwa didn't like being out in the bush alone. She never did.

Normally, the Bosnians were like the Croatians, their army was thrown together with poorly trained volunteers. It gave her a much-needed edge operating in enemy territory. But some of the Muslim foreign units were different. They were staffed by seasoned combat vets and trained by more advanced military organizations with experience in other conflicts. They were a higher caliber of soldier, and that made them dangerous foes.

Following the Neretva River, she managed to keep a steady pace. The river helped her move at night. The sound of the water guided her and masked the sound of her movements. The vegetation was also thicker and more consistent giving her better protection.

On the morning of the third day, she arrived at the rendezvous point exhausted physically and mentally. The days of playing cat and mouse in the bush had taken its toll. The rendezvous point was a small opening in the woods a short distance from the river. It was deserted. She had arrived a day early and didn't expect anyone to be there.

Following the instructions Augin had given her, Sauwa gathered nearby stones. She found a partially visible, yet inconspicuous location and started placing the stones to form an "X" with arrows pointing from two of the four ends. The marker was to be left by whoever arrived first. When the other party arrived, they would complete the formation by placing arrow tips on the other two line points establishing their identity.

Not wanting to stay exposed, she slipped into the bushes. Tired, she took advantage of her extra time and drifted into a light sleep. In the field, her mind released her from the nightmares of her past, nightmares that woke her to her own screams. She never slept deep enough in the field to have such dreams. Her nerves were too focused on the more immediate threats.

It was several hours before she caught sight of men, six in all, walking through the trees. At first, Sauwa thought them another patrol. The formation was lightly dispersed in a tactical way, and she could make out the outlines of rifles protruding from their arms. As the men came into view, she saw they weren't soldiers, not in the general sense. They were dressed in mismatched ensembles and looked as ragged as the Croatian boys back at her camp. Nor did they possess any better field skills.

She could hear them talking in Croatian and understood some of what they were saying. She had picked up enough of the language to know it was just everyday small talk. The words, even the slang, were somewhat comprehensible. She had heard such dialogue many times at the base or when transported on a mission. These men were her contacts. They had to be. However, this was not a good place for her to be hasty. As rough and violent as they appeared, she couldn't afford to be wrong.

Sauwa kept hidden and watched them. She held her AK-47 ready in case she needed to fight. The men were now in the clearing, mulling around lazily as if enjoying a day at a barbecue. Half the men rested their rifles over their shoulders, the rest drug them one-handed and slumped at their sides. They jabbered on, oblivious to everything except the ground below their feet, perhaps looking for something, perhaps not caring if they found it.

Finally, one of the men came across Sauwa's cross arrows. Loudly, he beckoned everyone over. A medium sized, muscular man, sporting long hair, a thin scruff for a beard, and a well-worn extreme metal T-shirt, marched over and slapped the announcer across the face. He followed up by pressing his index finger to his lips, then flashed the command to be silent to everyone. Instantly, the rest of the men, as unordered as they were, fell silent, fearful of disobeying the Metal Man.

After his order, the environment changed from a social gathering to a silent convent.

The Metal Man looked down at Sauwa's symbol and around the area, surveying it closely. He grumbled, knelt down and drew arrowheads at the end of the other two lines, stood up and presented himself to the trees, raising his hands as if to say, *Are you happy?* Then he rejoined the rest of his men who had gathered into a group several feet away.

It was not the best of circumstances, but Sauwa figured it was the best she was going to get for authenticating her contact. Taking a deep breath, she emerged from the bushes to reveal herself. To the men she could have been some monster. Wide-eyed and frantic, they grabbed for their weapons, which were inaccessible and awkwardly flopping against their bodies.

For a minute, Sauwa was sure this would end in a gun battle, until Metal Man jumped in and saved the situation, signaling his men to calm down. She was alone, Metal Man noticed. Not wanting to raise tensions, Sauwa lowered her weapon and pressed it gently against her body. Convinced that both parties were on the same side, Sauwa and Metal Man walked tentatively toward each other. Each reached into their coat pockets and pulled out a ripped piece of paper. They placed the ripped edges together to see they matched up perfectly.

Sauwa breathed a sigh of relief. These men were her contacts. She could see a similar look of relief on Metal Man's face. He spoke to his men and the atmosphere relaxed. Then he turned back to the plant-like figure before him. "I understand you prefer English." His speech was slightly broken but much clearer than what she was used to dealing with.

"I do," she replied.

Metal Man hadn't expected a woman for such a mission, but the voice he was hearing was too feminine to be a man's. He eyed her up and down. No, it had not been his imagination. The operative he was meeting was female. He blinked a few times trying to wrap his head around the revelation. "Are you…er…perhaps…er…with anyone?"

"No, I'm your contact," she replied with quiet indifference. "Just me." It was not the first time she had had such a reaction, and it wouldn't be the last.

Metal Man scanned the bushes hoping someone else would emerge and prove to be the real contact. No one else came forward. He stared at Sauwa, reluctantly. Nothing was said for several seconds as the two eyed each other.

"We're putting ourselves in danger just standing around in the open like this," Sauwa broke the stalemate. "We have units of the Muslim holy warriors lurking in the area. I saw them yesterday. They're not your ragtag militia types. They're trained professionals. Unless you want to stay here and wait to get ambushed, let's move out."

Metal Man waved his men back into the trees and beckoned Sauwa to follow. She did so at a careful distance. She swept the trees both in front and behind for signs of unwanted company. Nothing stuck out in the fairly open forests, so they might have been safe for now. Though, with the incessant talking and lumbering way they moved, it was a question of how long that would last.

Still carrying their weapons haphazardly, still inattentive to their surroundings, at the direction of Metal Man, however, the group cut down on the chatter and began to spread out as they moved through the trees. Metal Man stayed in the rear close to Sauwa. She couldn't tell if it was

63

because he was suspicious of her or if he didn't want her getting lost. In either case, he was one of the few in the group who was cognizant of the area around him.

At random intervals, they were met by sentries standing guard at a poorly designed observation post hidden behind a few trees and bushes. The guards called out to the patrol in Croatian, which Sauwa took for a halt and identify passcode. Metal Man replied, and the group was given leave to pass. After the better part of a half hour, the group came to a makeshift encampment.

It could have been a gypsy camp with a few covered wagons and beaten caravans, populated with a collection of about fifty men and ten women. Like the men in the patrol, they too were dressed in an assortment of military and civilian clothing.

Sauwa's group walked into the encampment and were immediately greeted by camp people who charged toward them as if they were long-lost loved ones who had been released from prison. Of course, given the utter brutality and human toll this war had taken, Sauwa could imagine that many of those going on patrol never returned.

The small celebration continued all the way into the encirclement of the camp. In the melee, Metal Man tried to keep close to Sauwa, not wanting to lose her. This was made difficult by the actions of a young woman who had grabbed hold of him, lavished him with an assault of kisses, and insisted he pay attention to her. Metal Man reciprocated with a firm embrace and slipped his arm around the girl's waist as they continued walking.

Inside the camp, the patrol disintegrated, the men vanishing into the sea of people. All that remained was Metal Man, who broke away from his young love and, to the girl's great dismay, motioned Sauwa over to a small caravan at the far end of the of the camp.

Sauwa followed until he stopped and knocked, in a respectful manner, at the door of one of the vehicles.

Whoever was inside was apparently quite important. A gruff voice answered. Metal Man reached for the knob and nodded his head toward the door. Cracking it open, he ushered her inside. Not sure what to do at that point, Sauwa entered.

The inside of the caravan was a strange mixture of salvaged furniture interlaced with the assorted piles of maps, photographs and various documents collected haphazardly on makeshift tables. At the center of it all was a large, jowly-faced man with a couple days of facial growth and a gut that protruded well over his belt line. He was hunkered into an armchair that looked totally out of place in the caravan. Despite wearing a more complete uniform than the other men, it was obvious to Sauwa he wasn't one for the field.

From his seat, the jowly-faced man was hunched over a long folding table with a grid map of their location spread out across it. How far it covered, Sauwa couldn't tell. But it was marked up heavily with a variety of different colors of ink and with little toys placed in specific locations. She assumed it was the tactical breakdown of where everybody was in the area or the best they could figure.

Metal Man stood quietly waiting. Sauwa followed suit. Eventually, the jowly-faced man sat upright in his chair. He had dark circles around his eyes and a sunken look that indicated he had not slept much in the last few weeks. He stared off into the distance until his eyes transferred to his two guests and displayed the first sign of recognition since they had entered. He said something in Croatian to Metal Man, who jabbered a few sentences promptly in reply. The jowly-faced man lifted his hand and nodded his head. A few more words in Croatian and Metal Man turned to the door, patted Sauwa on the shoulder as if to say she would be all right. Then he left.

"You are the one Rommel speaks of so highly." The jowly-faced man spoke in better English than what she normally heard.

"I wouldn't know," Sauwa replied. "I'm not exactly sure what he says about me to others."

The jowly-faced man chuckled. "He said you were modest amongst many other things."

"Are you sure you have the right person?" She cautioned. "In this war, with the communication system you have, he could have been talking about someone else. I'd hate to be here under false pretenses."

"You aren't." The jowly-faced man wrestled to get comfortable in his chair as he motioned her to a seat. "There are not too many female mercenaries in this war. And given your current state of dress, and the way you handled your-self in the field, Oleg was very impressed with you."

Tired, she dropped her camouflage field jacket to the floor, pulled off her hat and finally her Bergen. Relieved of her burdensome equipment, she sank into the adjacent chair. "Oleg? You mean the man that was just..." She pointed to the door through which Metal Man had exited.

"Yes," the jowly-faced man nodded with paternalistic pride. "I've known him for many years. He's like a son to me and is certainly a better soldier in this war than most who are fighting for our side."

His look suggested he wanted a response from her. She

said nothing, so he continued. "I imagine you know why you're here?"

"Yes."

"To train my men."

"I believe I'm here to carry out an assassination," Sauwa corrected him. She wasn't sure how much to divulge to a man she had only met minutes ago and seemed under a different impression.

"Oh, you're here for that, too. It's an Iranian military advisor who is your target. My people are the ones who have been collecting intelligence on him for Rommel. That is why he had you link up with us. However, when he told me they would be sending a specialist to deal with this affair, I suspected it would be the mysterious assassin — the Black Widow — who has dispatched so many troublesome Serbs and Bosnians over the last year or so. I imagine that would have to be you."

"I do the job I'm hired to do." Sauwa hated being talked to as if she were some sort of deified being. "I don't know about all the rest of what you're saying."

The jowly-faced man smiled. "Modest, I like that. However, let us be honest with one another. Oleg talked about how you caught his entire unit by surprise. According to his account, you were only a few feet from his men and no one noticed you until you revealed yourself. Looking at the attire you have just divested yourself of, I can imagine such a scenario."

"They weren't looking." Sauwa wasn't sure if the jowly-faced man's statement was intended to elicit an answer or not.

The jowly-faced man added a chuckle and wagged his finger as if he had just caught some deception or inside joke.

"You are right, and you noticed that didn't you. Though I must confess that a more experienced, better-trained force should have caught sight of you. You have seen what I'm working with. Look, you were out there all by yourself in enemy territory. You didn't get caught or discovered. I am inclined to believe the rumors about you."

"Putting stock in rumors can be detrimental in combat."

Maneuvering again for a more comfortable position in his chair, the jowly-faced man grunted. "I would normally agree. I do not place my beliefs off of anything but my own observations. However, with little else to go on and little time for a more detailed assessment, I have to get what I can from what I have to work with. Oleg spoke well of you and your abilities. You appear to be a very skilled veteran who is no stranger to the battlefield compared to the ragged appearance of those you see here. Or, for that matter, one who likes to play soldier by walking around in a fancy uniform that's more for show than practical fieldwork."

Sauwa wasn't quite sure how to respond. Nor was she exactly sure where this discussion was going. "Well, every conflict has its phonies and pros. It's a byproduct of war, I guess. But I'm here to eliminate someone. And…"

"I know what your mission is," the jowly-faced man interrupted. "I also know that you are not returning to Rommel's service after it. He asked me to aid you in getting you to Montenegro. This, of course, I can do. However, Rommel has heard of my concerns in past meetings about the poor state of my forces. We have no professional training and have survived more from luck than skill. With our problems, we needed help. We're fighting the Serbs again, which means a trained and well-equipped army and better trained Muslim fighters for the Bosnian forces. When he asked me to assist you with your mission, he also explained you would be available to help train us."

She didn't like the words coming out of the man's mouth. Rommel and Augin had neglected to explain this additional detail. At a time when she needed to be planning a serious assassination and making a speedy escape, training a guerrilla unit was completely out of the question. "I appreciate you and Rommel thinking so highly of me even though I don't know that I deserve the reverence. I wouldn't want to give you any false hopes with some misguided idea of my soldierly abilities."

The jowly-faced man fought his way out of his chair and managed to stand straight. He was an imposing figure towering over her. "Please come with me." He walked past her to the door. "They'll be fine here," he said as she knelt down to collect her things.

Sauwa ignored him. She packed her field kit into her Bergen. "We don't have that good of a relationship."

He waited as she threw it over her shoulder. With her rifle in hand, she followed her enormous guide out the door. The camp still looked more like a family outing than a military facility. Everyone was lazily walking about or sitting in collected groups enjoying food and pleasant conversation. Men carried their weapons haphazardly or laid them on their laps or against chairs. Scores of children ran about playing and presenting a distraction while older and younger women trotted about doing basic household chores. A few of the younger women, ones in their teens or twenties, were armed with rifles and wore some variance of combat attire similar to the men.

Aside from the poorly constructed observation post Sauwa had encountered on the way in, the camp seemed to possess very little in the way of security. What made for defensive positions would not have stood against attacks from explosive firepower, and they would have been easily seen by any half decent recce team. As her guide had said, it was only by luck that they had not been wiped out.

"You seem to notice some of the problems we have," the jowly-faced man said, interrupting her thoughts.

"Your camp definitely has a few problems," she replied continuing to look around. Along the way, people took notice of the new face. Sauwa had removed her black watch cap to cool her sweat soaked head and allowed her long black hair to fall wildly about her shoulders. The men did not miss a new young woman in the camp. Nor did the women, who eyed her with curiosity or suspicion. Sauwa and her guide moved around the circumference of the camp, which returned the to the jowly-faced man's headquarters. Without a word, he ushered her back inside.

"I understand your situation and concern." These were the first words the jowly-faced man said as he shut the door leaving them alone once again in his office. "You don't know us, and you want to get out of here. However, as you can see, we are not soldiers. Our village was attacked. Those you see are who I was able to gather together. Since then we have been trying to fight and survive out here as guerrillas as best we can, largely because the HVO units can't afford to house us. I became the leader because I had some previous military training in my youth. I do the best I can, but I fear it is only by God's grace that my people haven't been slaughtered. It is only a matter of time before we get caught and are murdered."

Sauwa took a deep breath and released a burst of air through her lips. "Sir, I don't like the rumor mill blowing my abilities out of proportion. You're betting a lot on someone you've just met and have made several profound assessments of already."

"Please call me Marko," the jowly-faced man said pleasantly.

"Marko," Sauwa said. "How do you see me doing anything any better? And, what about my initial mission?"

Marko moved past her to where he had a large marked up map on the folding table. "It will take some time for you to plan your operation. In the meantime, you will be living here with us. Give me two weeks for starters, a few hours a day to teach some basics and offer some advice on how we can make things better. When the mission is complete, you can continue more in-depth training while we plan our way to getting you to Montenegro. In return, if you find you need assistance, those who demonstrate good soldiering can help."

As much as she didn't like it, Marko had laid out something of a reasonable solution. He was also right. His people, while eager to fight, were not soldiers, and without some development would eventually be caught by the enemy.

Marko pointed to the map. "Both the Serbs and Bosnians have kept their activities away from here. That is changing. My people have begun spotting enemy patrols as close as ten kilometers. They've been sporadic and rare, but they are becoming more frequent. My people have exchanged gunfire with them from time to time. Soon we will be much more deeply involved in this war. If we can at least be better prepared, that will help."

Sauwa considered the communal dwellings and the gathering of raggedly dressed villagers. She was also aware of the patriarchal system of the camp with the women

71

attending to the laundry and cooking pots. "You know your men aren't going to take kindly to being taught soldiering by a woman."

Marko understood her concerns. His people had enough suspicion about foreigners who were coming to their country. "It will take some time to adjust to listening to a woman, but most of my men want to learn. They want to fight even if only to defend themselves." He scratched the stubble on his chin.

"Time is what we don't have," Sauwa snapped. "I have a mission, and your enemy will soon be at your door. I watched what Oleg had to put up with leading his patrol to come and get me. Most of your troops don't realize what they're up against. For a person to be a good soldier, they have to want to be a good soldier. I don't see that desire in your people."

Marko looked at her and planned his next words carefully. "They do want to fight. We've just never had any professional instruction. They may not look it, but these people have been willing to face danger to fight the enemy. Please don't give up on us."

Sauwa pursed her lips. She didn't like shouldering such a responsibility, especially since she felt she was being judged more on embellished myths and gossip than on firsthand accounts of her actual missions. Marko was desperate, and Rommel had sent her to offer some aid to him and his force. In this country, that was as close to a legitimate resume and referral as one could hope to get. "If we organize it right, and I have people willing to train, then I will give you what I can."

Marko nodded. "That will suffice."

7

Early morning the next day, Sauwa stood several meters outside the camp. The sun was little more than a pinkish red line breaking over the mountain peak. Alone, Sauwa felt the morning chill. She pulled her watch cap further down over her ears and zipped her field jacket up just below her neck as she waited.

Marko had promised he would collect his best people for her to train. He had asked for a day to arrange things. Not wanting to make things difficult, she simply gave Marko a location and time to meet the trainees.

As promised, they came right on time. Ten silhouettes walking in a line that snaked around the bushes and plants leading up to where she was standing. Oleg was leading the group. She and Marko decided, given the suspicions held by most of his people toward outsiders, the best way to train a squad would be to train a nucleus of men that would then train the rest of Marko's forces.

They were a ragtag looking bunch — just risen from their beds and hastily throwing on their clothes. But when they reached her, they immediately gathered around and went silent waiting for her to address them. Before saying anything, she looked the would-be trainees over, taking a moment to get a feel for who she would be dealing with. As she walked slowly past the group, she studied each one. Though the men were serious in their demeanor, she could see a few suspicious looks. It was easy to assume they were concerned about being trained by a foreigner. Foreign mercenaries had dubious reputations for signing on as skilled professionals and ultimately yielding poor results. She thought of Gerald and how many like him they might have seen.

Being a female didn't help in this regard. Among the suspicious were looks of disgust, as if this was some mistake, and they weren't about to be trained by a former army clerk. It was clearly going to be an uphill battle.

She began her course with lessons in basic patrol formations explaining the different types and setting everyone into them. She discussed noise and field discipline that should be adhered to on a mission. As her Croatian was not particularly good, Oleg served as her interpreter when she couldn't find the right words or say them clearly. This also helped mitigate any complications some of the trainees might have taking orders from a woman. They could tell themselves it was Oleg they were listening to, not her. He relayed her instructions as best he could and where he couldn't communicate well enough, a personal demonstration filled the void.

For the most part, the men followed her instructions and were mostly receptive to her. But as she started out with basic firing drills, one of the men — bullish, of medium height and brawny build — became belligerent.

Oleg went over to him to discuss the matter. The man

blustering in rapid-fire Croatian edged closer until his face was within a few inches of Oleg's. Sauwa waited for the shouting to end before she walked over to investigate.

Oleg didn't wait for her to ask. "He says he already knows how to handle a weapon, and this is all a waste of his time."

The belligerent man smirked at her. Sauwa eyed him for a second, realizing this was the test she had been anticipating. Without warning, the man drew a pistol and aimed it at her head. By now, this episode had drawn the attention of the other trainees, and she could feel all eyes on her waiting to see her reaction.

The man puffed out his chest. He smiled triumphantly, gun inches from her face. His arm was fully extended, weakening his control. She couldn't help but think him stupid for holding the weapon so close to his adversary.

In the blink of an eye, her hand came up from underneath and grabbed the barrel of the gun, while her other hand firmly seized the man's wrist. With a quick twist, she pulled the weapon toward the opening of his fingers and plucked it from his hand. In a rapid almost mechanical action, she brought the weapon parallel to her chest, pressing it firmly against her body as she angled the barrel toward the bewildered man. Leaping back a few quick steps out of his reach, she gripped the weapon with both hands as she looked coldly at her adversary.

He had just gotten over the surprise of what had happened when he looked up to see the young foreigner staring back at him with his own gun pointed at him. His face burned red with anger, and he moved in her direction intending to do her serious harm for this indignity.

The loud crackle of the gun firing and a bullet tearing up

dirt just short of his foot stopped him. He looked up to see the gun being angled at his crotch. Behind the gun stood a woman with the cold, dark stare he had seen in predators just before they killed their prey.

He heard the clicking of the weapon's hammer being pulled back in preparation to fire. He saw absolutely no hesitation in her eyes. Understanding his life depended on the next move he made, the man lifted his hands surrendering. He nodded his head in capitulation and backed away.

Accepting his surrender, she lowered the weapon slowly making sure his gesture was real. She then released the magazine and ejected the round in the chamber before throwing the gun to the ground.

The collective response around her was a universal bowing of heads. Everyone returned to their positions on the firing line. She had passed their test, no one would be questioning her ability.

Oleg looked stunned.

To her surprise, this small cadre proved a vastly different type than what she had seen. They were motivated and quick learners who soaked up her teachings with eager enthusiasm. They gained a reasonably good grasp of patrol movements, even going on extended patrols that took them around the greater circle of the campsite. They completed a few field craft maneuvers and basic drills in how to react to ambushes. Eventually, they worked on building skills on silent killing — something the Croatians practiced with enthusiasm.

The first live fire and maneuver with real bullets caused her to cringe. It looked like a cross between a cheap American action movie and a Muslim wedding celebration. Lack of any injury or death could only be explained by divine intervention. However, in short order, they went from a band of wild bandits to a group that could move and communicate with a fair degree of tactical proficiency. Soon, they were moving toward objects with a clean and coordinated cover by fire in which every other man fired a quick burst toward the perceived enemy while the man to his left and right moved up a short distance toward the objective. This leapfrogging pattern was repeated until they were able to move through their enemy's position.

Sauwa was able to advance to developing better attire for the field. Luckily, Oleg was able to procure some netting, old burlap, and some dark colored paint. It was her answer to the lack of combat fatigues. Cutting up the burlap and fraying it, they dipped the burlap in the different paint colors to better blend it in with the forest vegetation. They tied the burlap strips to the netting. Initially, Oleg had offered steel hooks and wire. The hooks and wire had the potential to shine so she opted for thin strings of brown rope which were more practical for concealment. They weren't the best camouflage suits, but they offered better protection than the bright T-shirts they had been wearing.

AFTER TWO WEEKS OF TRAINING, the trainees were beginning to show promise. As agreed, Marko arranged a recce to Jablancia, about fifteen kilometers from their location. They planned the patrol for sunset, allowing them to move more openly in the darkness. Initially, Marko had wanted her to take the squad with her, giving them some experience using their new training.

Thankfully, she, along with Oleg, persuaded Marko that

such a mission was premature. It could prove more costly than beneficial. Instead, Marko agreed to let Sauwa go with Oleg and another trainee, a former outdoorsman named Sasha. Sasha supposedly knew the whole area like the back of his hand and would be able to guide her through in the dark and in areas with no defined trails.

Sunset was less than an hour away. Like a non-commissioned officer in the South African army, Sauwa had ensured Oleg and Sasha spent the day getting ample sleep and being well fed.

In the hour before they were ready to step-off, she used the time to check gear for anything reflective, and that the Croatians taped down or packed tightly anything that would jingle or make noise. The team painted dark colors on the front of their faces while adding the lighter colors to the sides along the circumference. She checked that they didn't make their coloring too dark or unnatural or that the paint job on one-half was different from the pattern on the other side. These were all things that could potentially compromise a stealthy patrol. The final touch came when everyone donned their camouflage field jackets. The jackets weren't the best but, pulled up over their heads, they did the job of breaking outlines and blending in with the surroundings.

Sauwa also finalized the last details of the patrol with Oleg and Marko. After some argument, because Oleg wanted to use the more familiar trails over the less defined areas in the bush, a route was mapped out that seemed to work just as well. It would take them along the river line, to help guide them for the first six kilometers where they would be in territory still deemed to be relatively safe. Afterward, they would veer off two kilometers inland into the bushes where they would pick up a familiar area that they would follow the rest of the way to the town.

Sunset was in its beginning stages when the team stepped off. Staying within the tree line, the three moved along the river. She had taught hand and arms signals that would help reduce the need for conversation. Yet, like any tactical movement, verbal communication was still occasionally necessary. Keeping a seven-meter dispersion, the team moved through the grass and shrubs.

Sauwa was impressed. For the most part, the two guerrillas had taken her lessons to heart as they carefully observed their surroundings.

Bosnia was a land of mountains and high rolling hills. It had been a bone of contention that Sasha and Oleg wanted to take to the high ground of the hills to be able to observe better. In the darkness of the night, they were adamant they would be safe. Sauwa had to calmly explain that the hills offered no concealment, and they would be visible at a distance with the moonlight shining down on them.

"It's called skylining," she said.

Even walking along the side of the hills, they were still in the open on grassy fields and would be noticed by anyone in the area. They needed to keep to the base of the hill, out of the moonlight, and well concealed in the darkness and vegetation.

Arriving at the river break Oleg had chosen for the turnoff point, Sauwa brought the team to a halt. In the remaining sunlight, she could still use her hands to communicate. She had trained the Croatians to slowly drop to one knee, their weapons facing outward with every other man facing the opposite direction.

She had appreciated Oleg as an interpreter during the

training, and he was proving now to be an adept student when it came to her instructions. He remained silent, constantly switching his attention between watching her and watching the surrounding terrain. In similar fashion, Sasha kept his attention focusing forward and on the river.

Sound travels better at night. She closed her eyes, listened for alien noises, and heard nothing. After ten minutes, she decided the patrol was safe to continue and put herself and the team in a tactical triangular formation. She reduced the distance to three meters, keeping them apart but close enough to hear each other and see general outlines.

The patrol started off slowly, their feet rustling as they marched through high grass and navigated bushes that grabbed at their arms and legs. Between their inexperience and the darkness, the Croatian's frustration built as they struggled to understand Sauwa's hand motions. Somehow, she managed to convey what needed to be done without having to talk.

She had trained them to stop every two hundred meters for a five-minute pause to listen for sounds warning them of any enemy in the area.

Oleg grabbed her arm and pointed to a contorted looking tree. It was the marker for the location where they were to turn and make for the town. Rotating positions, Sasha became the point man. According to Oleg, he knew the area better than anyone. He had spent years as a professional hunter before the country's collapse. He was also one of the trainees who didn't seem to have a problem with not talking. With a nod from Sauwa, the lanky ex-hunter took off into the woods. She and Oleg followed behind.

Sporadic clusters of small trees and lush bushes broke up the otherwise open grassy fields of the high hills. As the space between hills narrowed, the team found themselves having to move higher up the slope. The further up they went, the thinner the vegetation and the more the moonlight exposed them.

While the moonlight helped the guerrillas see, it made the threat of skylining more of a danger. Sauwa moved the team back into a single column and took up the middle following closely behind Sasha. She directed him to stay as low on the hill face as possible where the moonlight wasn't focused and closer to the bushes where they could blend in with the landscape. It was a tactical game not easy to play.

8

The guerrillas arrived near sunrise. They were exhausted from the hours moving up and around the labyrinth of hills and the shrub line of the lower country. Sauwa estimated they had another thirty minutes before daybreak. The town was just in sight, the few lights still working provided enough illumination to give them a good outline of most of the town.

The moonlight had largely dissipated leaving the surrounding hills nearly black. Sauwa searched for a good location for their operation in the short time remaining. During an initial recce of the area, she wanted to get a good lay of the general landscape and military activity that went on. But, unfamiliar with the area, she didn't want to risk moving and finding herself in exposed terrain when the sun came up. As if reading her thoughts, Sasha touched her shoulder. He murmured something in Croatian. Oleg sidled up close to her from the other side and whispered into her ear. "He said, he knows these hills very well and knows where best to go to stay hidden."

She sighed, keeping her eyes focused on the town ahead. "Are there places I can get a good look at the town and its people?"

Oleg didn't have to repeat the question. Sasha murmured again. Oleg turned back to Sauwa's ear. "He says he knows what you need; he has hunted and trapped all over these hills. He will take us to where you can see and not be in danger."

Having no other option and not knowing what she was facing yet, Sauwa agreed. Sasha moved around her and knelt down scanning the town. Reaching his arm behind him he tapped Sauwa on the thigh, a sign to follow him. She rose to her feet. He stepped left and walked into a thicket of bushes. Sauwa followed closely behind with Oleg on her tail.

The morning dew dripped from the plants onto their clothing. Combined with the cold, sunless air, all three felt miserable. Sauwa kept close to Sasha who moved like a predator. It was clear he was now a man in his element. Meanwhile, she continued to look at the town, which came in and out of sight, vanishing behind tall grass or thick bushes as they progressed. She only hoped Sasha remembered the threat not hunting wild game and keeping his mind on not getting caught by armed enemy soldiers.

After three hundred meters, she grabbed hold of Sasha's shirt, stopping him in his stride. He turned back to face her and could see her cupping her ear. A reminder that they still needed to stop and listen, especially now that they were deep in enemy territory. They paused, listened. There was no sound aside from the singing of a few birds signaling the start of the day.

Sauwa ordered the movement to resume by giving a

slight shove to Sasha's arm. The lanky man moved forward, but this time with hesitancy. Apparently, the pause for listening had been a sobering reminder of what they were doing. His steps were more deliberate and cautious. Not that he hadn't been before, but now it seemed his nerves were getting the better of him. Sauwa began to worry. It was their first actual mission. They weren't just traipsing about in a relatively safe territory. She looked back at Oleg, concerned he might be falling into the same state of mind. He seemed to be handling himself better than his colleague, yet he had also shown signs that he realized the dangerous situation they were in.

The team pressed on, listening at appropriate intervals. However, where the Croatians had been slightly exasperated by the constant stopping, they now seemed to embrace the security stops, holding their breaths, waiting for any noise that told them the enemy was near. The first three stops had been quiet. On the fourth, they caught the sound of twigs snapping, then heard more sounds indicating movement was nearby. They heard a man's voice — the language clearly Bosnian — confirming their worst fear. The voice seemed to be giving orders.

Hunkered in a thicket of bushes, the trio waited silently. Sauwa took a series of slow, deep breaths to get her heart rate down and keep her nerves in check. Behind her, she could feel Oleg shiver. Ahead of her, Sasha tensed, becoming a statue.

She curled her camouflage cover around her and knelt down as low as possible in the hopes it would cover her legs and feet. She wanted to ensure the Croatians had done the same, but it would be too much movement while the

Bosnian soldiers were so near. The trio waited in complete stillness with as little noise as they could manage — something Oleg was having serious difficulty with. Tension rose when the Bosnians began to pass them. They listened to the sounds of many feet and the feel of their bodies scrapping against the very bushes that shielded Sauwa and her companions. A slight metallic clanking, distinctive to rifles, cut through the oppressive quiet, sending a chill down the spines of all three. Sauwa had been in this position many times in her life, more so since coming to this country. It was a frightening experience every time.

The patrol moved with a laziness that suggested men just coming off of a mission or ending the last round on a long security check. In either case, the tired sound of the few voices speaking and the way their feet dropped suggested they were not highly alert.

Light appeared along the eastern crest of the hills. Sauwa could feel the slight vibrations of Oleg shaking. She wanted to turn and slap him but resisted the urge hoping the men just a few feet away would not notice.

Finally, the last man passed them. The Bosnian voices faded as the patrol trudged away. When the voices were little more than a whisper, all three guerrillas took massive sighs of relief. Sasha clutched his chest as if he were about to have a heart attack, and Oleg fell onto his back gasping like a dying man. Sauwa raced to reassert control. With a finger pressed tightly to her lips, she indicated the need for them to stay quiet. Both men composed themselves remembering the present danger.

THE BOSNIANS WERE GONE.

She pushed Sasha to continue. Nervously, he moved to stand up, dropping once, when he heard a twig break, but he controlled himself and found his feet. Sauwa rose along with him, keeping close. Oleg remained on his back. She waved her hand to have him move, but he just lay on the ground shaking his head defiantly. She kicked his foot to punctuate her order. Slowly, the Croatian rose. She knew all too well that given the choice, he would have run back to camp. She gave him a second to understand such an option was no longer open. He could only press on with them.

Sasha and Oleg moved more slowly, their nerves clearly getting to them. They jumped at every sound they heard. In their eagerness and inexperience, Sauwa worried they would rashly open fire and alert everyone to their presence. But the few other enemy patrols they did run across were at a considerable distance and easy to avoid. Gradually, the Croatians began to relax.

True to his word, Sasha brought them to a spot along the face of a hill that offered a wide view of the town below and the surrounding area. Though along the side of a high elevation hill, the spot was nestled deep in the bushes and hid them perfectly. Lush as it was, the foliage also gave the protection needed for them to move about more freely. Using her binoculars, Sauwa observed the town.

Jablancia looked like what she had come to expect of Bosnia — bombed out buildings and piles of rubble. In happier times, it had probably been a nice place to visit — a collection of uniform, concrete, two and three-story buildings intermixed with small and mid-sized houses. The town was wedged tightly on one side of a plateau encircled by the river below and surrounded by high hills. It was connected to the outside world through a few bridges protruding from various points of the town that crossed over the winding river.

To her surprise, the atmosphere of the place was somber but more relaxed than she expected. Whatever fighting had gone on in the past had taken place a while ago. People went about their daily routines as if the war didn't exist. Soldiers half-heartedly walked the edge of the plateau periodically glancing around to keep up with expectations but not seriously contemplating a threat coming up the jagged ledge and steep hill. Beyond the few guards, the edges of the plateau were left relatively defenseless. The only serious effort made for their defense was at the entry points of the two concrete bridges that were still intact. The third bridge had been demolished by artillery fire, most likely from the Serb military.

The bridges were hives of activity with makeshift military vehicles and patrols of foot soldiers coming and going in between civilians doing business outside. The checkpoint consisted of a wood guard shack bundled under walls of sandbags next to another smaller wall of sandbags built up in a defensive position. A heavily powered, belt-fed machine gun was mounted on top. The guard's gate seemed to be more a gathering point. It was devoid of any real command structure, uniform protocols, or visible leadership. The guards were not a trained element operating with a practiced system but went about their jobs as if they had no clear understanding of what they were doing.

Occasionally someone who appeared to be in a position of authority showed up to check on the guards. From the look of the uniform, Sauwa assumed he was a junior officer. The officer did cursory checks and gave the hollow snaps and points of a commander going through the motions of asserting his authority. Otherwise, he performed cosmetic checks pretending he knew what he was doing. The guards changed after four hours. It was a clumsy display of hand-shaking, a whimsical conversation between friends, and the old guards gradually left. Like the previous guards, the relief force settled into a similar pattern of haphazard performance.

The trio spent most of the day in their observation post watching the bridge activity and the general bustle of the town. They sat through two more shift changes of the guards, executed every four hours, give or take twenty minutes. The officer in charge appeared to be the newest most inexperienced person among the guards...and the only recognized authority.

She then turned her focus to the buildings beyond the gate. From her position, she could look down on the whole plateau. The town occupied one side. Grass fields covered the rest. The buildings along the edge looked empty or were housing lower ranked civilians. She watched the movements of the soldiers and sketched the buildings they frequented, trying to figure out what places were being used for military purposes and for what reasons.

Considerable activity was concentrated near a cluster of small houses on the land next to a draw between two large hills. It seemed this was where most of the hierarchy congre-gated. Directly after making his checks, the officer in charge of the bridge guard reported to one of the houses. He would pay his respects to the men gathering around the house and enter hastily. A few minutes later he would emerge and continue with whatever business he had. It was the same procedure and location ever time, the one stable act in an otherwise unstable routine.

By early afternoon, Sauwa directed Sasha and Oleg to pick up and move locations. Sasha breathed more steadily now. Oleg still took each step with hesitation anticipating another close run-in with the Bosnians. He had not been happy when Sauwa made him place his weapon on safe. She figured it would make him useless in a gunfight should they come across the enemy suddenly, but the idea of a gunfight breaking out because of his irrationality was an even greater possibility.

Sasha steered them around the hill slope. Sauwa no longer had to remind him about stopping to listen for alien sounds. He was doing it all on his own. He was also more cautious about negotiating bushes, reducing noise, and being careful not to leave broken branches and plants that would draw someone's attention and give them a trail to follow.

Normally, she didn't like moving around in such lightly concealed terrain during the day. However, there were relatively few Bosnian security patrols except for the patrol they had encountered in the early morning. Not enough to indicate the Bosnians felt a genuine threat in the immediate area.

Nearly an hour and a half later, they rounded the hillside and came to another well-concealed observation perch with a better view of the Bosnian leadership's housing area. Using her binoculars, Sauwa concentrated on the main house, certain it was the headquarters. The houses sat along a road guarded at either end. The guards were more attentive and were restricting access, admitting only officers. The men roaming about the houses wore uniforms hosting leadership insignias.

A greater number of soldiers patrolled the land routes around the lower half of the hills. She saw another defensive position built of sandbag fortifications and protected by more belt-fed machine guns—the same type as those guarding the bridges — pointing down the draw between them. They were Belgian Fabrique National 240 Golfs, used generally by the militaries of the North Atlantic Treaty Organization. She could only assume they were part of the illegal weapons shipments supplied by the Pakistanis. Defensive positions lined all the main entry points of the land connection, the only direct means in or out through the hills. They were skillfully established, maintaining interlocking fields of fire that could sweep the entire landscape, offering no visible means for an enemy to mount a frontal assault.

Oleg shifted his position, restless. Sauwa ignored him.

She had noticed a couple of senior commanders walking around one of the defensive positions in the company of a man dressed in civilian attire. The civilian was waving his hands as he spoke describing something to the Bosnians. The civilian motioned to the defensive position and the area in front of them. The Bosnian commanders nodded their heads and moved down to one of the machine guns instructing the gunner in positioning it better.

Finally.

Sauwa narrowed her focus. She recognized the civilian from photographs she had seen. Selim Abhajiri may have dressed the part of a diplomat or businessman, but his mannerisms and behavior were those of a soldier — an officer, a high ranking one, judging by the way he commanded the men around him. From his hand gestures, Abhajiri appeared to be advising the Bosnian commanders on their base security plan. Sauwa would bet the defensive line along the land connection was his work. The fighting line looked to be new, the sandbags only recently put in.

The contrast between the lax security at the bridges and the far better operation at the land connection led Sauwa to believe she was looking at the Iranian's first project. Logic dictated that, in time, he would heighten security around the entire base. Doing so would eventually make infiltration that much harder.

Abhajiri never stopped moving as he walked the line. He made sudden and unpredictable shifts in direction, veering off to different sides creating a lazy zigzag pattern. It took her time to realize he was doing this deliberately. His movements were those of a man anticipating an assassination shot from a distance with a long rifle. Unceasing, unpredictable movement while out in the open made sniper considerations impossible.

Oleg and Sasha grew more impatient. The long night and day and hours kneeling in shrubs had taken a toll on the two men. The boredom of having nothing to do wasn't helping either. They were becoming complacent and struggling to stay awake. Their attentions were focused more on finding a place to get comfortable and less on their surroundings. On a few occasions, Sauwa found herself having to kick and nudge the men to get them to stay alert. She was also struggling to keep awake and focused on her recce as the day wore on.

Abhajiri retreated back into the row of houses used by the commanders. The guards at the entrance parted to create an entrance as he brushed past them. Sauwa no longer harbored any doubts of who the Iranian was. Walking down the road, he disappeared into the second to the last house. An hour later he emerged wearing a new shirt and sipping from a bottle. He leaned up against the house taking his time to relax. It was the only time since Sauwa had caught sight of him that he had been stationary, but he was protected from any long distance shot by buildings on both sides. Thus, confirming her initial suspicions that he was a highly trained professional operative fully aware of the possible sniper locations around him. He would not be an easy target.

IT WAS NEARLY SUN up when the trio reached their camp. They were greeted by a crowd of excited countrymen happy to see their loved ones. As the crowd mobbed her two companions, Sauwa quietly slipped off toward Marko's trailer. She was tired and hungry, but she wanted to have a quick discussion with the guerrilla leader.

Marko was standing just outside his office enjoying a cigarette when he saw the mercenary covered in her strange camouflage garb. She could have been playing the role of a forest creature in a low budget movie.

"You should eat and get some rest, my dear," he said with a note of paternal sympathy. "You look like you're going to fall over any minute."

She must have looked as bad as she felt.

"We need to talk," she said.

Marko moved aside and held the door open for her. She stepped inside quietly. Throwing off her camouflage field jacket and hat, she dropped her Bergen to the floor with a thump. She didn't wait to be offered a seat before she plopped into the nearest chair. The guerrilla leader made no protest as he passed her to take his usual seat. "What is so important?"

Massaging her forehead to keep her mind lucid, she fought the fatigue overtaking her. "The Iranian. How did you obtain the information on him?"

Marko shot the mercenary a look of confusion. "A few of our people have good standing and move about the area relatively freely. They shot the photos and made notes for our file."

"And the Bosnians have no difficulty with them being Croatian?" Sauwa found it all irregular given the deep ethnic tensions between the factions involved.

Marko nodded. "Some merchants have the means to obtain things that are not easily obtainable in this war. That has a tendency to create forgiveness even in some of the staunchest enemies."

Sauwa still distrusted Marko's plan. "The Iranian is advising the Bosnians all right. They're developing their base defenses as we speak. Those information sources you've been relying on are going to dry up in the not too distant future. It won't be long before you're flying blind. I would advise that you move your base to a more defendable location. Watching this guy from a distance, he seemed to know what he was doing, and he was definitely turning the Bosnians around as a fighting force. It won't be long before they start running more aggressive patrols out here. When they do, they will find you. This place is open to attack, especially with the Iranian advising them on how to run an assault."

At first, Marko looked like he was humoring a petulant child. He studied her — the hardened sincerity pressed on her face — and his own expression turned serious. He reminded himself that this was the professional advisor he had asked for. And, she was giving him her professional opinion. "Very well, where do you suggest we go?"

"I need a better understanding of the terrain," Sauwa explained. "Let me take some scouting parties out to see what I can find. It will be good practice for the troops. They'll be confronting the enemy sooner than you think."

Marko ruminated as he sat in his chair, uncomfortable with the news he was receiving. He didn't look forward to fighting professional soldiers with people who were barely learning how to handle a gun. "How well are the trainees coming?" He needed to hear some reassuring news.

Rising to her feet, a persistent ache permeating her body, she stretched out her back. "They're coming along well for what I've been able to teach them. They're eager and attentive. They absorb the training and are taking it seriously, but it's only been a few days of basic tactics with no idea how much time I have to train them until they have to be put into action."

"Whatever you can give me will have to suffice," Marko replied in a defeated tone.

"I've made some sketches and taken notes from the recce." She pulled out a disorganized pile of documents from her coat pocket and proceeded to stuff them into her Bergen. "I was hoping I could use your office to plan my mission."

The Croatian nodded absently. His thoughts were stuck on the mercenary's report. Sauwa gathered her gear and rolled up her camouflage field jacket. She tied the bundle onto her Bergen and lifted it onto her shoulder. "Could you leave the notes and sketches with me for my review?" Marko asked, his hands out as if begging for a handout.

"When I'm here using your office, you can review them. But I need this information for planning my own mission, and I can't afford to have it lost," Sauwa yawned. Though tired, her voice resonated with cold finality.

Wearily, she exited the office and made her way down a slight hill to a collection of tents where a few campers were gathered together in a semi-circle. Sitting in the middle of them were a group of women. They laughed and gossiped and passed around cups of tea and bowls of soup ladled from large kettles simmering over an open fire.

Sauwa walked into the circle and plopped down next to a couple of young girls barely out of their teens. Half dead and feeling little ability to move, she eyed the kettles with a look of despair. She was both hungry and thirsty, but her body was refusing to let her stand up again. Such a simple act was now a major life decision.

One of the young girls, who went by the name of Enya, went over and fetched one of the bowls from a pile and dipped it into the soup kettle. She followed the same routine with a smaller metal cup and the tea kettle. She returned to where Sauwa was laying and handed them to her. "You must keep up your strength." The girl's English was quite good. She had spent time attending school in England when she was younger.

Taking the cup and bowl, Sauwa nodded. "Thank you." The soup was potato mixed with a variety of indigenous herbs and vegetables and ladened with an abundance of salt. In the weary state she was in, it tasted delicious. She washed it down with the tea that flowed down her parched throat with a heavenly delight. Only in such conditions could one appreciate such simplistic meals as if they were high-end delicacies.

"We need you functioning," Enya said with a mischievous, girlish smile. "Oleg has been bragging to the men about your adventure. He spoke of your mission sneaking about the highly guarded enemy facility. He speaks as if he were like that American cinema character, Rambo. He is now acting like a seasoned commando telling everyone what it's like in combat behind enemy lines." The young girl might have suspected some exaggeration or fallacy to Oleg's account.

Sauwa chuckled, shook her head and sipped her tea. *This was how the legends start,* Sauwa thought to herself, devouring the last of her soup and washing it down with the last drops of her tea.

After the meal, Sauwa, at Enya's and a few of the other girls' insistence, walked down to a small pond the ladies used for washing.

The girls took turns standing guard while the others stripped naked and bathed. The water was naturally cold, but it was worse in the early morning. Sauwa shivered as she slid into the water along with a few of the other girls. Rubbing the bar of soap over her body, Sauwa scraped at the camo paint cemented on her face. The mud beneath her feet was slushy and unnerving as she walked about in the slimy substance wondering what things she was coming in contact with.

The bath ended with Sauwa dunking her head in the cold pool. It was a relief when she leaped from the water onto the grass. Her shirt from the night's mission served as her towel. Hastily, she dressed in her fatigues. Though tired, she returned the courtesy by taking up guard while Enya and the others took their turn in the bath.

When they were done, Sauwa slipped back to the quar-

J. E. HIGGINS

ters assigned to her — a big, green canvass tent that housed most of the young women. Picking a free spot, she rolled out her bedding. Tucking her weapon and gear where it was easily accessible, she fell back onto the ground and within seconds had fallen asleep.

9

Threeweeks... The next few weeks went off in a relatively normal routine.

Sauwa spent her time taking the trainees through assorted battle drills dealing with "react to contact","react to ambush," and how to move in larger sized patrols with advanced teams or with flanking teams covering the sides. The trainees continued to learn quickly. They understood too well what they were preparing for. The lessons were also facilitated by Oleg and later Enya bridging the language gap. What phrases and words Sauwa did understand were hardly enough to be conversant and were not enough to deliver the detailed instruction she needed to give.

Such attentiveness and determination allowed Sauwa to progress to more complex concepts such as deceptive moves aimed at leading them or their enemy into traps with decoy actions. From there, they covered ambushes, starting out with the basic linear forms and graduating to the more advanced forms, such as L-shaped and V-shaped. As her squad of trainees became more proficient with their new skills, they began to train the rest of the fighters in the camp. They were behaving like professional mercenaries themselves, speaking as though the knowledge they passed on had come through hard lessons learned on the battlefield.

They also, at her request, moved their campsite to a new location. After a few patrols with the trainees, Sauwa found the ideal location deep in woods along the river. A canopy of trees shielded them from anyone looking from surrounding hills. A wall of thick bushes grew all around the area like a labyrinth that would deter most foot patrols.

Based on Sauwa's advice, Marko set up observation posts a mile down on each end along the river to serve as an advance warning of an enemy patrol by boat. Sauwa had walked along the river a mile in both directions. Amidst the virtually impenetrable wall of trees and shrubs that guarded the waterline, she found a few weak points where an enemy could penetrate after they passed the observation posts.

Using an old trick taught to her by her uncle from his Rhodesian bush war days, she set about with some of the Croatians making rows of sharp pointed wooden stakes. She had them placed into a dugout part of the ground, set in lines three rows deep encompassing the distance of the entryway, covered by a painted sheet of burlap, and finally covered with some leaves and shrubs. The trick was having the enemy come in, step on the burlap and fall or step into the bed of sharply pointed stakes. It would slow up an infiltration and lessen the need for guerrillas to guard the area. As a precaution, they repeated the procedure and set up another identical trap a few meters away — a second surprise for an enemy continuing their advance.

The Croatians were made to leave their trailers behind after sanitizing them for anything an enemy force might use for intelligence purposes. This did not go over well. Marko, in particular, nearly cried when Sauwa informed him that he had to leave his cherished office and settle for a tent.

It was an argument she fought hard to win. They were a guerrilla band with limited weapons and women and children to protect. If the enemy mounted an attack, they would have no real means to defend themselves. It was vital that the camp remain as hidden as possible. That meant dispensing with larger, more cumbersome things that would leave trails or be more easily spotted from a distance. Sauwa had won the fight, but she still suffered vengeful stares from many who hated giving up their few luxuries.

In between the camp relocation and her training duties, she found time to go on a few more recces to build more intelligence against her target. She attempted only one more recce on the enemy base before deciding her concerns were well-founded and security was becoming tighter. The lax and disorganized operation she had first seen had been replaced with a much more efficient and developed set up than what had existed a week ago. The guard posts were better established as were the machine gun positions defending them. Every bridge had a set team with an identified soldier in charge of operating from more established protocols.

In the same period, true to her prediction, security at the town began to tighten up on the Croatian merchants and workers who had been the lifeline of intelligence for the guerrillas and the Croatian forces. Reports came back that the Croatians coming in and going out were now searched thoroughly and many were being denied access to the town altogether. Even inside the town, Croatians were given escorts who stayed with them at all times. They were barred from many sections of the city, especially anywhere near the houses where the Bosnian command operated. Abhajiri certainly knew his business and was onto the growing security threat the Bosnians had for so long overlooked. Although this setback didn't end the intelligence connection, it certainly limited its effectiveness and general significance.

And just like the bridges, the external security was becoming more cumbersome. Twice in her second recce, she nearly stumbled upon a couple of hidden observation posts manned by Bosnian soldiers. They were set up to cover identified avenues of approach. Trying to maneuver with so many hidden observers would be impossible, particularly when trying to make an escape. Sauwa ended the recce with the understanding that taking her target at his base camp was entirely impractical. The problem was she didn't see any other truly viable option.

When not training or out on a mission, Sauwa spent much of her time in Marko's tent pouring over maps and photos of the area and the notes she had jotted down on each recce. She read and re-read her notes and scoured the maps, telling herself she was missing something. But no matter how many times she repeated this exercise, the answer was the same. She gave up on the base and pondered a roadside operation. Eventually, she determined she needed a different location altogether.

Her other missions consisted of studying the vehicle convoys along the road systems. What she hadn't noticed in her first recce was the paved roadway that cut along the edge of one of the hills overlooking the river. The Bosnians ran several logistical trains over this road every day. It was a lifeline for much of their operation. Strangely, for as much traffic that passed by, she was surprised by the remarkably scarce amount of security that accompanied it. Neither had she failed to notice how little heavy firepower accompanied the convoys themselves. In each case, the security seemed to be relegated to a complement of soldiers riding in the back of a single large troop carrier.

The truck was always covered, which meant the soldiers had no visibility outside. In the event of an actual attack, they would have to get their bearings as they leaped from the vehicle while under fire. Even better, they were all concentrated in a single location. With enough firepower focused on them, they could be neutralized quickly, leaving the rest of the convoy defenseless. It would be a good start for a guerrilla force looking to step up their campaign.

With this in mind, she reviewed her notes and what she got from the dossier. The Iranian was, by all accounts, a field man who took his job seriously. What if they could create an attack hitting the convoy hard enough to warrant a serious response and force the Iranian to come out of the base to review the situation?

As she pursued the idea, she realized there might be a second option for her target after all and began to formulate a plan.

Selim Abhajiri had a long career fighting in support of Iran. It had started in his youth when he first joined the thousands of young men answering the cause of the Islamic revolution in the initial stages of the war with Iraq. Luckily for him, the extensive education he had received in Great Britain's Eton College and later the prestigious military academy at Sandhurst, had spared him the fate of so many of his generation. Young men — poorly educated peasants pulled from the countryside — lost their lives as martyrs being sent across open minefields, charging into Iraqi machine guns or delivering explosives as suicide bombers. It was a desperate response by the government to combat a much larger, better equipped, and better trained Iraqi army.

What few combat units the Iranians could muster and train were in urgent need of competent leadership after Ayatollah Khomeini had purged the military ranks of most military officers. Abhajiri suddenly found himself an officer in the newly formed Iranian Revolutionary Guard, the Pasdaran. The next ten years saw his career fluctuate between the brutal slaughter of the border war and a series of special assignments to the Mediterranean that took him to the clandestine training camps run by the elite and secretive Force 17.

Force 17 was the special commando unit of the Palestinian military wing. Developed by the infamous terrorist leader, Ali Hassan Salemi, the unit had received extensive training from several of the world's best commando units: the Soviet Union Spetsnaz, North Korea's naval combat assault units, East Germany's naval combat swimmers and Egypt's and Morocco's own commando units. Force 17 quickly became the response to the Israeli commando assaults being staged in Lebanon conducting a series of successful infiltrations of their own against the heavily guarded Israeli coastline.

In late 1979, while the revolution was taking over Iran, agents of the Revolutionary Guard approached the Palestinians with a request to help set up and train their own commando unit. This unit would be used to hunt down and eliminate those identified as counter-revolutionaries. At the time, for certain political reasons, the Palestinians declined the request. By the mid-eighties, tension in the Mediterranean had become dire as Israel invaded Lebanon, then the Palestinian stronghold. Desperate for allies, Force 17 began informally opening its training to select members of the Revolutionary Guard and the Iranian supported Hezbollah.

Abhajiri had been one of the few fortunate enough to attend the advanced commando training, at which he excelled, taking part in a few commando missions to gain experience.

He had not necessarily planned on a military career. Sandhurst Military Academy had been more of his father's idea. Abhajiri proved to be an adept soldier, demonstrating his abilities numerous times on the battlefield and eventually advancing into the officer ranks in the Revolutionary Guard's elite al-Quds Special Forces unit. Since the end of the war in 1988, he had been part of Iran's covert strategy, operating in clandestine missions abroad or assisting with training and organizing his country's allies.

Now in Bosnia, under some meaningless cover that was supposed to give him a reason to be out in the middle of a war zone, he was performing his duty yet again.

He had had many such covers in his life. What was he supposed to be this time? An agricultural specialist? A trade and commerce advisor? Or was it something else? He only needed to know enough to explain his being where he was. And that was a war zone in a country in chaos.

Leaning back in a creaky, wooden chair that sounded as if it would break any second, he watched the frenetic actions of those in the planning office from his place in the corner. The soldiers of the Army of the Republic of Bosnia and Herzegovina shifted from table to table reviewing their charts, maps, and any recent intelligence reports. They had come a long way since he had arrived several months ago. Back then, the headquarters looked like a badly organized archive of documents spread about in forgotten piles. Intelligence reports were non-existent and each commander planned from their own maps without talking to each other. As a result, units created redundancies and duplicated missions that wasted time and resources.

It had been a fight, but gradually Abhajiri had managed to turn things around. He organized a more fluid system, establishing a general map where all forces and their locations were identified. He implemented evening briefings to ensure all commanders were aware of the missions going on around them, so the Colonel in charge could better direct resources and make decisions. The Iranian also persuaded the command to develop a more sophisticated intelligence system by having units report back to a designated intelligence officer to be debriefed when returning from a mission. This was a step up from the previous arrangement, whereby soldiers would recount their mission over meals in the mess tent.

Thankfully, while many of the officers were resistant to change, the Pukovnik (Colonel) commanding the unit was interested in bettering the disposition of his operation. The Colonel took the Iranian advisor's ideas seriously. In the last few months, the Bosnian forces had scored several key victories against the encroaching Serb forces, driving them back and securing the immediate area.

Colonel Hvardic Mjovich, satisfied with his victory dispatching the Serbs, now wanted to direct his attention to the Croatian guerrillas operating in the area. A little less than a year ago the Croatian and Bosnian leaders had decided to realign themselves after the Croatians broke the first alliance to side with the Serbs. Bad blood remained among the rank and file levels and fighting between military units persisted. Colonel Mjovich had little love for the Croatians, who he regarded as opportunists and traitors. Whether his government had ordered it or not, he continued to engage the Croatian fighters.

Abhajiri had tried to dispel his Bosnian hosts of such a notion, judging it as a waste of time and resources. However, the troops shared the Colonel's attitude, and it was in their interest to keep such hostility alive to better their own relationship with the Muslim Bosnians. Abhajiri had decided to let the issue go where it would.

Draining his tea, the Iranian took one last look around the planning office. Determining matters were well in hand, he stood up and made his way to the door.

Outside, the chilled air caught him off guard. He wrapped his coat more tightly around his body and raised the collar to keep the cold air off his neck. He crossed the road and gazed up at the surrounding hillside. The trees covering the lower portions of the elevated areas made him nervous. Too many comrades had survived vicious battles only to die in the safety of a base camp by a well-aimed shot from a sniper. One had died less than a meter away from Abhajiri while in the middle of a conversation.

Snipers in this war were used heavily by all sides with great effectiveness. Yet, outside the cities, commanders tended to focus more on the conventional military threats — the severity of artillery barrages or the slaughter brought on by heavy machine gun fire — and not consider the lone gunmen firing single shots from a distance. To them, snipers were an annoyance, nothing more, so when Abhajiri had broached the issue with the Bosnian command, it received only mild attention.

Once across the road, Abhajiri entered a house like the one he had just left. Inside, men with senior insignias on their uniforms were having a meeting. This was the strategy center for the command. In the room he'd just left, officers gathered day to day information and moved pieces on maps. This room was used to discuss the longer-term strategies and plans for their area and situation.

Colonel Mjovich sat at the head of an elongated wood table like a king presiding over his court. Flanking him were his senior officers. Further down the table were commanders of the various sub-units. The mood was somber, not festive nor defeated. At the moment, the room was still, except for Mjovich, whose finger tapped rhythmically on the table.

"Anything of interest to report?" The Colonel broke the silence. His question was directed at Abhajiri.

"Nothing you don't already know," Abhajiri said casually. He rounded the table and took a seat directly across from the senior commander. "The Serbs are still in retreat. So far, they are showing no sign of building any counter-offensive. I still advise keeping their feet to the fire and remaining relentless in your push."

The Colonel continued tapping his finger as if he were composing a musical piece. "I concur. Ensure all priority is given to that effort. I don't want to give those bastard Serbs a chance to regroup. In less than a week, we should have this area fully under our control."

Heads bobbed along the table, accompanied by wide toothy grins of satisfaction. This had been the news these men had wanted to hear for almost a year.

Mjovich looked over at the Iranian and gave him a complimentary nod of the head. The Colonel knew it had been the counsel of his foreign associate that had been the decisive factor. Through Abhajiri, they had effectively neutralized the guerrilla elements working behind their lines on behalf of the Serb army, the Jugoslavenska Narodna Armija (Yugoslav National Army) or (JNA). Abhajiri had also been instrumental in aiding in the planning and coordination that turned the tables on what would have been a Serb victory.

"Now comes the next part of our business," the Colonel scratched his salt-n-pepper beard. "The Croatian scum must be dealt with. We have sightings of armed bands of Croatian guerrillas in the area. Until now we have overlooked them in our area because they haven't been much of a threat."

"Disorganized nuisances really," snorted one of the junior commanders.

"Exactly," Mjovich smiled but only for a moment. "We are supposed to be in an alliance with the HVO bastards again." The room returned to silence. All eyes were on the Colonel anticipating his next words. "Just because politicians make peace sitting across a table in comfortable offices doesn't mean the men fighting and dying can so easily forget such betrayal."

The support in the room for the commander's words was palpable. "I don't care what some piece of paper scribbled with a bunch of ink says. They betrayed us because they wanted more land for themselves. They're greedy and treacherous, and I want them off Bosnian land just as much as I want the fucking Serbs gone. Now is the time to discuss our second front in this war. We need to intensify our campaign against the Croats. Up 'til now, you have had mild engagements with them. From this point, your orders are to engage the Croatian military or suspected guerrillas when you see them. I think it's time we begin the next phase — initiate a more active seek-and-destroy mission."

Abhajiri remained silent throughout these pronouncements. He did not feel it prudent to interrupt during such emotional tirades. He didn't deny the grievance and suspicions the Bosnians had for the Croatians. The Croatians had broken the initial alliance and allied themselves with the Serbs with the understanding they could carve out their own land in the deal. He certainly did not object to the continued hostility against the Croatian army, the HVO. His own government wished to promote any rift that would isolate the Muslims from other factions.

It was the campaign against the alleged guerrillas that concerned the Iranian. There hadn't been much conflict thus far with the Croatians residing in the area. And, Mjovich and his subordinates seemed to have a very liberal definition when it came to who they described or considered *guerrillas*. At a time when the Serb army presented the greatest threat, he thought the eagerness of the Bosnians to commit to such an aggressive measure was dangerously unwise. But Abhajiri had always opted to choose his words and moments carefully. This time was no different.

After riling his men, Colonel Mjovich moved to discuss the planning. "From the reports we have received, these guerrillas have taken to setting up encampments in the forests. We need to locate these camps. Once we do, we can take measures to eradicate the threat. I have been conferring with our esteemed friend." He waved his hand in the direction of Abhajiri. "He has helped us devise a strategy to more efficiently execute this operation so that we are not clowning around out there."

The Iranian gave a reluctant and awkward bow from his chair not knowing how else to respond.

The Colonel pressed on. "Please, sir, if you would. What is your advice?"

All eyes were now on the Iranian waiting for his wisdom. His initial thoughts were to explain the sheer stupidity of the plan and encourage them to abandon the idea. He envisioned second and third order effects they may not be prepared to deal with. But it was not the right time.

He rose and walked over to a large map hung across an entire wall of the house. "Right now, what we need to be focused on is the intelligence portion of this operation. As the commander has stated, we have begun to focus on these guerrillas. We know little about them other than they exist and are operating in our forests. So far, they have been active only against the Serbs and even then only on a small scale. We need to figure out their level of training, capabilities, and any support they are getting from the HVO or whether the HVO is directing them at all. We can figure this out by capturing a few of these folks and getting the information from them. Next, we isolate the areas where these camps might be located. If we control their movement, we can marginalize their threat. Close them off gradually before locating their camps and eventually neutralizing them entirely."

The room was a chorus of congratulatory hums and grunts. Colonel Mjovich smiled, a broad grin glowing from under his thick beard.

Having satisfied his audience, the Iranian returned to his seat. The meeting returned to the issue of the Serbs. They finalized the last details of their plans regarding the campaign. It ended with the officers feeling confident and anticipating the satisfaction of a victory. The room emptied except for Abhajiri and Mjovich.

The two men stared at each other.

"I have some reservations about your plan," Abhajiri said simply.

"The Croats?" the Bosnian snorted. "I understand you think it might be too early diverting more resources to dealing with them."

"It's not that," the Iranian cut in. "I just feel that the Croatians have not presented any threat so far, nor does it look like they plan anything from all accounts we've received. I fear that if we pursue this agenda, we might exacerbate a problem we don't need."

"Don't need!" Mjovich blurted. "I do appreciate your advice. My officers and I have benefitted greatly from your council. But this is not your country, and you don't understand the politics. I don't want to wait until these guerrillas organize enough to be a threat, and the Croat leadership decides to betray us again."

"That's assuming they do," Abhajiri responded. "I know I'm not from this land. However, I do know the Serbian army is still the most powerful foe you have. They're still the best trained, best organized, and certainly the best equipped. I don't trust the Croatians either, but you're both more formidable working together than being at odds. Taking steps such as this not only goes against the order of your own leadership, it risks creating a rift with an ally you need right now."

The Bosnian began chewing his lips as he lowered his gaze to the man across the table. "We don't need the Croats as allies, friends, or supporters." He barely kept from growling. "We need to be leery of them and that means making sure they don't have the means to easily turn on us!"

"That prophecy may be self-fulfilling if you pursue this course," Abhajiri cautioned knowing he was treading a dangerous path with his host.

Mjovich rose slowly from his chair with his eyes fixed on the table in front of him. "I have listened to your views. My decision is final. You are here as an advisor to help us fight our enemy. I suggest you do so."

With that, the Bosnian marched out of the meeting room leaving the Iranian alone with his thoughts.

The tension was high. Sauwa could sense the anxiety amongst the Croatians as they lay prone in the thickets, covered in their camouflage suits under layers of fallen leaves. The last few weeks of intense training and rehearsals had prepared them for this operation. Set up in a linear ambush formation several meters away from a grass field, they waited. Training was over, this was going to be their first actual combat mission.

Reports of patrols in the vicinity had been filtering back to them for the last couple of weeks. Sauwa had undertaken a few personal recces to see for herself. She had watched the line of Bosnian soldiers walk this route multiple times in the last four days. The timeline was desultory, but there was no deviation from the established trail. A well-beaten path in the grass field ahead confirmed this. The patrols usually consisted of eight to ten men. They never used any follow-up units for protection. Sauwa thought this was the perfect mission to initiate the Croatians.

They began settling into place in the wee hours of dawn.

It was the only time she was sure they wouldn't need to worry about an enemy patrol. Sauwa brought the squad through the woods to avoid giving away their position. She wanted an additional ambush team set up several meters down the trail to catch any retreating Serbs or provide backup in case another squad was following her people. Her uncle and Fort Doppies had taught her that ambushes could easily go wrong if the ambushed target is not swiftly killed. Sauwa opted to keep the plan simple for their first mission. The guerrillas were too anxious and inexperienced to trust with too much complexity.

Oleg, since the first recce operation to Jablancia, had started to think of himself as a seasoned professional. He had been Sauwa's interpreter while conducting training and had gone on a dangerous mission close to the enemy strong-hold. He was playing instructor to the rest of the guerrillas, and his head had swelled even more. Oleg constantly tried to correct everyone as if he were in command. The other Croatians had come to see him in this light. Oleg had become a little difficult to deal with while she was trying to set up the group's first ambush. Sauwa let him have his moment. She figured he would be playing the role for real shortly.

Nestled deep in the trees, Sauwa kept her attention focused on the lumpy patches in front of her — they were supposed to be her forces. Whether they could perform had yet to be seen. During the three hours they had been waiting, she confirmed the machine gunner initiating the attack hadn't fallen asleep. She also risked checking on some of the others to stop them from moving around. Luckily, the Bosnians didn't arrive when she was doing so.

The Croatians were exhibiting a stronger resolve than

Sauwa had anticipated. For the hours they had lain in wait, she expected the nerves to be hitting hard. She had expected some vomiting or even losing a few men trying to run away from their first experience with combat. First-time operators getting excited or unnerved could become dangerous liabilities. To her surprise, they held firm. Perhaps it was their dire situation — when a person's back is to the wall, they find the resolve to fight.

The rustling of shrubbery broke the monotony. Sauwa couldn't tell if the Croatians understood what was happening and didn't dare do anything to alert them for fear of alerting others. The rustling became heavier and was soon accompanied by the voices of several men talking. The conversation was loud enough that, even at a distance, the language was indisputably Bosniak. By now her team had to know the moment had arrived.

Deep in the thickets, Sauwa readied herself. Her eyes darted from the ambush site to the line of her camouflaged guerrillas as she anticipated the nervous twitches and movements that would inevitably alert the oncoming Bosnian patrol. The rustling bushes and voices grew louder. The Bosnians seemed unconcerned about the degree of noise they were making. The patrol acted bored and tired. The tone of their conversation sounded irritated and defeated. She assumed they had been on patrol for some time. Despite being experienced, the Bosnians were still quite primitive as a fighting force and tended not to implement the best field discipline.

The Bosnians slowly poured from the tree line looking more like a group of weary travelers than a military patrol and walked haphazardly into the open field. Their weapons were draped over shoulders or dragged by one arm. A short fellow in the middle of the group wore the insignia of triangular stars of a Kapetan though he didn't act like it. He did not seem to care a bit about his troops' behavior.

Sauwa tensed and clutched her rifle tightly. Her apprehension was as much for her own troops as the Bosnian soldiers. So many things could go wrong in an ambush. It took one soldier seeing something in the trees and alerting his comrades before the ambusher became the ambushed. She feared her troops would start to shake or give into other habits that would give them away.

The Bosnians were in a long line out in the grass field sitting like ducks at a carnival shooting gallery. As they neared the point where the machine gunner was waiting, Sauwa hoped the gunman was paying attention and ready to do his part. The Bosnians were so close now that a failed ambush would have deadly consequences.

Trying to focus was difficult. Sauwa's mind raced through all the different possibilities of what could go wrong, and how she would react to them if they did. She found herself taking short, deep breaths to keep her own body under control.

The eruption of machine gun fire thundered as bullets tore from the bush line. Within seconds, the ambush party joined in with the machine gunner, and the tree line was ablaze with gunfire exploding everywhere. The Bosnians, taken completely by surprise, stood frozen as the bullets ripped into their bodies. The Kapetan, who only a short time before was oblivious to the world, was now running about screaming wildly to a non-existent audience. His unit began to break apart with men running in every direction trying to get away.

Picking up her rifle, Sauwa took aim at the officer and

firing off a burst hit him squarely in the chest. As scared and frantic as he was, it took the Kapetan a few seconds running around before he clutched his chest and slowly sank to the ground. Entirely leaderless the remaining Bosnians stopped to fire off a few sporadic bursts of return fire in a vain attempt to retaliate. Doing so sealed their fate.

Sauwa chose targets the furthest targets away knowing her Croatians had not mastered their weapons well enough to take long-distance shots. One of the Bosnians was running the long way out of the field. He was not zigzagging but running in a straight line. He was less than fifty meters out, but it was still beyond the marksmanship of her novice guerrillas. Another target had made it back to the trees but had stopped to look back. A burst from her rifle brought him down instantly.

In less than twenty-seconds, the gunfight was over. The silence was haunting. Not even the sound of birds chirping could be heard. The once green fields were awash with blood stains and littered with corpses. There was no time to assess the situation before Oleg jumped from his hidden position and began shouting for everyone to search the bodies. Acting like a bunch of excited children they started to rush in unison out into the open.

Exasperated, Sauwa leaped into action screaming at her pupils to hold steady. Confused, the Croatians looked at her unsure what to do. Oleg, his face red, approached her. "Woman, we must hurry and collect what we can!" He was bitter that she was contradicting his self-bestowed command.

"We need to move carefully," she explained. "Place some people in security on our flanks. If we get caught by unforeseen threats, we will have some protection."

Oleg stared at her for a time; he was quite aware that all eyes were on them both. The mercenary held her position staring back at him. Finally, nodding his head and waving his hand in the air, he turned and began instructing some of his people back into the trees to provide security. The rest immediately raced into the field to begin pillaging the bodies. Sauwa trod lightly. She knew Oleg was becoming dangerous with his arrogance, and she tried to keep up the appearance of being merely an advisor.

The few Bosnians still alive were executed on the spot. The guerrillas couldn't afford to take prisoners or leave witnesses to provide dangerous information. Sauwa's stomach turned as she heard the gunshots after the desperate words that could only be pleas for mercy.

Sauwa undertook searching the body of the Kapetan for any vital documents while the Croatians collected all the weapons, ammo, and all the military supplies they could. She investigated the Kapitan's uniform as if it were a Chinese puzzle box. Searching through it, she managed to find a bundle of documents stuffed into a leather pouch strung along his tactical web belt. She didn't take time to try and review it, she would do that back at camp.

Oleg, at Sauwa's suggestion, began calling for the guerrillas to fall back into the wood line. The whole exercise lasted no more than five minutes. The Croatians jaunted somewhat leisurely back toward the bush line with Oleg leading the pack playing the role of triumphant hero of the day feeling confident from their victory. Sauwa looked about nervously. This was the most critical moment in an ambush. Everyone was exposed and vulnerable, and they had no idea if the gunfire had been heard by anyone else or if any enemy forces were on their way.

This notion was definitely lost on the guerrillas who were too wrapped up in their own triumph to understand the danger they were still in. Sauwa followed behind them looking back at the blood-drenched field. She kept waiting for enemy troops to emerge. Thankfully, no one appeared. Despite his derelict behavior, Oleg did maintain the exfiltration route Sauwa had mapped out after she and Oleg had recced the area earlier. It ensured they followed a path within covered foliage and led to a well-protected rally point they could easily defend if they found themselves pursued.

The trouble was that feeling the excitement and triumph had made it hard for the Croatians to contain their jubilance. Some were already bragging loudly about their exploits. Far from curtailing such behavior, Oleg began promoting it by building on the momentum. He began touting the episode as an example of Croatian superiority over the Bosnians which resulted in a chorus of cheering. Sauwa tried to catch Oleg's attention and have him contain the noise. She'd motioned with her rifle and body toward their surroundings — an unspoken reminder of the danger still present. All the lessons of field discipline were be being entirely disregarded.

Arrogantly, Oleg responded with a simple yet condescending smile as he goaded the others to continue enjoying their victory. He even began singing one of their traditional victory songs. He was soon joined by the others. Only Sasha seemed to take her warnings to heart and remained quiet and alert.

Anticipating the gradually heightening noise level would lead to a bad outcome and unable to get control over the guerrillas in their moment of excitement, none of the Croatians noticed Sauwa slowly falling back even further. They marched on in ignorance as they sang ever louder with their

new feeling of self-confidence and invincibility. Such oblivi-
ousness was only proving the validity of her concerns. She
lamented not having Sasha with her. He usually provided
the right counter-balance to Oleg's abrasive arrogance.
Having been with her on that first recce, many of the guerrillas tended to revere the former hunter. And, unlike Oleg,
Sasha didn't seem to milk his new found fame.

Looking about the trees and foliage, she tried to conceive
where the greater threat might emerge. She assumed the left
side would be less defendable for the Croatians. Veering to
the left she skirted the guerrillas' left flank. If an enemy came
up behind them, she would be able to give warning. If a
counter attack occurred by more enemy forces, she could at
least distract them coming up on their side. Either way, she
would be of far better use protecting the weak spot on the
current path.

The guerrillas were a considerable distance from her, but
Sauwa could still see them well enough to keep up. Because
the noise they were making gave her a perfect means to
follow them, she didn't really need to stay close. She
clutched her weapon and trekked slowly amongst the trees
and bushes looking for anything suspicious. Her mind ran
through the scenarios of what could plausibly happen. The
singing was loud enough she could clearly make out the
words. Sometime later she was going to have a *discussion*
with Oleg in private. A conversation with the self-styled
combat expert was going to find rather humbling.

Almost to the rendezvous point, she heard a gunshot. It
wasn't the slight crackle associated with a traditional automatic. It was the cannon-like boom from a high caliber rifle.
The exuberant singing had been replaced with an equally
loud chorus of screams. The Croatians were in trouble.

Picking up her pace, Sauwa began moving in the direction of the gunfire. She could already hear a barrage of wild return fire. It seemed like the guerrillas were firing blindly in response.

Sensing it was a sniper by the lack of follow-up fire coming from the booming weapon, she moved up hoping the gunman had hit his target and moved on. A professional knew better than to stay in the same place after a shot. It was the amateur who stuck around and tried to rack up kills leaving muzzle flashes and enough time for people to spot their location.

Another cannon-like boom dispelled her of this notion — the sniper was racking up kills. This report prompted another wild barrage of gunfire from the Croatians confirming the sniper had been successful yet again. This time, however, Sauwa was able to determine a general location of where the sniper's shot had to have come from. Despite the Croatian gunfire tearing through the bushes she continued to move ahead looping around in the hopes that she would come up behind the shooter. She imagined in her absence, Oleg would actually have to be a leader for a change rather than just play one.

The cannon-like boom echoed loudly in the air. This time it was louder and closer, and Sauwa started to close the distance. Again, it was followed by an uncontrolled barrage of return fire that didn't even seem to come close to the sniper's position. She saw him at a distance — a shadowy silhouette of a person tucked closely to a cluster of trees. The rifle, a long powerful looking piece, was perched nicely in the pocket of a tree branch. The shooter may have been an excellent shot but, as she surmised, he was not a professional sniper. He didn't have much in the way of deep camouflage and was relying on the trees and shrubbery to conceal himself. He did not change positions after each shot — which would prove to be a fatal mistake.

Moving up a little to close the distance, Sauwa sank to one knee as she sighted in her rifle. With the sniper in her sights, she fired a single round in his direction. The shot hit within inches of his head smashing into the tree branch next to him. Taken by surprise, the sniper fell back blinded by the shards of wood that flew into his eyes. Dazed and confused, he rose to his feet in an attempt to wipe the debris from his eyes. Doing so he automatically turned in her direction presenting a full silhouette. She took her kill shot. Firing at center mass she watched as the sniper clutched his chest and fell backward.

"Cease fire! Cease fire!" She screamed hoping the Croatians would at least recognize her voice and stop shooting.

"Mercenary! Is that you?" It was Oleg's voice; he had never gotten Sauwa's name and had generally begun referring to her as *mercenary*.

"Yes, it's me. I got the shooter so stop firing!"

A few more shots rang out from the Croatian side. Like the rest, they were wild and shooting blindly. "Stop shooting!" She heard Oleg yelling angrily. "We're coming to you," he shouted at her.

"I'm making my way toward the shooter," Sauwa called back. She hoped the guerrillas would hone in on her voice. She carefully approached the location of the sniper. She watched carefully for any movement that might indicate danger. There was nothing. The sniper's body was sprawled over a bush that had kept him artificially propped up.

She could hear the rustling of bushes as the Croatians neared her position. "I'm this way!" She called out assuming

Oleg was amongst those coming. There was no actual response, but the muttering hinted at both anger and fear.

The sniper's body was soaked in a thick pool of dark blood. She instantly identified the uniform as that of the Serbian army. When she found him, Sauwa imagined the camouflaged figure had been lingering until shortly before she arrived. A black knit baklava covered the man's face except for his eyes. Usually, she would have checked for a pulse to ensure her target was dead, but the blank stare from his lifeless eyes looking off into nowhere told her enough. She had seen enough dead men up close to know the difference between a decoy and the real thing.

By now, the Croatians had found her as they trotted through the trees. She didn't have to look to know their guns were out and pointed squarely at the dead sniper. She felt Oleg move up past her as he reached to grab the sniper's throat and press the barrel of his pistol at his head. Her presence no longer necessary, Sauwa shifted her attention to the tree where the sniper had taken up his position.

The rifle he had used had fallen against the tree. It was an old-time German Stg 44. Initially a standard issue rifle in World War II, it was quickly adapted for use as a sniper rifle making it the first ever rifle to be used for such purposes. It wasn't the best weapon for what she was looking to accomplish, but it was better than her current options.

Taking the weapon, Sauwa began looking it over. Despite the chips on the wood stock and general wear from decades of use, the rifle was in relatively good condition. The previous owner, lying only a few feet away, had maintained the weapon with great care. The rifle also hosted a 3.5x power PU Scope, a common model used for this type of rifle. It was preferable to the less durable 4x power PE scope. It was a good find. Sauwa retrieved the ammunition pouches from the sniper. They were loaded with several five round magazines. Given the few rounds expended, the sniper had just gotten started on his mission.

Turning back to the Croatians, she saw they had already ripped the baklava off the dead sniper and were grumbling angrily. She imagined they were bitter over the fact he had died before they could kill him slowly in revenge for their lost comrades. Rifles in hand, Sauwa joined the group surrounding the dead man. Oleg still had his Makarov automatic pressed to the dead man's head. He spat out an angry litany of phrases Sauwa could not make out.

The shooter looked to be in his early thirties and had a knife scar across his face. The scar looked to be the result of a bar fight rather than from combat. His uniform appeared to be Serbian; a fact that fueled the rage of the guerrillas. They hated the Serbs even more than the Bosnians.

Firing an unnecessary round into the sniper's head, Oleg exhibited a satisfied look as he holstered his pistol. While he didn't voice it, his facial expression registered a look of gratitude and humility when he glanced at Sauwa. He realized he had allowed his new popularity to go to his head. When the group rejoined the rest of the patrol, Sauwa saw two bodies sprawled out on the ground. The older man was Sasha — the hunter and farmer, then briefly a soldier. The other victim was a girl barely sixteen years old. She had seen her entire family die from this war. It was a sobering moment for the remaining Croatians as they looked at their dead comrades. For a short time, they had felt a sense of power in this horrific war, and it had gone to their heads. They had paid a terrible price.

The guerrillas loaded up their fallen — their demeanor

changed. Oleg's attitude had altered from the arrogant combat expert who knew everything back to the cautious professional she had first met. He walked up next to her as the squad collected themselves and prepared to move out. From his facial expression, the deaths of the girl and the old man were something he took as his fault. The patrol continued their journey; this time in complete silence and moving in a more tactical way.

German Stg had come into her possession after a raid on a Serbian Chetnik campsite. It had been found by one of the Croatians while rummaging through a pile of dead bodies. But the Mosin-Nagant 91/30 sniper's rifle would be even better. This was a stroke of luck for Sauwa. It was the best weapon she had been able to obtain. It had been the weapon Sauwa had been looking for to complete her plan.

The Russian made Mosin-Nagant 91/30 was a mass-produced infantry weapon with a history of military service going back to 1891. During World War II, it had been adapted to serve as the premier weapon for Soviet snipers and proved to be so effective it continued to see action even now.

While not appreciated by urban practitioners who regarded its wood stock and twenty-nine-inch barrel as cumbersome, rural snipers found its durability and long-distance accuracy of nearly 600 meters a serious benefit for engaging targets from a safe and distant vantage point. That it was cheap, mass-produced and used extensively all over the world meant that they were easily obtainable for militaries and guerrilla organizations that didn't have a lot of money or connections.

Burrowing into the dirt, she stared at a single tree standing alone in the center of a field. Peering down the scope, she focused her attention through the sighting hairs on a vertical, thick black arrow centered between a broken, horizontal line on a single piece of paper with a large black dot drawn in the middle of it. The paper had been nailed to the trunk of the tree and was just short of 500 meters away. It wasn't the preferred way she wanted to familiarize herself with her new weapon; however, in the interest of limited training areas, resources, and time, she worked with what she had.

Sighting in, she peered through the scope to see the white paper and the blur of the black mark fixed within the center of her crosshairs. Closing her eyes, she took a deep breath. She exhaled slowly until all the air was out of her lungs. She opened her eyes to see the cross-hairs had sunk just below her target. The scope was not the ideal one, especially at such a far range — it was still better than nothing. Adjusting her rifle slightly to get it back on sight, she squeezed the trigger gently until she felt the recoil of the round being fired. Like the sound of a cannon being fired, it was ear-shattering. Thankfully, she enjoyed the benefit of some hearing protection by using melted wax wedged into her ears.

Pulling back the bolt, she ejected the spent cartridge. Across the field, Enya came rushing out from a place far off to the side. She examined the target for a moment then reached for a small walkie-talkie and called Sauwa. Her voice crackled over a like contraption as she reported, "You grazed the tree an inch to the left of the paper."

Not bad for a first shot, Sauwa thought to herself. She raised her eyes from the rifle muzzle to adjust the windage dial a few clicks. She was relieved that the trouble had not been with the elevation. The scoping system did not have a normal means to make such adjustments. The 3.5x PU system of Eastern Europe did allow a shooter to correct for elevation. The original Soviet scope models came from the factory already zeroed for elevation. Later replicas of the scope and weapon were not produced in the same manner leaving the shooter to have to estimate to compensate.

Having made her adjustments, Sauwa radioed her companion that she was getting ready to fire. She watched as the young Croatian bolted across the field disappearing into the safety of the tree line. With Enya out of danger, Sauwa reached down and picked up another cartridge. Forcing it into the chamber, she closed the bolt until she heard the click telling her it was locked in.

Once again she raised the rifle until she had a solid position and her eye was peering down the scope at the ground ahead. It took her a moment of searching before the target was again in her sights. Shutting her eyes, she again exhaled all the air out of her lungs, opened her eyes and adjusted the sighting lines of her scope and gently squeezed the trigger a second time. The trigger was tight and tended to stick which was another reason it wasn't the ideal weapon for her task. The report of the shot being fired shattered the harmony of the quiet surroundings. The hardwood of the weapon's shoulder stock punched violently into the pocket of Sauwa's shoulder radiating more agonizing pain.

Enya was on the radio asking if it was all clear. Still

reeling from the recoil, Sauwa ejected the spent cartridge from the rifle. She reached for her radio and notified Enya it was all right to come out. Enya ran into the field and checked the target. Seconds later she confirmed the shot had hit the corner of the black dot.

The exercise continued for another few shots until the rounds centered in the black. Despite the Mosin-Nagant not being the ideal sniper rifle, Sauwa was able to maintain a relatively decent consistency. When she checked her handi-work, Enya excitedly showed her the tight grouping within the black dot.

This information was a mixed blessing for Sauwa. She had seemingly mastered the rifle well enough to carry out her mission at the required distance. On the other hand, she did not relish the need to use the weapon again.

Tearing the paper down, the ladies made their way back to the base camp. Enya was looking down at the target and dancing about with girlish playfulness. "I have never seen such shooting," the Croatian exclaimed. Sauwa was oblivious and didn't reply. She was focused on her plan. She had her method, her weapon, and now she needed a location.

Sauwa returned to the camp exhausted. It seemed as though the last several days had been nothing but field work and rifle practice. The wood shoulder stock was uncomfortable. She had tried to find some type of padding that would mitigate the problem, but her luck with resources had run out. Her arm was hurting terribly from the shooting practice. Ideally, she would only require a single shot.

Moving past the two sentries dressed in camo netting, blacked out face paint, with their serious and expressions, they looked like young men trying to project an image of hardened fighters. The ladies walking by elicited a growling statement from one of the young sentries. Sauwa didn't understand him, though she could assume from his look and the way he said it, that it was an order of some sort.

Enya looked back. Her girlish look and mannerism were replaced by a scowl, and she replied with equal harshness. The young man fell back slightly unprepared for the response he had just received, but he quickly recouped and maintained the same intense gaze as the two women passed by.

"What did he want?" Sauwa was curious.

Enya's face returned to the pleasant expression she normally displayed. "He told me how dangerous it was for us to be out there and ordered us to get back to camp. I basically told him to fuck off."

Oleg greeted them as they entered the camp. With arms extended and a big grin spread across his face, he trotted over to Sauwa. Since the run-in with the sniper, he had developed a greater sense of humility. He had become less self-absorbed with his soldierly abilities and adopted a more humble role. He had thanked her for saving the lives of his friends who he had foolishly led into danger. Now, he treated her like a patron saint. He certainly became a better student soaking up her training with a renewed enthusiasm — a man determined to right the mistakes of his past. "My saint, my saint," he said as he wrapped Sauwa up in his arms with a warm hug. "I have good news. We have hit another Bosnian patrol. This time we made a good escape, no mistakes."

"Good, congratulations," Sauwa replied happily. It was the first operation the Croatians had undertaken without her.

She was pleased with how well they were coming along as a force. Oleg turned and waved his hand toward a large pile of weapons — his trophies.

For Sauwa, it was a personal achievement. Her interest was in Marko — how happy he was with the progress his people were making. If he thought they would be able to carry out missions without her, she would soon be able to leave for Montenegro.

The guerrillas were celebrating their recent victory. Men and women danced and drank their few reserves of alcohol. Across the way, overseeing the pile of captured equipment, Marko walked about with the composure of a general surveying his army. Breaking from the engaging Oleg, Sauwa casually approached him. A look of satisfaction was on the guerrilla leader's face.

"You have done well," Marko spoke first not waiting for Sauwa to broach the subject he knew she wanted to discuss. "Your training has exceeded my expectations. I thank you."

"Not at all," she replied quietly. "I'm glad to hear you are satisfied with my services. I assume that when I complete my other mission, you'll assist me in getting to Montenegro."

"Of course," Marko turned his head to face her. "My people are getting to where they can operate without your assistance. When you have finished your other responsibilities, I will arrange for you to go with a consignment of my men who are going south to obtain supplies from the markets along the border." He looked down to see a look of confusion on her face. Understanding her suspicion, he continued. "I promised you I would get you as safely as I can to the border. It just so happens that since our closest neighbors are as war-ravaged as we are, necessary supplies are not easy to obtain. This situation makes it necessary to obtain needed material through the criminal markets in the South making getting you there a necessity."

"Necessity, how?" Sauwa asked. Originally, if the guerrillas kept their word, she was going to be moved along a chain of guerrilla camps until she reached the border. This plan was an unexpected twist, especially the part about getting her there being a necessity.

Marko responded, "It will be a dangerous journey. The contraband my men obtained from the enemy convoys has given us the opportunity to barter for needed resources. Getting the contraband to the needed destination will be dangerous and require great skill. Though my people are better than they were, they are still naïve and would benefit from your experience guiding them on this journey."

In the last few weeks, the Croatians had carried out numerous ambushes against Serbian military supply convoys. The Serbs were the best-equipped military, enjoying unfettered access to the vast arsenals of the now defunct Yugoslav People's Army from the heyday of the cold war. The fruits of such raids yielded better equipment than the Croatians could obtain. The equipment taken from the Serbs stocked the guerrilla's own armaments and left them with an excess they could now offer in trade.

"I can't promise miracles." Sauwa felt nervous about being handed another unwanted responsibility that was so important to the Croatians. She looked at Marko. His eyes were warm as he looked at his people dancing. Their happiness was gradually developing into a celebration.

"I'm not asking for them," he responded. "I'm asking for the best people I have to undertake this mission. The world of shadows and intrigue are still new to my people. Whereas it is the world you live in quite comfortably."

Sauwa took the heavy man's insinuation as an insult even though she knew Marko had meant his statement as a compliment. He was remarking on the natural way she excelled as a mercenary. It wasn't the world she wanted, and she resented the very idea that he thought her so comfortable in that world. Still, she could understand Marko's concern. Sending his people on this mission was dangerous for them.

"Even if I did get them to the border," Sauwa sighed, "they'll be on their own coming back."

Marko nodded. His eyes were still fixed on the now full-blown party. "What they learn from you making their way south will have to do for their training when returning. At least you will get them through the first part of it, and that's all I ask for."

She found a strange respect for the older man. He genuinely wanted to protect his people in a conflict that was brutal and nasty. Like the others, Marko also benefitted from Sauwa's training. She had spent many nights in his office planning out missions and developing strategies. Through her, he had in his own right become a far better field commander to his guerrillas. And, unlike Oleg, the developing capability of the group had not gone to his head as he remained steadfast in his professionalism.

The Croatians danced about merrily as they celebrated their victory. A young man, who could not have been more than twenty, bounded up to where Sauwa was standing. He stopped before her and gave her a gentlemanly bow. Then turning to Marko, he spoke something in Croatian. Marko responded with a shrug as he waved his hand in her direction. "He wants to know if you will dance with him."

Sauwa was a little surprised. Since her arrival, the young men stared at her from a distance but largely avoided her. When her abilities became known, they became even more apprehensive about being around her. She had noticed the young man earlier. He had stood with a group of his friends eyeing her. The friends had goaded and pushed the young man just before he approached her. She guessed he had been bragging about being able to charm the mysterious foreigner and landed in trouble. Now, he had to make good on his professed abilities.

Slowly he raised his hands to waist level and gave her a casual, friendly look as he cocked his head to one side. Marko added, "You should know the young men of the camp have a bet going as to whether Dovac here will succeed."

"Just a dance?" Sauwa asked suspiciously.

Marko chuckled, "Just a dance."

With nothing more to say to Marko, Sauwa looked at the young man and shrugged as she lowered her Bergen to the ground. She took his hand and headed out to join the others. In the distance, she watched the widening eyes and astonished looks of the young men and teenage boys as their comrade walked out to dance holding the hand of the woman mercenary. The triumphant strut displayed as he looked back at them was not lost on her either.

He turned back to her and slowly they began to jump about as Sauwa struggled to learn the dance routine being performed. Dovac helped her, and she gradually began to get the hang of it. The two danced and a few times Dovac reached over and took her by the waist as he led her around.

The boys looked envious as Sauwa and Dovac danced. Marko watched with the eye of a protective father guarding his child. Sauwa wasn't quite sure who Marko was protecting. She also kept a close eye on her Bergen that remained by Marko's side. She was more comfortable with her new companions then she had been with her old unit. However, she remained vigilant. The men she worked with were all utterly untrustworthy.

An hour later the festivities started to wind down. Exhausted, Sauwa made her way to her tent. Dovac had given her a nod of appreciation before returning to his friends to receive a hero's welcome. She slipped through the thick canvass covers that guarded the entry. Enya was lying on her collection of blankets. "So, was marriage proposed?" She smiled at Sauwa with laughter in her eyes.

"Not yet," Sauwa replied as she dropped down on a collection of blankets next to Enya. "I wouldn't rule it out though." She struggled to get comfortable between the blankets and the makeshift cot that was kept a few inches off the ground. "I think some of these guys would like to know me more permanently."

Enya smiled. "I imagine they would. Sex is something that is sought in many situations. And, young men are always in competition to prove themselves. The foreign, pretty girl is the exotic being that they all strive to obtain."

"I know," Sauwa said. "I see them stare and whisper. Funny they can bravely handle a gunfight but fear the ever mysterious and elusive woman."

"No," Enya interrupted. "Just you. The female mercenary who trains guerrillas how to fight like professional soldiers. It's something they find intimidating and at the same time alluring."

Sauwa chuckled. With all that had happened in her short life, she grew up fast and often forgot she was still very young. She looked at Enya who was laying in her blankets continuing to chuckle. Sauwa began to feel the exhaustion overtake her as she sank into her own bedding. She had barely felt her head touch her rolled-up coat before her eyes closed.

13

The deep baritone of Colonel Mjovich's voice made his shouting sound more like an opera singer's than a command. Selim Abhajiri stood quietly in the corner and listened to the Bosnian commander deliver his speech. The Iranian kept a stoic pose that guarded against revealing his thoughts. Though the Colonel's voice was clear and loud, his oration was little more than an unintelligible rambling covering everything randomly from strategy to his own political and philosophical views of the world and the conflict. The reason he could arouse his men's passion despite his inaudible rambling is that he spoke with such fervor.

Abhajiri looked at the men surrounding the wood podium where the Colonel stood. He studied them carefully. Despite their camouflage fatigues and tactical webbing, it was easy to see that none of these men were soldiers by trade. They were a group of peasants and factory workers thrown together to create something of an army. Most had never even handled a firearm until they were suddenly standing against an enemy in brutal combat. At a time when the Serbians were on the rampage intent on expanding their own territory in the old Yugoslavian country, such makeshift armies were the only thing standing against them.

The Iranian felt a deep respect for the fighters he viewed. They had endured serious hardships in horrific battles, betrayed by the Croatians, who wanted to expand their own territory, plus arms embargoes that had left them nearly helpless against their enemies. Despite the time constraints, lack of equipment and the brief time he had been able to work with them, he had seen some great improvements. However, they were still sub-par from what he would have liked to accomplish.

The best combatants for the conflict had been several hundred foreign fighters who had come to the country to fight in support of their Islamic brethren against the Orthodox Christian Serbians and the Catholic Croatians. Many were seasoned veterans from previous conflicts in Afghanistan or more recently Chechnya, where they had encountered the powerful Soviet/Russian army. Many had enjoyed the opportunity to further their training in Taliban-controlled Afghanistan. Since the end of Soviet occupation, it had become a haven and training ground for Islamic revolutionaries.

Abhajiri enjoyed the support of these seasoned fighters who augmented his less capable Bosnians. Still, they seemed to be religious zealots, and he remained suspicious of them. Colonel Mjovich continued his monologue. It became ever more theatrical. He moved about and skewed his speech into something of an evangelizing sermon. The performance seemed to captivate his audience. The Iranian tried to hide his ever-growing boredom. The whole event appeared like grand-standing.

The speech ended with the soldiers chorusing in unison some slogan professing their country and their faith. The colonel left the podium like a rock star leaving the stage his soldiers cheering loudly. He walked past Abhajiri who casually followed him. They slipped down a walkway between houses and turned into a door guarded by a large man who looked like something out of a cheap horror movie. The planning room was lined with maps across every wall. Three radios were manned at all times by attentive clerks writing every message onto paper and uniformed men surrounded several tables reviewing the contents on top.

"I think it went very well," Mjovich said smiling victoriously as he removed his long black trench coat and passed it to the horror movie guard.

Abhajiri said nothing. He continued to follow the colonel to one of the tables. Ignoring the Iranian's obvious silence, Mjovich continued. "The men seemed properly motivated. Hopefully, they will express such energy on the battlefield."

The Iranian nodded halfheartedly but remained silent. Mjovich sensed his guest had a lot on his mind and pushed the issue a little further. "From your silence, I assume you do not agree."

Realizing he was not going to escape the impending argument, Abhajiri ran his tongue across his teeth trying to collect his thoughts. "It was a little strident." He held back telling Mjovich it was mostly incoherent ramblings. The parts that were concise and articulate emphasized the colonel's favorite topic — Bosnian nationalism and the dangers of the Serbs and Croatians. Abhajiri found the topic distressing.

"Strident?" The Colonel snorted. "How can you say such a thing? In combat, a commander must often motivate his men."

"Yes, normally I would agree." Abhajiri began but was not sure he wanted to continue down this road. "However, much of your rhetoric had a staunchly nationalistic blend. The kind that in my experience leads to calamitous results."

"I was merely voicing the sentiment held by the majority of my countrymen." Mjovich was now looking the Iranian squarely in the eye. "How can that be wrong?"

Abhajiri stood fast and held his own commanding presence. "When you speak of the Croatians as traitorous enemies out to steal land, you seem to forget they're your allies. I have advised you several times that it is not prudent for you to antagonize an already fragile relationship. Just because you have continuing hostilities with certain Croatian factions, it does not infer you can extend those hostilities as part of a personal crusade."

"I was motivating my soldiers and reminding them of a people that we should not trust easily." The colonel tried to meet the Iranian with his own commanding presence. "And, as I have already stated, I was motivating soldiers. Something I'm sure you have done in your own conflicts."

Abhajiri sighed slightly trying hard to mask his growing exasperation. "Patriotic motivation is at times healthy. But in the field, I need soldiers operating responsibly, not a mob of vigilantes on a crusade to exact revenge. In the long term, it will only create bitter hatreds that will make amicable reconciliation impossible. The Croatians are going to be here long after this war is over. If you want some viable lasting peace, your crusade of revenge can't go on."

A long-time warrior fighting in numerous Muslim causes, Abhajiri might share the hardened views of the Bosnian Muslims and their desire for a state free of Christian interference. Mjovich remained silent though he focused an intense gaze on the Iranian. His body swayed strangely from side to side. By the pinched look on his face, the Bosnian commander was angry, but he didn't know how to respond. Abhajiri held fast to his own unyielding posture as he waited for the conversation to proceed or end abruptly.

Abhajiri may have sympathized with the Muslim cause, but he was a soldier first as well as a pragmatist who understood the delicate situation of the region better than most. He was not one to succumb to longtime hatreds and vendettas that seemed to encompass the thinking amongst the indigenous elements. He wanted to win a war and go home. He did not want to win a victory against one dangerous foe to have another emerge and continue as a destabilizing element long after the Serbs left.

Deciding he didn't want to pursue the issue, Mjovich turned on his heels and walked over to the largest map on the wall. "In the last few weeks, the Serbians have suffered a series of attacks on their convoys. We suspect that it is Croatian guerrillas doing this."

"I'm aware of the reports," Abhajiri replied. "My understanding is that the attacks were successful."

"Too successful," the colonel snapped as he retook control of the conversation. "Only a few months ago, the Croatian units operating in this area were thought to be groups of untrained peasants with a few rifles. Now, it seems that is no longer the case."

"I agree," the Iranian responded. "They have clearly been receiving professional military training making them much more formidable."

"Who do you think is helping them, HVO?" The colonel asked.

"Our intelligence suggests they are in touch with units of the HVO," Abhajiri replied. "They might be receiving training from them. I have scanned a few sporadic reports we received recently indicating a mercenary is working with one of the groups. The reports mention little other than a foreigner, a female foreigner, seems to have been directing many of these operations."

Mjovich's eyes widened. "A woman mercenary. I don't believe such things."

"Do you believe the sudden success rate of these guerrilla attacks?" The Iranian looked directly at the colonel.

"Then what do we do next, advisor?" Mjovich asked.

"Their operations have been largely focused on the Serbs." Abhajiri scanned the colorful map of the area of operation. "I know of only one attack against Bosnian forces that may have been their doing."

"Yes, a patrol of our men was the first experience where we realized the guerrillas' capabilities." Mjovich was abrupt in the way he explained it.

"I am aware," Abhajiri replied in a calm quiet tone. "I'm also aware they have largely concentrated their efforts on our mutual enemies and that has served us. We should be careful how we approach this."

The colonel was eyeing the map, looking at the Iranian out of the corner of his eye. "So, your advice, advisor, is to do what? You would have us simply let these guerrillas run free because they're not inconveniencing us the way they are the Serbs."

The Iranian shook his head slightly. "In time, you will have to deal with these groups. However, choose that time wisely and ensure a viable strategy so you don't kill one faction only to create ten more."

"You seem gravely concerned with appeasing the Croatians on the auspice that the insurgent conflict will only proliferate." Mjovich turned to face the Iranian and looked him squarely in the eye. "You seem so sure that this rabble could present something more."

Abhajiri kept his focus on the colonel. "The Israelis learned a valuable lesson when they invaded Lebanon. They pushed out the Palestinians to the adulation of the Lebanese people, Shia, Druze, and Christians alike. Then due to their own repressive policies and excessive military responses, it wasn't long before they had created a hated backlash. These policies laid the foundation for a nasty guerrilla movement. When I was there, I found no shortage of recruits willing to fight against the hated Israeli occupiers. Israel is still in Lebanon today. The enemies they fight there are not Palestinian, but Lebanese who are entrenched and continue to threaten them."

"An interesting current events lesson," Mjovich replied with a sneer intending for the Iranian to notice it. "Still, you compare your well supported Hezbollah allies to the ragged Croatians. Not an association I would draw. These people could be dealt with more simplistically and, I believe, we should do so."

Abhajiri turned and began to approach the map the colonel had been eyeing earlier. "If you haven't noticed sir, your landscape is filled with high rolling hills and several places with good forests and vegetation. The Croatians you love to think of as foreigners have been here as long as your people. They are an entrenched people and as familiar with the land as you are not to mention the number of villages they populate. I would not consider this land an ideal area in which to wage a guerrilla campaign. Operating in it is not easy. Under the circumstances, although you might feel they are poorly armed peasants in ragtag armies, I would remind you that your own forces are not in any better shape."

The colonel's facial expression became distorted with a look of irritation. Evidently, he did not appreciate the foreign advisor reminding him of his own weaknesses. Abhajiri didn't care. He had balanced the colonel's fantasies of power with the reality of the situation long enough. "If you start waging your campaign against them, you'll turn a force you can't control against you at a time when you already have limited resources."

Mjovich said nothing. It was hard for the Iranian to tell what the man was thinking. Hopefully, he was digesting the advisor's words, but his anger was actually building momentum. Abhajiri decided not to press the issue. He had said his piece.

Finally, Mjovich spoke. "You may have a point. For now, our attention and resources should be focused on the Serbians. Still, my Arab friend, I feel you are an optimistic fool who is entirely too trusting of the Croatians."

Abhajiri nodded respectfully to the colonel. He had temporarily won a battle. Not against Mjovich, who he knew still harbored the misguided belief that his forces were far better than they were. And his hatred for the Croats was still overriding his better judgment. The Iranian had won his battle. The real prize — the men and the other officers standing about pretending not to listen to the conversation. Mjovich, for all his stubbornness, could read the political climate in the room. For the moment, it was not with him. Deciding the time was not right for his cause, he decided to back down.

14

After weeks of planning and watching, Sauwa was able to rule out several options for carrying out her assassination. The Iranian advisor had proven to be a far more elusive and difficult target than those she had previously dealt with in Bosnia. She decided her only viable means to make her shot would be from a long distance. The question then became how to get her target to stand stationary long enough to do so.

Having performed several recces in the last month, she had become quite familiar with the landscape. She had also become equally familiar with the way the local Bosnian forces operated in the area, not to mention the Iranian himself. The Iranian was a hard target who infrequently ventured out of the boundaries of the town making it difficult to establish a pattern that one could plan from. When he did venture out of town, his mode of travel remained irregular adding to the confusion. This made targeting a specific convoy or vehicle utterly pointless. It was an exasperating exercise. She had been unable to find a weakness she could exploit.

After prolonged and close observation, she found a niche she could possibly work with.

When Abhajiri arrived at a location outside of town, it was usually to observe and advise on a problem or to help direct a more complex operation going into effect. It was here she found the Iranian vulnerable. Whether to observe or direct, the Iranian was in a place where he was forced to leave the protection of his vehicle and stand stationary out in the open for a short time.

It wasn't the ideal plan, but it was the best option she had. The difficulty was to create a situation that would guarantee Abhajiri's presence.

A paved roadway connected the town to the rest of the world. It was well kept and frequently used for Bosnian supply convoys. It also ran tightly alongside the base of a chain of high peaked hills and a crest well above the bottomland on the other side. It left little room for the vehicles to maneuver.

In her previous patrols, Sauwa had scoped out a site where the road wound around a circular hill. Above was a carpet of trees and bushes that wrapped the hill's midsection. On the other side was a steep dip leading into a deep ravine. It would be the ideal site for an ambush.

Along with Oleg, she led a force of the Croatians to the base of the rounded hill and placed them just a little further past the bend. Not wanting to leave any trace of their existence and alert the enemy, the group headed down the road and crossed into a denser area. After hours of maneuvering through trees and brush, the group arrived at their destination.

Sauwa remembered her uncle's teachings. When it came to ambushes, one identified the approach, the setup and the means of retreat. She had looked the area over thoroughly to determine the best method of setting up. The thick carpet of trees protected them on the hill overlooking the road. Topping the hill, Sauwa led her guerrillas fifty meters short of the bend and stopped.

She left the force positioned around an easily recognizable tree as she, along with Oleg and another person who went by the name Targa, moved ahead.

The incline of the hill was difficult to navigate. It was still a little muddy, and Sauwa and her comrades had come close a couple of times to losing their footing and sliding straight into the road. More disconcerting was that the ground was too steep and unstable for anyone to operate from. As with most ambush situations, the ideal terrain was generally more of a fantasy than a reality and this location was no different.

Scouting around the bend of the hill, the two Croatians expressed frustration at her continued disapproval of possible set up locations. They were either open and noticeable or they were entrenched and would prove too awkward to operate from. For Sauwa, it was the experienced understanding of how vulnerable ambush units were and how easily the tides could turn in the heat of battle. It was essential that she stay patient.

Having gained his own experience from previous missions, Oleg was determined to find good locations and moved about diligently eyeing the ground. Targa was a young man not yet twenty years old. He was energetic and motivated but lacked patience causing him to get bored and just go through the motions.

Eventually, Sauwa found a location she thought was

workable. It wasn't perfect, but it offered enough of every-thing to make it viable.

Rounding up her comrades, she dispatched Oleg to retrieve the others while she set Targa into position. The young man had only been on a few previous missions and was acting with the giddy excitement of a young man going on his first date. He didn't like the idea of being made to lie down on the moist ground among the wet leaves and prickly branches. He wanted to stand and be ready to charge into combat like he'd seen in action movies. It took a bit of persuading for Sauwa to get him to comply, which, in the end, he did with irritated reluctance.

Oleg returned flanked by two more people. Sauwa went to work placing them as Oleg went back to grab two more. It wasn't wise to have so many people visibly standing around. They gradually placed people into position two at a time while leaving the bulk of the force staged a good distance back in deeper cover.

After placing the first ten, she left Oleg to finish making last-minute adjustments while she grabbed the remaining members. She turned back the way they had come until they found a spot for the eight people a few hundred meters down from where they could cross.

The ravine proved arduous as she and the others inched through the shrubs and thickets, practically side-crawling with their hands and feet along the steep edges. Even though it was only a couple of hundred meters, it felt like they had been moving for endless miles when they finally got to their destination.

Placed several meters beyond the bend in the road, the squad awkwardly tried to position themselves. Carefully she traversed the steep ground as she moved to ensure her people were well placed. They were far enough behind the bend of the hill that they didn't need to worry about being seen by someone looking at the hill crest. Hopefully, their camouflage suits would be enough to mask their bodies from anyone who might see them from across the ravine.

The L-shaped ambush formation she had set up wasn't ideal.

Despite their previous experience, the Croatians had not yet undertaken such a complex attack. She had purposely kept them to more limited operations where she could better manage everyone and limit the responsibilities for anyone else. Even the few successful operations the Croatians had managed to carry out without her had still been simplistic and amateurish in their undertaking.

Sauwa worried about how easily it could all go wrong with so many moving parts. Since the incident with the sniper, Oleg had become far more attentive and disciplined as a soldier. Still, she remained concerned about him over-estimating his abilities. But it didn't matter. She was set in and unable to go back and check on him.

Nearly two hours had passed in which nothing happened. Sauwa remained cognizant of the man perched next to her designated to handle the Soviet model rocket-propelled grenade launcher. The rest of the team were staged several feet below to avoid the force of the back blast.

She could see they were bored and showing signs of complacency. She wanted to throw something at them to wake them up, but she knew better. Besides, they would only be back to their complacent state within minutes.

The sound of the engines was a distant hum when she first heard them. Gradually they developed into a chorus of growling roars as the trucks neared.

Giving the man next to her a hard shake, she felt him jump to life from his light doze. He turned to her with a blank face beading with sweat as he realized the time was growing near.

Kicking her foot into the ground, she allowed the loose dirt to fall on the guerrillas several feet below her.

A middle-aged man in his mid-fifties irritatingly shook his head as dirt clumps fell on him. He looked toward Sauwa with a grimace, but the look quickly changed to one of concern when he too heard the roar of the engines. He nudged the man next to him who was already alert. The line of guerrillas came alive and agitated as they heard the vehicles drawing near.

Concentrating her attention on the road, she raised her head just enough to peek over the edge. She could hear the trucks. They were a distance away but approaching rapidly. The man next to her with the grenade launcher in his hand began to tremble.

The growth of over-brush lining the road afforded enough concealment for the grenade launcher to be sighted in and set up. A canvass cover lined with branches from bushes lower down on the hill finished masking it. It was not visible when the first truck came around the bend.

The man with the grenade launcher continued to shiver. Sauwa gently squeezed his shoulder to help calm him; it had only a slight effect. She edged closer to him, tightening her hold as the moment was imminent.

Her mouth was inches away from the man's ear, her eyes looking down the road. She didn't want to commence action too early while out of range of Oleg's group, nor too late where the enemy was too close, and they would be in the blast radius when they fired. Making an educated guess, she pointed to a place in the road she judged would be the time to start the attack.

She could hear the click of the gunner cocking the weapon as he readied for her order. The trucks neared, and Sauwa tried not to let her mind run through all the things that could go wrong in the next few minutes: would Oleg keep his people controlled, or would they jump the gun, or would her rocket gunner lose his nerve and freeze up at the wrong time. She tried to put such thoughts out of her head and remain fixed on the timing to launch the attack.

It was almost time, the trucks coming closer were now sounding like a cacophony of beasts descending upon them.

When the first truck rounded the bend and was starting to straighten out, Sauwa yelled into the gunner's ear. The earth echoed with a loud, snapping bang as the grenade launcher fired. The air became clouded with a suffocating grayish smoke. The blast tore into the engine block and exploded with a terrible ear-shattering detonation. Another thick cloud of smoke and steam emanated from the engine as the truck ground to a halt.

Sauwa didn't have to look to know that the guerrillas were quickly scrambling up the hill. Throwing the muzzles of their weapons over the edge when they came to the road, they were soon laying down a base of fire at the Bosnians exiting their vehicles responding to the disabled truck.

Another explosion echoed loudly. This time it was the truck in the back, the one housing the security detail. Seconds later a barrage of gunfire hailed down from the hill above.

Oleg had managed to stick to the plan and everything seemed to be working. One by one, the Bosnian soldiers dropped to the ground in widening pools of blood.

Confused, taking heavy fire and their entire security detail roasting in a blazing conflagration, several Bosnians abandoned their trucks and ran toward Jablancia. Others ran the other way attempting to escape around the bend, only to be cut down by gunfire from Sauwa and her group.

Watching them run, Sauwa waited until they were some ways down the road before blowing the whistle hanging around her neck. She continued blasting high-pitched sounds from the whistle until the gunfire died down and eventually come to a stop.

With the attack over, Sauwa stepped cautiously out from her hiding position. "Move out! Move out!" She shouted. Oleg shouted in Croatian, repeating her order.

Rustling in the bushes followed and several guerrillas emerged from the tree line of the hill out onto the road with Oleg leading them. In similar fashion, Sauwa beckoned some of her own team out from their positions to move up and cover the road. Normally she would have left a security element in the ambush spot; however, the awkwardness of both locations made that impractical. She posted teams of three at each end of the road to engage and offer harassing fire if the enemy should arrive earlier than anticipated.

Oleg ordered the rest of the guerrillas to move on the trucks and grab the equipment based on Sauwa's previous instructions. They usually took the valuable equipment and resources for their own supplies. This time, they hurled it all over the side into the ravine.

Sauwa was surprised the order to toss the equipment didn't elicit protests. However, the equipment the Bosnians had was sub-par compared to what they found from captured Serbian stores. The Croatians decided it was better not having to lug all the junk home.

15

A hard-hitting ambush had not yet befallen the Bosnians so close to Jablancia. It would still have the intended effect, looking like a normal ambush to obtain supplies. Hopefully the attack would create enough havoc to demand the Iranian's presence.

Oleg and his people quickly unloaded the trucks. "We have this under control," he told Sauwa. "We'll be out of here soon. You should go and prepare."

Not wanting to leave the guerrillas at such a time, yet understanding that her time was limited, Sauwa nodded to Oleg.

She walked past the destroyed truck and the security team posted at the turn of the road and moved to the edge and down into the ravine. She worked her way off the steep ledge ensuring she left no trail marking her destination.

The trees and bushes soon became an opening to a field of grass allowing her to increase her speed. Sticking close to the bushes, she veered off some more to further distort her line of movement. She skipped across a small creek at the base of the ravine, shivering as the cold water splashed against her boots and lower legs, then climbed up the other side.

Back inside the thickets, she headed in the direction of the ambush. She was exhausted by the time she got to her destination. She was now at the ravine about 200 meters across from the site of the ambush.

Feeling her way on the ground around the bushes, she found the canvass roll she had hidden prior to setting up the ambush. Pulling it out from its hiding place, she untied the two strings holding the bundle together, rolled it open and examined the Mosin-Nagant 91/30. She had taken great pains not to risk damage to the battle sighting of the scope.

Next, she retrieved her Bergen from underneath the same shrubbery.

Crawling toward the edge of the ravine, she took some time to look around. Coming down the ravine, Sauwa had been careful to circle around the long way taking the most vegetated path to ensure she didn't leave any trail that would lead to her position. She knew the Iranian would immediately check for any signs that enemy forces, predominantly snipers, would still be in the area.

Satisfied she had left no such evidence, she grabbed her rifle and Bergen and set about looking for a shooting position.

She slid further back, masking herself within the darkness created by the trees, and found a location behind an old tree and berm that provided a dugout she could nestle into. Various shrubs and bushes helped conceal her and still offered her an adequate view of the area on the other side.

Placing the Bergen so it was easily accessible, she rested her rifle across the berm stabilizing it against the tree. She didn't want to consider taking such a risky shot from a prone position. She wanted as much stabilization as possible. The rifle scope rested forward of the bolt making it awkward to sight through. It was just another problem with which she'd have to cope.

Across the ravine, she could see the Croatians had just finished up. The trucks, with their green canvass covers, were engulfed in flames. Even from her vantage point, she could see that the tires were flat from guerrillas slashing them.

Oleg was busy gathering his force. She watched as they moved slowly down the road one or two at a time, disappearing into the trees like ghosts as if they'd never been.

SAUWA LEANED against the berm and waited. She had learned long ago that the key to sniping was patience and not allowing fatigue to set in. She occupied herself with a small meal and taking sips of water from the steel jar that passed for her canteen.

She heard the sound of trucks roaring down the road an hour later.

Slowly and methodically she picked up her rifle, gripping it firmly as she tucked the butt tightly into her shoulder. She sighted in through the scope at the truck that had been destroyed by the RPG round. She made the tactical assumption that this would be the location the Iranian would most likely stand stationary the longest.

Her head was so far from the scope it allowed her to see the total sight picture of her scope and avoid sight parallax.

Still, she felt her neck stretching to ensure her eye was properly meeting the scope.

The point of the thick, black arrow appeared vertically in the scope and stopped halfway in the center. It was fixed on the driver's side door of the destroyed truck.

She could feel her breathing getting stronger and sought to control her nerves. The nagging, intrusive thought of this turning ugly ran through her mind. She tried to take her mind off the problem. She would have only one shot, and it would be from a considerable distance using a rather primitive rifle.

She scanned the area to see what the Bosnians were doing. A large green military truck had arrived. Behind it were two smaller tactical vehicles encased in makeshift metal covers that served for additional protection. The larger truck stopped at the end of the convoy of deserted vehicles, while the two smaller ones moved past it to the head of the convoy. They drove past the destroyed truck Sauwa was sighted in on, then pulled into a V-shaped security position with their engines coming together diagonally.

For the next several minutes, everything seemed to stop. The vehicles remained still and no one inside them moved.

Sauwa's hand tightened on the wooden stock of her rifle. She was alert to the unpleasant possibility she could have been spotted. Gradually she allowed such thoughts to die down as she continued taking deep, calming breaths. Her more rational mind, now back in control, reminded her that it was a simple precaution Bosnians were taking. Inside they were scanning the immediate area for signs of another impending ambush. Confident in her assessment, she felt her nerves calm.

She readied herself.

Five minutes later the back doors of the two smaller vehicles swung open and several uniformed men emerged. They were all in identical green, leafy patterned camouflage fatigues. A few men looked over the remains of the ambushed convoy while the rest moved to the front of the security vehicles to take up guard positions.

Apparently leading the convoy, a man with a salt and pepper beard shouted to the men in the larger truck. Sauwa couldn't make out what he was saying. Seconds later, the canvas cover on the larger truck opened and more men clad in the same camouflage fatigues jumped out.

The men ran over to the man with the beard and formed a loose ring around him as he waved his hands and issued instructions. Since everyone was dressed alike, Sauwa found it difficult to identify Abhajiri, which was probably the group's intention. Then the group quickly dispersed to assume security positions along the road.

Sauwa noticed one man lingering around the bearded figure yet keeping a good distance from him. She initially thought he was a bodyguard of some sort based on the way the man moved around. As she watched, he began to move casually trying to remain inconspicuous.

He looked over the exploded frame of the destroyed first truck, then turned around and proceeded to the edge of the ravine where Sauwa had staged her team. He knelt down, and looked over the site.

This man peaked her interest because of the way he moved freely compared to the rest of the micro-managed soldiers. Like the rest, he wore a scarf around his head that covered the lower half of his face. She checked to see if there were any other potential candidates for her target. None seemed to fit the bill better than this man.

Her suspicions were confirmed when she saw the commander approach him. The commander, who until then had been barking out orders and had everyone else racing to his beck and call, approached the mysterious figure allowing him to acknowledge his presence before saying anything. The two behaved toward each other more like equals than commander to a subordinate.

Positive she had the right man she sighted in on him and waited for the right moment.

ABHAJIRI EYED the entire spot where he was sure the ambush had been initiated. The indents where the man with the grenade launcher and his leader had waited until the right time were deep and unmistakable. He also found the torn-up grass and shrubs where the rest of the squad hastily climbed up to add to the operation.

"What do you think?" The deep voice of Colonel Mjovich interrupted his thoughts.

The Iranian took a few more glances at the scene before answering. "This was not an amateur job." His attention remained fixed on the ravine below. "I would say they recced this area well and planned quite thoroughly for this ambush."

He rose and twisted so he was facing the ambushed convoy. Looking at the last truck in the convoy carrying the convoy's security escort, he saw it had been destroyed by a rocket-propelled grenade and not simply burned like the rest. "They hit the lead truck to stop the convoy and initiate the ambush. With a second force, they hit the last truck knowing it carried the guards. It is apparent they had been watching us for a while and learning about our operation. The question is why?"

"Because they are targeting us!" Mjovich growled angrily at what he thought was an obvious answer.

Ignoring the colonel, Abhajiri continued studying the site. He racked his brains trying to piece together what had happened and who could have done this. The Serbians couldn't have done this. They didn't have a very strong presence in this general area, nor was this the type of ambush they would generally use.

"It had to be the Croatians. I'd wager it was those guerrillas we've been hearing about. But they've been targeting the Serbs. So why start attacking us all of a sudden?"

"Because you can't trust those slimy bastards! They want to destroy us, that's why," shouted Mjovich bitterly.

As the colonel had nothing intelligent to add, Abhajiri addressed his energies to studying the ambush. Turning toward the hill above, he scanned it as if expecting some mystical answer to appear explaining everything. That Mjovich was eyeing him with irritation did not go unnoticed.

"The ambush was started by the team staged in the ravine," Abhajiri explained. "Then another team in the hill above followed up by attacking the rear and catching the convoy in a crossfire. Whoever was leading them knew what he was doing."

Frustrated Mjovich began to speak. He had barely uttered a word when he heard a distant rifle report. He stopped when a wash of warm liquid sprayed his body and face. He wiped his eyes to regain his vision just in time to see the Iranian drop to the ground in a puddle of his own blood. There was a sizable hole visible in his upper back.

Frozen with shock, the colonel stood like a statue looking in horror at Abhajiri lying dead at his feet. The shouts of his men were like echoes in the distance as he tried to figure out what the noise was, where it was coming from, and what to do.

Finally regaining his faculties the colonel shouted, "Sniper! Sniper! Take cover, everyone!" He didn't even realize he was moving until he felt the road against his face, and Abhajiri's blood oozing between his fingers as he made his way behind the cover of the destroyed truck.

He climbed to his feet and attempted to regain his composure. Looking around, he saw his men diving for cover behind the other vehicles.

On his order, soldiers fired across the ravine. Unsure of exactly where the shot came from, their gunfire was wild and sporadic.

Mjovich peeked over the tire he was hiding behind in a vain attempt to locate the assassin's position. His eyes darted as he looked about not even sure what he was looking for.

The chorus of gunfire laid down by his men tore into the bushes across the way. The colonel couldn't see anything but convinced himself that they had to have killed the sniper. He ordered his men to cease firing. He looked across the ravine and then down at the body of the Iranian advisor.

"This is why I warned you of the Croatians," he murmured with a mixed feeling of terror and vindication. This whole situation proved his point — the Croatians were a threat.

IN THE CONFUSION, Sauwa managed to escape. After her shot hit the Iranian, she took advantage of the chaos that ensued and lowered herself behind the berm. She discarded the cumbersome rifle in the bushes to make it easier for her to travel, grabbed her Bergen and low-crawled a good distance away before she heard the barrage of gunfire.

She could hear and feel bullets flying over her and stayed low to the ground, the bushes and low plants swiping at her as she maneuvered through them.

About a hundred meters away, Sauwa felt she was deep enough in the woods to maintain concealment. Slowly rising to her knees, she looked around.

She could no longer see the ravine let alone the other side. The thickness of the vegetation was dense enough she felt comfortable going the rest of the way on her feet. She continued watching her surroundings to ensure she wasn't exposing herself. Then confident she was safe, she quickened her pace.

16

There hadn't been much of a celebration or much of a break. Sauwa had barely returned to the camp when she was accosted by Marko. He didn't waste time with pleasantries and came right to the point. "You have concluded your mission. We need to get everything ready to move my cargo."

In between her other duties, Sauwa had been planning the cargo move for some time. She had predicted Marko would demand the movement immediately after the assassination. He was rather eager to obtain the goods his people needed desperately. He was also anxious about this first mission. It was so important for his people, he wanted it led by the experienced South African mercenary. He wouldn't have her expertise to rely on much longer and was determined to gain as much benefit from her talents as possible.

Tired and wishing to enjoy a hot meal and some sleep Sauwa wasn't in the mood for conversation. She wished Marko had waited until the next day for this conversation. However, knowing he wouldn't wait, she motioned him to follow her as she led him back toward his quarters. She wasn't about to discuss such a delicate matter out in the open.

His exasperated look was evident to anyone watching as he followed her. The image of the Croatian and the South African looked like an irritated father chasing after a petulant daughter. They made it back to his tent at the far edge of the camp. Along the way, Marko grabbed a couple of his more trusted men who he left to stand guard as he followed her inside.

Sauwa had already made her way over to the large map spread out on the table as Marko came inside. She had spent so much time in the private office of the guerrilla leader that walking into the restricted area was second nature. She was intent on getting the briefing over with as quickly as possible. Marko stepped over to where she was and peeked over her shoulder to get a better look.

"The way I see it," she began, ignoring the fact that he was less than a few inches from the back of her neck. She could feel his breath down on her neck. "Going over land is out of the question. Between the Serbs and our situation with the Bosnians, any land route would invite trouble. These days there are enemy ambushes and patrols everywhere."

She didn't have to look back to know the man was grimacing at her report. "Then what do we do?" His deep voice expressed a demand for an answer.

"The river," she replied curtly as she pointed to a thin blue line that weaved across the map. "The Neretva River is the route we should take." Sauwa waited for Marko's comments. There were none so she continued. "Rivers sit along large swaths of thick vegetation and forests. Because they are so thick and cumbersome, no one emphasizes patrolling them or worrying about them. Neither the Serbs nor the Bosnians have anything in the way of river patrols which will make things a lot easier. For added protection, I plan on moving mostly at night to avoid any unexpected patrols or prying eyes that would cause a problem."

The guerrilla leader remained where he was; his breath still heavy against her neck. "Even so, you'd be sitting ducks out on that river should you miscalculate and are actually accosted. You have nowhere to go."

"They are generally hard to monitor from land and the fast pace of the currents would make it even harder to ambush us. We'll move through the towns and cities we come to at night to bypass any security. Like Jablancia, I would assume the security will be focused on staving off attacks from land, so it shouldn't be a major problem. To aid us we'll need a boat for hauling the equipment and another smaller boat that can run ahead and scout for any possible threats." Sauwa pointed to the line denoting the river. "Boatmen and fishermen still use the river as a means to move about. I figure if we use a normal raft or flat bottom boat, we should be able to sail through even the shallower waters."

Marko said nothing though his breathing had become lighter. Sauwa took this to mean he was getting more comfortable with her plan. His arm reached around her with his index finger landing on the map where the river was identified. His finger slid across the paper as it followed the wiggly blue line finally ending at the point where the river came out into the Adriatic Sea. "But the river doesn't end at Montenegro."

"No, it goes through Croatia into the Adriatic." Sauwa

had anticipated this observation. "That's another reason I like the water. The Neretva River stays well within Croatian territory while in Bosnia and keeps us where the enemy still works but with limited means. We then enter into Croatia where we will be exiting into the open sea. From there, we ride the coastline staying in Croatian waters until we hit Montenegro. I like this route not just for our immediate safety, but also as a long-term plan if you are thinking about making any future runs. As I see it, this is the safest way to get there."

"Any attempt to move over land would undoubtedly place us in the gravest danger. It would also mean having to travel some distance into Serbian country where we would certainly be caught. Afterward, assuming we don't run into any unforeseen problems, your men should be able to take the same route back. This plan should work as a long-term supply route."

Marko's breathing again grew deeper. Sauwa kept silent as she waited while the guerrilla leader was thinking her plan over. She thought about moving out from under him to avoid the discomfort of him breathing down her neck. She decided against moving to avoid disrupting the man's thinking. It was an unpleasant several minutes between his breathing and the silence. Then feeling his head move behind her, she figured he had come to a decision. "Well, what do you think?"

Marko rose, leaving Sauwa a means to step back. "I think it is the most logical plan we have. What will you need?"

"As I said, we'll need boats that are big enough to meet our needs for this mission." Sauwa rubbed her face. "I'll need some men who would know how to pilot such crafts, and Oleg or Enya to serve as an interpreter." She looked around the tent as if expecting some further information to materialize from the display of documents lining the tent's covers. "As for the rest, we'll need weapons and supplies. We can calculate the amounts when we have the boats. I realize our resources are limited, so if we have to work with what we have, we focus on getting down the river. We'll be well within Croatia by the time we have to contend with the Adriatic. It should be easier to negotiate a more suitable means of water travel from the locals. I will be honest. I don't like how this plan is based on too many assumptions and not enough hard facts."

Marko's face broke into a toothy grin. "Yet once more, you have proven yourself a most valuable asset for my people's cause. It is a shame you are leaving us."

"I hope that's not an invitation to stay," Sauwa asked somewhat nervously.

Marko shook his head. "I wish it were so. I would feel so much more comfortable with you here aiding us. However, this is not to be. I am aware of the conditions that brought you to us, and why you will not be returning to your old unit. I've been told they have been hindered considerably by your absence. I also know that a mercenary fighting against his or her will can be more dangerous than the enemy we fight. This is also why I would not think of holding you against your will. Someone like you, with your skills, also comes with your own motivation."

Sauwa didn't argue. The unspoken words between them were that she had been preparing her escape and movement south in the event that Marko reneged on their agreement and tried to keep her. Both quietly agreed that this was the best option for all sides.

With the guerrilla leader satisfied with her plan, Sauwa

departed his tent and made her way to where a group was gathered around a kettle burning on an open fire. The aroma was not something one would describe as alluring; nevertheless, it smelled delicious to a starving mercenary who had been traipsing through the bush and fighting the enemy all day. She had no sooner arrived when Oleg, standing next to the pot, grabbed a metal bowl from a pile of bowls and poured a ladle full of the warm, mushy substance into it before handing it to Sauwa.

She nodded her appreciation. He tried to get her to stay and join everyone in the conversation. Waving, she politely declined. She stepped away from the group and sat on the ground a distance away. Her stomach was growling loudly with a demand for sustenance. It was a dish comprised of meat from the latest hunt and vegetables that were whatever wild plants had been gathered in the woods. A little salt and some herbs made it more palatable. In her current state of hunger, it tasted like a five-star meal. She wasted no time in consuming everything in her bowl.

Sucking down the last morsels she went back for a second helping. The group had largely disbanded leaving only Oleg and a few others to enjoy the small fire. Ladling another scoop into her bowl, she plopped down on the ground next to them and resumed eating. This time she ate more slowly enjoying the warmth and taste of the second plate.

"You are showing your human side," Oleg warned sarcastically. Sauwa chuckled in reply, as she realized she was practically sprawled out on the ground. A long day of combat and trekking around the rolling hills had taken its toll. It was in sharp contrast to the image she had unintentionally built up amongst the guerrillas. An image of being some kind of superhuman combat soldier who never seemed to tire and was constantly ready for action. Now she was feeling the exertions of the day catching up with her as she began feeling the soreness and felt her eyelids getting heavy.

"What will your fans think?" Oleg pursued his original question with the same sarcasm.

"I guess they'll just have to be disappointed." Sauwa leaned back against a chair one of the older men was sitting in. "I'm sure they'll survive."

Oleg chuckled as he relayed her response to the rest of the group sitting by the fire. The older members rumbled with laughter while two of the younger ones gave her a shocked look. Sauwa caught the look of shock but decided to ignore it. She had no interest in becoming a celebrity. She finished her meal and leaned back enjoying the peace of the approaching night and the warmth of the fire. One of the gawkers, a young man in his late teens, was still watching her. She noticed but felt it wasn't worth acknowledging.

The older man who occupied the chair Sauwa was leaning against paid no attention to her. He seemed drained of any energy and had become mesmerized by the fire. Eventually, he stood up and started to leave but not before unfolding a wool blanket he had at his side and draping it over her. He muttered something to her in Croatian as he started to walk away. Slightly bewildered, Sauwa looked around confused. Oleg leaned forward to offer an interpretation. "His wife made that blanket. He gave it to you as a gift for all that you have done in helping us. He also was berating you. He said young ladies shouldn't fall asleep in the cold."

"Well then, I wish I could offer my thanks properly." Sauwa felt a little disheartened that she had been given such a gift and said nothing. But the man had already disappeared. She figured she would express her appreciation when she saw him later. The group began to dwindle until it was just Oleg, some of the younger people, and her. The young man who had been eyeing her the longest had been sitting by nervously biting his lip as if trying to work up the courage to say or do something.

With everyone else gone, he was now able to speak up. Turning to Oleg he quickly spat out a litany of words that exited his mouth faster than machine gun fire. Sauwa watched this event with mild curiosity. Even when the young man nodded in her direction indicating the conversation had something to do with her, she was too tired to worry about it. Oleg blinked several times at the young man. Whatever was being discussed obviously took him by surprise. He apparently was uncomfortable being part of the conversation.

In her semi-lucid state, Sauwa assumed the young man must be asking to propose to her or something. A question she would politely rebuke if there was a need to do so. Oleg was taking his time before explaining the conversation to her. With the glances the young man gave him and the continuing nods in her direction, he finally conceded. "Micha has a request," Oleg began. He looked back at the young man as though giving him a chance to back out. The young man's face beamed with excitement and a twinge of concern as he looked over at her. Whatever it was he wanted, he certainly felt it was important. Oleg continued. "You are getting ready to leave us. Micha wants to go with you. He wants to be a professional mercenary like you."

Sauwa looked at the young man trying to hide her confusion. At first, she thought she was hearing another sarcastic joke. She studied Oleg's face to see if he was playing with her. She expected him to crack a smile and say that young Micha really wanted something more intimate. Oleg's face didn't change, he remained deadpan in his sincerity. She then looked at the young man. His face was slightly distorted as he nervously awaited her answer.

Micha had gone on a few missions and with what little training he had he operated relatively well in the field. Still, he was a novice learning basic infantry tactics. She turned her gaze back to Oleg. "Oleg, are you serious? Why the hell does he want to become a mercenary?"

Oleg shrugged. "He thinks he has tasted battle. He doesn't want to return to the life he had as a farmer. He sees you living the life of intrigue and adventure, and he feels he's cut out for that life. He thinks you have trained him well so far and can train him to be a world-class soldier. In short, Micha doesn't want his old life when this war is over. He wants the life you have."

"No." She looked over at the young man and violently shook her head at him. Before she could say another word, Oleg chimed in. "Can you and I take a walk?" He leaped to his feet. Sauwa threw off the blanket and struggled to stand up. Her muscles were sore and achy, so she was a little slow. She had no sooner made it to her feet when Oleg took her by the arm and escorted her away from a nervous Micha.

Once out of earshot, Oleg turned to Sauwa. "I understand your hesitation, and I agree with your response. But in this case, you need more tact."

Sauwa looked even more confused. Oleg continued. "Remember the sniper who attacked us that day when my ego got some of my people killed?"

Sauwa nodded.

177

Oleg twisted his hands slightly as he found his next words. "Sasha was one of the men killed. He was Micha's grandfather — the man who raised him."

"Oh shit!" Sauwa said with a sigh.

Oleg went on. "Since then, he has been on his own with no other family. He has envisioned himself fighting as a soldier. He thinks this is the path he wants to continue. To him, he is not making this request lightly. He doesn't have anything or anyone to go back to after the war, and he thinks his destiny is as a mercenary."

Sauwa gritted her teeth. "Oleg, this is my life," she said as she waved her hand in all directions of the camp. "Here, living in makeshift camps, living off whatever I can get my hands on. I'm a wanted fugitive in several countries and some very dangerous people are after me. When I leave you, I have no idea where I'm even going."

"To him, you lead a glamorous life of adventure — an adventure that takes you all around the world. While I know you have to decline his request, I'm only saying that with his only family dead and nothing to look forward to when this is all over, he needs something to hang on to. He has been giving this a lot of thought. I'm only asking that you do not just dismiss him as some kid with a childish plan."

Sauwa sighed, "What do you suggest?"

"I'm asking you to take him seriously and let him down easily so he doesn't feel like you're mocking him." Oleg looked at her sympathetically. He was not just concerned about the young man's ego. Oleg had never gotten over how his carelessness had gotten some of his people killed.

With a shrug and a hand wave, Sauwa nodded in agreement as she motioned for them to return to the fire and the young man waiting in anticipation. When they returned,

Micha was standing up awkwardly fiddling with his fingers. Through Oleg, Sauwa calmly expressed her dismay that she could not bring him along. She phrased it explaining her own precarious situation and told him she did not know where she was going or how she was going to get there. Currently, she didn't even have a job once she left, and it would be impossible for him to follow her. Micha lowered his head, his disappointment quite clear. Yet, he seemed to have understood well enough. Mustering as much dignity as possible he wandered off to join his friends.

Sauwa looked at Oleg, who returned her glance with a nod as his means of saying thank you. Tired and feeling guilty, Sauwa grabbed her Bergen and her blanket and slowly walked toward her tent.

———

COLONEL MJOVICH WAS GNASHING his teeth as if he was a wild dog preparing to defend his territory. He paced slowly across the floor of his meeting room like a predator preparing to strike. That was the exact tone of the meeting as his staff stood poised and silent unsure what to do or what was going to happen.

"This has been a disaster," he growled through his teeth. He was of two minds as he looked at his terrified staff. They had lost a skilled military advisor who had made them a far more effective force. Abhajiri's guidance had helped them become more victorious against a better trained and better equipped Serbian force. He had been a true Muslim patriot coming to the aid of fellow Muslims in their dire need. However, Mjovich had found the Iranian's constant calls for restraint and reconciliation when dealing with the Croatians to be utterly naïve. "We've been seriously crippled by this assassination, and this has happened at a time when the Serb bastards are at our throats."

"What is our next step, sir?" One of the young officers dared speak up during the colonel's tirade.

Mjovich's smile was sly and sinister in response to the young man's question. "I know this was a Croatian plot. It was too well planned and too professional to have come from the Serbians. No, this was the Croatians using one of their foul mercenaries. I'm sure of it. As elaborate as it was, it could have even been that Black Widow that supposedly exists."

"Are we believing the myth, sir?" Another officer gulped.

The colonel shook his head. "I don't know. All I know is that our Iranian friend is dead, and I can only think the Croatians are the reason why. They only prove, yet again, what traitors they really are. And, I do intend to make them pay."

17

A few days later Sauwa inspected a long, flat-bottomed boat that looked as if it belonged in a museum. Marko stood next to her his eyes sparkling as if he were looking at a yacht readying for a luxury cruise. "I have found you a boat." His voice betrayed the excitement he was obviously trying to conceal in front of his mercenary.

Sauwa stepped forward to take a closer look. The boat was indeed old yet its hull was in remarkably good condition. Stepping onto it, she felt the wood slightly give as she walked over to the motor in the rear. Like the boat, the motor was something of a relic from the cold war — a model from the sixties-seventies time period. However, relic that it was it had been well maintained by the previous owner and looked to be in acceptable working condition.

That Marko was able to obtain a boat at all was a miracle. That it was big enough to carry a few sizable boxes and crew made it even more unusual. Where he got it was a question she was not prepared to ask. The problems involved were the same regardless of whether they stole it or obtained it from a legitimate source. What troubled Sauwa was ensuring the craft would meet their needs. Pulling the cord the motor turned over immediately. The motor came to life with a loud irregular grumble and a growling burble emerging from the water.

She could feel Marko moving behind her as she scrutinized the boat. "So far the boat looks adequate for our needs," she said.

"I'm glad you approve," he replied. "Getting it was not easy."

"Nothing in this war is." Sauwa was still bent over the side studying the motor. "However, in this case, we're doing a lot with very little."

"You understand the situation well," Marko chuckled. "Sometimes, I think better than many of my own countrymen."

"I just understand fighting a desperate war," she replied as she rose and turned to face the guerrilla leader. "When will we be ready to leave?"

Marko scratched his chin as he slowly looked around. "I intend to have everything loaded within the next few hours. As you and I discussed, my hope is that you will be leaving at sunset."

"I don't like moving at night," Sauwa lamented. "Still, this area is controlled more by the Bosnians and the Serbs than your people. If we move by night with limited illumination and running the boat at low speed, we should be in Croatian country by morning. It's not quite out of harm's way but certainly in friendlier territory. We should then be able to maneuver easier."

"To be honest, I never truly considered the river as a means of transport," Marko said in a way that was meant to be complementary. She could also sense he was looking for some greater reassurance of the mission's success.

"Whether it works or not is yet to be seen." Sauwa knew this wasn't what the guerrilla leader wanted to hear. She also had learned from experience that new ideas tend to sound better in theory than what emerges once put into practice. Despite all her planning, she remained cognizant of the fact that several things could easily go wrong. It was not lost on her that she had developed this plan with limited information and other responsibilities consuming valuable time. It was not an ideal situation.

Marko rolled his tongue across his teeth as he tried not to reveal his high state of nervous tension. He wanted to hear a more optimistic assessment from her. Sauwa moved past him making her way to the front of the boat. She took a moment to examine the smaller craft moored along the river-bank just a short distance ahead.

"That is the boat for your forward team." Marko automatically explained without waiting for her to ask questions. "Like this one, the smaller boat should also be capable of making the trip down the river."

"You aren't a boatman by trade are you, Marko?" Sauwa interjected cutting the guerrilla leader off in mid-sentence.

"No, I'm afraid I am not," was Marko's chagrined response.

Ignoring his obvious discomfort, Sauwa continued. "We have to make it down a very long river with a constantly changing depth and then might still need to use these boats to navigate the coastline."

"I, myself, am not a sailor," Marko spoke up. "However, I am sending some men with you who are. They have traveled these waters for many years and know them quite well."

"Well enough to get all the way to the Adriatic?" Sauwa made no attempt to hide her skepticism. And Marko's face again displayed an uncomfortable look. "They know it well enough," he responded gruffly.

Sauwa nodded in acknowledgment. She reminded herself that they all had to work with what they had. That Marko was able to scrounge up some people who knew something about riding the river was a much-needed break. "Well, if everything is as ready as we can make it, we'll be shoving off tonight."

"Good," Marko replied with a gentler voice. "I guess in a few hours we will be saying our last words to each other." His eyes became soft as he looked at her in a paternalistic way. "If I don't have a chance to say it later, many of us including myself will miss you. You have not only been a great mentor to us, you have also been a good friend."

His words took Sauwa off guard. She smiled warmly as she looked him in the eye. "I have also appreciated your hospitality and your friendship."

"I only regret that we could not offer you a permanent home." Marko placed a hand on her shoulder. "I know that outside our country you are a fugitive and highly sought after by some powerful governments. For all that you have done for our cause, you should have been rewarded at least with our protection so you could have a home where you could find peace. However, it is not to be, and the only reward I can offer is to give you a means to escape before your enemies are at our door."

"I thank you for the kindness you have shown me." Sauwa touched Marko's hand in an affectionate way. The conversation ended with both of them leaving the boat. Marko continued back to camp as Sauwa went to check the smaller boat. While it was still daylight she wanted to make a thorough inspection.

———

IT WAS ALMOST DUSK when the final five wooden boxes were loaded onto the larger of the two crafts. Sauwa was standing by in a pair of brown worker's trousers, an oversized grey knit sweater, and black knit watch cap. A charcoal grey flannel coat completed her attire. The clothes weren't simply intended to help disguise her while on this mission but also serve to help her when she escaped into Montenegro. Her fatigues would not help her disappear as easily.

She reached behind her and pulled a weapon from her waistband. The Zastava M57 Tokarev pistol she had been given was in fine working condition. It had been the primary weapon of the Yugoslav army up until the 1990s. In light of the number of recent attacks on the Serbian army supplies, it had become a premier weapon for the guerrillas as well.

Fingering the left side of the pistol, she felt it to make sure the safety was on. She pulled back the slide enough to verify she had a round in the chamber. Rifles and grenades would be carried under cover. Her concern was having something she could reach quickly in close quarters or to address potential threats that they might meet along the way. She had told Marko she expected a civilian disguise would deter prying eyes, but they both knew it had only a fifty-fifty chance as most forces shot at ethnicity, not uniforms. Her hope was that after tonight they would generally be in Croatian controlled territory ensuring less chance of enemy contact.

The guerrillas had finished with the final crate and had

draped a large canvass cover over the top. Then they added a few bundles of large netting and some fishing gear. At first glance, it would appear they were fishermen and their equipment was simply piled in the boat. She supervised the operation carefully, paying close attention to any details that might attract unwanted attention.

She heard thrashing in the trees behind her. Turning around she saw Marko arrive followed by an entourage of men clad in similar attire to her own. This would be the crew going with her. Directly behind Marko was Oleg. He was waving the others to the boat while he and Marko joined Sauwa.

"Everything all right so far?" Oleg asked with a big grin while rubbing his hands excitedly.

"We're as good as we're going to be," Sauwa replied in a noncommittal tone. "We'll still be taking a serious risk."

"When aren't we?" Marko spoke up. "No matter how we do this, the situation will be the same."

"Are these are the men going with us?" Sauwa looked at the motley crew moving toward the boats.

"They will be security for this mission," Marko explained. "They will be the group in charge of future supply runs after this. As to your earlier concern, they have had experience navigating this river all the way to the sea."

"Well, let's check our communications," Sauwa said as she tucked the pistol back into her waistband and reached into a box containing two small walkie-talkies. Handing one to Oleg she walked several paces away before pressing the button and speaking into the contraption. "Testing, testing."

Oleg's voice crackled over the receiver as he replied. "I read you. I read you very well."

She walked back to where the two men were standing.

Marko looked satisfied. "Remember these only have a short reach, fifty meters at best. So don't get too far away from the cargo boat."

Next, they pulled some small flashlights from a box. Illumination was essential for moving in the pitch darkness. It was also a good draw for enemy attention. They had a mixture of small flashlights that they could use for most of the journey. The hope was that their flash wouldn't be powerful enough to be easily seen by anyone patrolling the hills, but would provide enough light to at least see anything in front of them. They had a few larger, more powerful flashlights to be used in the event of an emergency. After a quick check and finding all the flashlights were in good working order, Sauwa took one of the walkie-talkies, a big flashlight and a smaller one. She handed the rest of them to Oleg who went over to the larger boat to distribute them to the others.

Marko placed his hand on her shoulder. "When you get to the border, we have friends there with good connections to the black-market networks. They will assist in getting you with people who can help you get to where you need to go."

"Then I guess we're ready," Sauwa sighed. Marko's promise of contacts to the border sounded questionable and did little to comfort her. She reached down to retrieve her Bergen. Throwing it over her shoulder she gathered the rest of her equipment and headed for the smaller craft. The sun was getting lower, creating a beautiful dark pinkish sky. She wanted to take some time to enjoy the sight but knew she couldn't.

She was barely in the boat when Oleg joined her. "This is it," he said his voice still holding a hint of boyish excitement.

Sauwa didn't reply. Her mind was occupied with other things, not the least of which was a small rope bracelet she wore on her wrist. It had been a going away present from Enya, the only friend Sauwa could remember having in a long time. She played with it nervously as she looked back and thought about how she was now bound, once again, for a life of uncertainty. The last year she had been living in a hellish war zone, but at least she was no more hunted than anyone else with whom she had fought alongside. She was not a fugitive here, and her past crimes were of no concern to anyone around her. It was a strange freedom she had enjoyed. When she crossed into Montenegro all that would change.

Dropping her gear into the smaller craft, Sauwa walked the few feet over to the larger boat. Oleg was waiting with the rest of the men. He approached her as she neared. "Well, we've checked all the gear," he began. "The lights work, and the guns are covered but accessible if needed in a hurry. I checked the fuel in the motor, and it's filled to the top. We only were able to find enough fuel for one reserve canister for each boat." Oleg nodded in the direction of the smaller craft. "I don't know if we'll have enough for the entire voyage."

"We work with what we have and improvise the rest," Sauwa explained with a shrug. Even though the supply raids against the Serbs had yielded an abundance of useful resources, the guerrillas were still lacking many things. Fuel remained in short supply, and Sauwa was surprised they were able to find any working hand-held radios with full batteries, no less. It came as quite a relief that the radios worked when tested. They were the only communication devices the Croatians had. If they hadn't worked, the crew would have been unable to communicate between the two boats as they rode the river at night.

Sauwa looked over the crew of men standing before her. They were mostly older men in their mid-forties. A couple of men appeared to be at least fifty. Regardless, she had worked with them all on one mission or another and knew them all to be strong and able. A couple in the group had their issues working with or taking orders from a woman. It didn't matter. For this journey, Oleg would be presented as the one in charge. She was simply an advisor offering her services when asked.

At the end of the line of men, she spotted a much younger man who was trying to hide his face beneath the hood of his coat. It took her a couple of seconds to realize it was Micha, the boy with whom she had spoken to a few nights before — the wishful adventurer. "What is he doing here?" Sauwa turned and quietly whispered to Oleg.

"He volunteered for the mission," Oleg replied in an equally hushed tone. "Marko nor I felt there would be any problem. He's proven himself capable the times he's been on a mission."

"He also wants to go with me when I leave," Sauwa reminded him. "That he was so adamant makes me a little uneasy about him coming."

Oleg lowered his head to be closer to her ear as he whispered. "We have to leave shortly. It's too late to get a replacement. If you send him away, we have to explain it to Marko who won't like making such a change at so late an hour."

Pursing her lips, Sauwa eventually capitulated. She looked over at young Micha, whose tight facial expression reflected he had a good idea of what their hushed conversation was all about. She smiled and nodded at him pleasantly. His face relaxed into a beaming smile as he dropped the hood of his jacket back revealing his whole face.

With everyone assembled, and only minutes until they stepped off, Sauwa explained the final instructions to Oleg. "We keep the boats moving at medium speed. We should use only the small flashlights to see ahead and reserve the larger ones for emergencies. Every thirty minutes on your order we cut the engines so we can conduct an audio recce and listen for any sounds that might alert us to a threat. If we come across any potential enemy patrols, we keep the motors off and drift with the current until we're out of danger. The same goes for any towns or cities we pass, we keep the motors off and move past paddling quietly."

Oleg nodded as he turned back to the men and explained everything in Croatian. His orders were met with a chorus of complying grunts and head nods. One of the men spoke up with his hand tentatively raised. Cocking his head slightly toward Sauwa, Oleg interpreted. "They want to know what should be done if we are attacked?"

Turning away from the men, she tilted her head back in Oleg's direction. "As we're in the lead boat, we'll most likely make the first contact. If confronted, we act like we're just looking for a place to fish. We'll give a squawk on the radio to let them know they need to park along the bank until the issue is resolved. Everyone keeps weapons hidden, and we'll try to move without any conflict."

"If it comes down to violence, you and I will initiate the shooting and the others should try to move past us while we provide cover fire. Should the fighting prove too intense, we will improvise on our next course of action from there. No matter what we have to protect the cargo from damage. They must keep it out of harm's way at all cost."

"In the event we get ambushed, rivers are also incredibly restricting. It will make it easy for the enemy to hit us. The enemy can easily plan ambushes that we won't be able to avoid. That said, the lead boat will move no less than seventy meters ahead. If we take fire we will pull forward and establish ourselves on the opposite side of the river. The following boat will stop short of where the ambush point is, pull up on the same side of the river, disembark, and assault through it. We'll provide cover fire from the other side of the river.

"Once we've cleared the ambush, we have to continue moving up on foot along the banks a good distance to make sure we aren't going to encounter anyone else."

Oleg lifted his head and repeated her instructions in Croatian. His orders were once more responded to with grunts and nods. The group disbanded with most of the men returning to the larger boat. One of the older men stayed back and moved up to meet Oleg.

"This is Smolesk," Oleg said, as he brought the man forward. "He has fished and sailed the river since he was a boy. He will be with us to help navigate the waters."

Sauwa looked the man up and down. Smolesk had a round, pudgy face that matched his equally round, pudgy gut that was quite visible under a baggy wool sweater and equally baggy field coat. His mustache was so thick and unkempt that it hid his lips entirely. "Pleased to meet you, Smolesk," Sauwa bowed slightly to the older man.

Smolesk didn't wait for Oleg's interpretation; he replied cheerfully in Croatian. That his lips appeared not to move under his mustache made him look like a cartoon character when he spoke. He was a happy, affable sort that Sauwa liked instantly. The trio started back toward the smaller boat. As she turned to leave, Sauwa caught sight of Micha. The young man was looking at her from the bow of the larger boat. He was about to step in her direction when he was stopped by one of the other Croatians who took him by the arm and pulled him back on board. He continued to stare at her as if watching the love of his life walk away.

Stepping into the smaller craft, Smolesk moved back next to the motor so he could steer. Sauwa and Oleg quickly took one more inventory of equipment. In addition to the radio and flashlights, they also carried three Kalashnikov rifles loaded with thirty-round banana magazines. They stowed an additional twelve magazines, four for each rifle, and two boxes of grenades. Marko and Sauwa had discussed using a grenade launcher instead of the East European grenades that were of generally poor quality and unreliable.

Despite Marko's insistence, Sauwa turned down the grenade launcher. She would have liked it, except it was too big and awkward for such a small craft and would be far too difficult to adequately conceal. The grenades would have to do. The rest of the inventory consisted of some food to get the trio through the night, a pair of wooden rowing oars in the event the boat motor wasn't usable, and a map in a plastic bag with all the towns and cities they might come in contact with marked.

Sauwa knew that the river boasted numerous inhabited places along its shores. Aside from Mostar, which was one of the biggest cities in the country, she had little knowledge of the others. Smolesk waved his short, pudgy finger over the map and began speaking something in Croatian as he pointed to the various ink stains denoting the locations. She looked up at the kindly older man and gave him a shrug reminding him she had limited understanding of his language.

"He was explaining that most of the villages are small

with very few people or buildings," Oleg interpreted. "So, aside from Mostar, most of the places should be easy to pass without much difficulty," Sauwa said as she looked at both men waiting for an answer. Oleg quickly interpreted for Smolesk who promptly turned and nodded back to her in reply.

"All right then, let's get moving," Sauwa ordered as she went to untie the boat from the large rock mooring it to the pier. Smolesk took the cue to start up the motor. He pulled on the cord a couple of times before the motor came to life and water began to gurgle and spray mists. Pulling the rope away from the rock, the boat was now free and began to slowly pull away from the shore.

Looking back, Sauwa and Oleg watched as the men in the larger boat followed suit. The ropes securing the boat were rolled in and they followed the smaller boat into the river. Both boats were flat-bottomed making it easier to pass over the shallower parts of the river. As an added precaution, the boats were lined along the sides with of old tires cut in half to allow a buffer when navigating around the sharp, jagged rocks. As the current became a little stronger, it slapped against the side splashing large drops back onto the occupants, continuously annoying them. The journey was finally underway.

18

Darkness descended leaving the world around them in pitch blackness. The guerrillas had enjoyed a full half hour of mild light from the retreating sun before they were navigating with nothing more than the weak illumination of their tiny flashlights. Sauwa sat at the front of the boat holding the light as she carefully scanned ahead for any protruding rocks or debris while ensuring they stayed on the river rather than too close to the aligning bank. Behind her, Oleg stood with one of the oars ready to use if he needed to push the boat around any obstacles. Aside from a few near accidents earlier, the ride had gone relatively smoothly.

Every so often, Sauwa diverted the flashlight to look quickly at her watch. True to their plan every half hour they cut their motor and signaled back with a radio squelch to notify the second boat do the same — the time was 19:00 hours. Sauwa nodded to Oleg, who turned and ran his hand across his throat giving Smolesk the order to cut the motor. The boat instantly went silent. Squelching twice on the walkie-talkie, Oleg looked back hoping the other boat was following suit. In the blackness, the only evidence the other boat was still there was the slight glow of the other flashlight. Between the noise of the river and the low sound of the motors, it was impossible to tell.

Sauwa had redirected her attention and light to observing in front of them. The lack of visibility also meant that her other senses became more acute to compensate. The water was calm now leaving an eerie silence. She could make out distinct sounds, such as twigs and branches cracking from someone or something moving along the land nearby or whispered tones of people talking. The quiet river made it easier to hear potential threats. It also made their own movements more noticeable as the thrums of their motors could be heard. The darkness continued to offer protection because they could not be seen aside from a mild illumination.

At the allotted time, Sauwa nodded back to the two men. The motor came alive, and Oleg sent another squelch to the second boat. Both boats began to move steadily again. The narrow beams of the small flashlights continued to provide their only means of forward sight. A few times Sauwa spotted a tree in the river or a collection of rocks protruding from the water. Oleg easily negotiated around the obstacle by using the paddle while Smolesk radioed back to alert the others.

Sauwa was continually tense as she kept a lookout for an attack. She hated that they were entirely vulnerable on the water. She had initially assumed that rapids would move them too fast for an enemy to lock them down. But the virtually lifeless water presented something totally different. They would be too slow to move quickly past any enemies they encountered. Even if they cranked the motors up to full speed, they would be sitting ducks and virtually defenseless to any enemy that caught them out in the open. In the dark, moving too fast with the lack of illumination could easily cause them to crash into something. The only real hope she could imagine would be that the thickets and rocky terrain would make it nearly impossible for an enemy on land to intercept them.

Midnight came and the silence of the night was suddenly shattered by the sound of multiple explosions going off in rapid succession shaking the earth and rising in spectacular displays of colorful lights in the distance. The explosions were followed by a loud barrage of machine guns going off wildly in what sounded like multiple directions. What worried Sauwa and the guerrillas was the gunfire was going off just a short distance from the river. A few times the sparks from the heavier guns could be seen lighting up the nearby pockets of trees.

"Should we dowse the lights?" Oleg's voice broke her concentration, and Sauwa felt him hovering near her. His breath was hard and rich with the flavor of nervous energy. She knew he was hoping she would flip off her flashlight and instruct him to order the same for the boat behind them.

"In this darkness, we'd crash," she replied to Oleg's obvious dismay. "Which means we keep going and hope we bypass this battle, or we move to the thickets and wait to move at dawn."

Neither option offered much relief to Oleg. In either scenario, they risked being embroiled in the midst of what was turning into a hellacious firefight. Sauwa continued holding the flashlight and searching the river ahead. She could feel Oleg slowly crawl away from her as he returned to his original spot. Behind her, she could hear the voice of

Smolesk saying something in hushed tones to Oleg and grunt slightly after Oleg's reply. Apparently, he wasn't happy about the decisions either.

For the next thirty minutes, the fighting fluctuated between intense exchanges for short periods to intermittent exchanges of shots between sides. The bombardments could only be from Serbian artillery and remained concentrated somewhere off in another direction far from the river. Lighter gunfire remained close making it clear the warring factions were moving. The situation soon became more complicated with the sound of men shouting and running through the trees while laying down fire as they moved. The voices were loud enough that at times pieces of their conversation could be heard clearly. Sauwa couldn't understand what was being spoken but knew instantly that the language being used was not Croatian or Bosniak — it was Serbian.

She felt her heart race as she quickly turned off the flashlight. She didn't need to tell Oleg. He had no sooner watched her than he was already on the walkie-talkie instructing the following boat to do the same. Both Sauwa and he looked back just in time to see the scant beam of light vanish.

"Kill the motor," Sauwa commanded softly. "With Serbs this close, we can't chance that they won't hear us."

Oleg relayed the order to Smolesk who promptly cut the motor. Oleg picked up the walkie-talkie to explain to the rest of the band. In seconds both boats were dead quiet and drifting slowly while the battle raged only a short distance from them. No one spoke as they waited nervously anticipating what might happen next. They heard the voices of Serbian soldiers as they moved closer to the shoreline. All it would take was one artillery round landing too close and lighting up the area long enough for the Serbs to spot the boats on the river or even someone shining a flashlight in their direction.

Sauwa stood at her post her head turned toward the shore and the direction of the battle. She could feel the boat slightly vibrating and realized it was Smolesk shaking with fear. She wanted to try and stop him but decided it would be a wasted effort. Instead, she fixed her mind on strategizing for her next step should they be discovered. They had no information on where they were and no idea how extensive the battle was. There was no way to estimate how long they would be in danger.

The current was light and in the absence of the motor, the boats were little more than inching along. In the absence of any light, Smolesk was navigating blindly, and Sauwa feared what would happen if they should get thrust up onto the bank. They would suddenly become sitting ducks. Another major concern was the second boat. Though none of the men was the hot-headed attention seeking type, she figured they had to have already dug out their weapons in preparation for a fight. As inexperienced as they were, it wouldn't take much for one of them to start firing. She didn't like the situation but without knowing what they were up against she was hesitant to make any move beyond what they were already doing.

The situation was quickly made worse when it appeared the Serbians made contact with someone who wasn't their friend. Suddenly, the land was awash with gunfire as the Serbs engaged with whoever they were fighting. The darkness along the bank was quickly disrupted as guns began firing erratically lighting up the bank with flashes of white and red tracers. Screams and shouts erupted from all over as the two forces closed in on each other. Soon Sauwa was listening to another language being shouted by numerous voices she recognized instantly as Bosniak. It was clear to her that the battle on land was being waged between Serbs and Bosnians.

With the current truce between the Croatians and the Bosnians that could be a good thing. However, given the situation the guerrillas had with continued hostilities toward the Bosnians, either side was likely to kill them at first glance.

The shooting intensified as it became obvious the armies on the bank were much larger than initially thought. To make matters worse, bullets were soon flying over their heads in massive waves and tearing into the surrounding water. It was only a matter of time before they were going to get shot.

She looked behind her to see both men hunkered down in the boat trying to take whatever cover they possibly could get. "Call back to the other boat!" She screamed at Oleg's silhouette. "Tell them to turn on the motors full blast and have them use the big flashlights. We're going to make a run for it!"

Oleg screamed back to Smolesk in Croatian, and the older man quickly scrambled to start the motor. As he did, Oleg was already on the walkie-talkie issuing orders to the other boat. Sauwa grabbed for the larger flashlight. She waited until she heard the motor roar to life. Once she did, she flicked on the light and aimed it toward the front looking down and ahead. Almost immediately the boat was speeding through the water.

"They're following us!" Oleg shouted.

She looked back to see the powerful beam of light as the other boat followed suit. Onshore they heard shouts and screams. Bullets continued to fly over their heads and into the water near them, but it was impossible to tell if they were intentional or just misdirected rounds from the existing firefight.

"They've spotted us!" shouted Oleg. "I can hear someone commanding their troops to fire on us!"

"Tell our people to fire back and keep going!" Sauwa cried. She wanted to offer cover fire for the larger boat, but it would have been futile. In this instance, it was better not to offer another obstacle for the larger boat to have to navigate past quickly. Behind them, she could see the second boat unleash a barrage of gunfire toward the left bank. Grabbing a grenade from one of the boxes, Sauwa fingered it in the dark as she felt around to get her bearings while she used her forearm to steady the flashlight. Pressing the spoon tightly as she gripped the checkered metallic object, she pulled the pin. Taking a deep breath, she raised her arm and hurled the grenade as hard as she could. Jumping back down she focused the flashlight back on point as she steadied herself. A second later a thunderous blast erupted behind them as the grenade exploded on shore. She didn't look back to see where it hit.

"Good work!" Oleg shouted. "You were on target. I think it killed some of them!"

Sauwa didn't respond, she was now entirely focused on the river ahead. Speed was their only hope for survival. Smolesk navigated the water with the precise expertise of a true seaman. It was amazing to see such skill from the man with so little light available and under heavy gunfire. Bullets continued to fly over and near the boats, but they kept going nevertheless. At an elevated speed, the boat was pounding heavily into the water with waves splashing into Sauwa's face. It was running down her shirt and freezing her body. Still, she held her position.

The boats continued knifing through the water until the storm of bullets began to dissipate and the rattling of gunfire faded away. The only remaining sounds were the boat motors roaring over the water. Making a judgment call, Sauwa instructed Oleg to slow the boats down. Oleg hesitated at first, then relayed the order to Smolesk. The boatman eased the motor to a slow cruising speed. At the same time, Oleg was on the walkie-talkie issuing a similar command to the following vessel. Sauwa heard shouting from the communicator that she could only assume was an angry protest. Oleg relayed his command again, this time in an equally angered growl. Seconds later, the boat, that had been speeding up to them began to slow and gradually fall back to its original distance behind them.

With the noise dulled significantly, Sauwa listened carefully. Artillery blasts and gunfire were still going off in the distance. However, none of it seemed to be happening in their immediate vicinity. "I think we escaped them," Oleg said with relief.

Sauwa didn't reply to the Croatian. Instead, she held silent as she continued to listen. Her chief concern was that while they had escaped the middle of one battle, they could still be deep in hostile territory with forces from one of the armies still lurking about. She listened intently for the slightest hint that they were not alone, but ready to give Smolesk the signal to accelerate the motor at any time. Time passed and nothing occurred. The two men sat nervous and impatient, not knowing what to do as they watched the movements of their leader.

Satisfied that they were alone, Sauwa turned back to

Oleg. "I think we're out danger, I don't hear anything unusual."

Oleg breathed another sigh of relief as he turned to explain things to Smolesk who responded in equal fashion. "What now?" Oleg asked as he wiped his brow with the sleeve of his coat.

"We keep moving until daybreak," Sauwa said. Her attention was still focused on the river ahead. "We can't see anything now, and I don't want to take a chance that we're still too close to that action back there. We'll keep moving until light. Then we need to find someplace to tie up while we assess casualties and any damage. From there, we'll decide what to do. In the meantime, we keep going."

"Do we go back to the smaller lights?" Oleg asked, still a little edgy.

"Yes," Sauwa replied, hesitantly. "We've made our presence known to the very people we're trying to avoid. The question is can we hope to disappear again. Tell the other boat to go back to the smaller light, and let's hope we can stay hidden."

Oleg relayed the message back to the other boat. As he did, Sauwa switched out the bigger light once again.

THE EARLY LIGHT of the dawn was little more than a crack emanating from the crest of the mountain range. After the long night without sleep and the adrenaline-pumping excitement, Sauwa could barely keep her eyes open. She was drained of energy and freezing from the water that had earlier poured down her shirt. Her only saving grace from catching a cold or worse was Smolesk throwing a blanket over her shivering body.

Despite her exhausted state, she held firm keeping watch and directing the flashlight to guide them. Oleg had already drifted off to sleep sometime back. Smolesk started to wake him, but Sauwa deterred him. She felt it better to let him sleep now to enable him to function later. The trailing boat continued following at a respectable distance. Since the gun battle, they had remained quiet with no radio communication. Sauwa could only wonder how everyone was holding up after last night.

Looking over at the darkened shoreline, she remained concerned about the possibility that they could have been pursued. After hours of silence with only a few alien noises that had momentarily attracted her attention, she was convinced they were relatively safe. She looked out at the black waters that were starting to sparkle as sunlight began to touch them. It was a hauntingly beautiful sight.

As the sun started to provide better visibility, Sauwa began searching for places to tie up. The banks on both sides were lined with thick trees and dense undergrowth. Suddenly, she saw a spot with a collection of thick overhanging bushes that presented a place they could conceal themselves. Better yet, it was on the other side of the river from where they expected trouble. Kicking Oleg awake, she allowed little time for him to totally revive as she pointed out the location and instructed him to contact the other boat.

Fumbling for the walkie-talkie that had been lost somewhere in his clothes, he managed to find it and relayed her orders. A voice crackled from the receiver. It sounded as though the man talking was as tired as the occupants of the smaller boat. Slowly the boats drifted to the other side. Once there, they weaved into the thickets of overhanging bushes.

The sun was still barely up allowing just enough illumination to see the general vicinity. As the second boat came into view, Sauwa could see instantly the two motionless figures laid out in the center of the boat. And two more were clutching obvious wounds. Leaving Smolesk to tie up the boat, Sauwa leaped onto land and, with Oleg following closely behind, inched her way along the riverbank for several feet until she was able to set foot on the larger craft. Two of the men helped her and then Oleg aboard.

Kneeling down she began to examine the injured men. Between the darkness from the shadows of the overhead shrubbery and little illumination from the sun's early stages of rising, visibility was limited.

"Why didn't you tell us you had taken casualties?" She asked, directing her question to no one in particular. Oleg, who was right behind her spoke in Croatian, she assumed he was repeating her question. One of the injured men who groaned as he spoke replied.

Placing a hand on her shoulder, Oleg leaned toward her ear. "Roughly explained: we were on the run, had narrowly escaped a horrific gun battle, and we weren't sure we were still near the enemy. We weren't exactly in a position to do much, if anything, about it."

It was a logical assumption. Even now, she wasn't sure they were out of danger. Reaching over she gently took hold of the bicep the man had been clutching. Having trouble seeing, she asked for a flashlight. Oleg addressed the crew and in seconds a light was flashing on the man's wounded arm. He had slid his coat off leaving on his long-sleeved collared shirt. The blood-soaked sleeve and the tear across the side where the bullet passed left an easy marker to find. Ripping the sleeve further, she wiped away the patch of drying blood that had started to cake around the wound.

To her relief, she saw that the wound was little more than a graze; it had barely cut into the muscle tissue. She gave it a quick dose of alcohol from a bottle of vodka. Her action was met by a reflexive recoil from the men watching and the patient gritting his teeth as he endured the stinging pain. A cloth lightly soaked in vodka was tied neatly around his arm to finish the job.

She turned to the other wounded man to see that Oleg had already begun treating him. Sauwa paused realizing he was attempting to demonstrate leadership in front of his men. She didn't want to make the mistake of asserting herself too obviously. After all, Croatian men still tended to take a dim view of women giving orders. That they acknowledged her skill as an expert soldier was the only reason she was tolerated when asserting any leadership. This was a liberty she was careful not to abuse.

"He has a stomach wound," Oleg said, as he turned to Sauwa. "He's lost far too much blood, and it's doubtful he will live much longer."

Shining the light over the wounded man, Sauwa saw a thick pool of blood forming at the man's feet. It was being fed by streams of red liquid pouring over his pant legs onto the boat's floor. Looking up, she saw the man's face was looking drained and waxy. Even in the limited light, Sauwa could see Oleg's facial expression as he looked at her. It was an unspoken plea for help. Climbing over the gear and minding the feet of the dead men, she worked her way over to him.

Instructing Oleg to get the man onto his back, Sauwa

reached for the nearest piece of cloth, which was someone's discarded shirt. As Oleg worked to get the man onto his back, she busied herself wadding up the shirt and saturating it with vodka. The action met with the same bridling sounds as before. Seeing that the man's shirt had already been lifted to expose his wound, she pressed down on the wadded shirt applying pressure to the gaping hole. The man passed out. Sauwa ignored him as she took a knife and began cutting the pants of one of the dead men. She eventually was able to slice off a long strip that she tied around the wounded man's stomach to secure the shirt. The dampness of her clothes and the chill of the morning once again made her shiver with cold.

"Have him lie as still as you can," she explained to Oleg, "or he'll risk moving the bullet inside him and possibly puncture a vital organ if he hasn't done so already." Sauwa then leaned back to catch her breath. The sun had risen enough that she was able to see the faces of the men around her clearly. They all wore looks of despair. This was only the first leg of their trip, and they had lost two of their comrades and been virtually sitting ducks in a horrific gun battle.

Oleg returned to where she was sitting. "Can we speak somewhere?" He sounded almost desperate, and he looked concerned. Nodding slightly, Sauwa slid to an upright position, crept across the boat, then moved onto land. Oleg followed. She started toward the smaller boat but was stopped by his hand gently touching her shoulder. She turned back and saw him nodding his head landward. Together the two moved silently up the bank and further into the trees.

When they were out of sight of the rest of the men, Oleg turned to her. "Do you think we can keep moving on the river?" His voice sounded edgy and nervous. He clearly needed an answer.

Sauwa was quiet for a time as she collected her thoughts and assessed the situation. Finally, after keeping Oleg in pained suspense, she answered. "In the absence of any other viable option, we should keep to the river. It's our best means of travel."

"But after last night," Oleg responded, "the Serbs had artillery and seemed to be a much bigger force than what we anticipated. Which means we don't know anything anymore. And, they probably sent patrols to follow us."

"You're right," Sauwa cut in. Her eyes peered at Oleg with intensity. "They were locked in a battle with the Bosnians, and we don't know who or which group is where. We also don't have any other viable means of travel. Even if we did have trucks we could seize, we still have to navigate the same land the enemy would be controlling. All of which keeps us in the same dangerous position. Right now, the river is still the best option we have for the time being."

Oleg went silent. He wanted a different answer, but he knew Sauwa was right. Sensing she needed to explain further, Sauwa continued. "Remember, whatever concerns you have, keep in mind that both sides were engaged in a serious conflict as you yourself pointed out. We need to assume that they were too busy dealing with each other to be too concerned about some mysterious group of boatmen that briefly came upon them in the course of their battle."

Oleg ran his tongue over his lower teeth creating a bulge in his lower lip. He was clearly disgruntled and nervous. He, like her, understood the risk of the venture they had undertaken. The attack last night was being treated as if it were entirely unexpected. "I don't like this. I don't like this at all."

He finally spoke, shaking his head and pacing back and forth. "No matter how this goes, I feel that we are now taking too much risk." He looked back at her as if expecting to hear Sauwa concur with his assessment and possibly give him a reason to turn back.

With his eyes focused intently on her, he could see she was rubbing her hands over her shoulders as the cool air moved against her damp clothes. He knew she needed to change and get warm, but he needed an answer. He didn't want to be the one to make such a decision, not alone. He needed to tell his men that last night had been all for naught, and they were going home; or that even after they had narrowly survived, they were going to continue. The greater problem was what he would tell Marko if they came back empty-handed. Having the professional mercenary agree with him would certainly make the decision more acceptable in either case.

The look in his eye said that he wanted her to agree with him. Sauwa instead shook her head. "You know I have a vested interest in all this," she began. "I'm not saying a thing regarding your decision. You have a deathly injured man that needs treatment and most of your crew is still reeling from last night. If you decide to turn back now, I won't stop you or raise a protest. However, that means we also part ways here and now. I have to get out of the country, and this was supposed to be my means to do so. If you're no longer continuing on, then let me grab my things and that will be the end of it."

Oleg was taken by surprise. It was not the answer he was looking for, nor was it at all what he expected. Standing there watching her face, he was mystified to see that it was blank of any judgment or unspoken emotion. She was simply waiting for an answer as if she were entirely indifferent to whatever response he was about to give her.

Oleg deliberated over his next move. His greatest concern at that moment was the thought of navigating the waters back upstream without her and knowing what possibly awaited them. "We need to go on, I guess."

"Don't do it on my account," Sauwa, cut in. "If you're only doing it because you feel you owe me something..."

"I'm not." He replied calmly cutting her off in mid-sentence. "You have done a lot for my people, and we owe you a great deal. I'm also doing it because I feel we have to. We're in a war, and we run a risk no matter which way we go. And, our injured man, if he even survives, is not going to find much help back at our base camp. At least not compared to what kind of treatment we can get him if we can get further down the river." He noticed she was now shivering. "So, what do we do now?"

"We need to take inventory of our current situation," Sauwa replied. "Now that the sun is shining, we can have a better look at what damage we sustained. I also think it would be advantageous for us to give everyone a few hours of rest before pressing on."

"Do you think that's wise?" Oleg was concerned.

"Honestly," Sauwa began, "it's necessary. We also need to acquire some intelligence on what we're up against. That can best be answered by running a quick patrol a little way ahead. The rest of the men can get some sleep while some of us have a look around."

Oleg folded his arms as he nodded. It was a good idea. Finally acknowledging that Sauwa was in need of some dry clothes, he directed her back to the boats. Returning through the foliage, they found the men solemnly contemplating the bodies of their fallen comrades. They had moved to the boat to see if the man who had taken the gunshot to the stomach had joined the line of corpses spread out on the floor of the craft.

Taking on what was going to prove a difficult task, Oleg began explaining the new plan to his men. As he did, Sauwa trotted over to the smaller craft. She found Smolesk still perched at his station. He was looking as sullen, unsettled and melancholy as the men in the other boat. Disregarding the men around her, she began to remove her damp clothes. She had spent all night shivering and was saved from freezing only by Smolesk's blanket. After being forced to endure her chilled condition while planning with Oleg, she was in no mood for modesty. Stripping down to her cotton underwear, she found that amongst the older men, she was relatively ignored as they directed their attention between mourning their dead comrades and listening with dismay to their leader's orders. From their scowling, the news was not being taken very well. The only eyes she caught taking notice of her were those of Micha trying to look indifferent but was still casting an occasional eye in the direction of the foreign beauty now scantily clad.

She hung her clothes over a few nearby branches to help them dry. The only other clothes she possessed were her combat fatigues that she had stuffed in her Bergen. Happily, she found that the Bergen had missed the splashes of water that she endured during their hasty getaway. The dry clothes felt pleasingly warm the moment they touched her body.

19

H er tactical camouflage fatigues weren't ideal, as they prepared to set out to discover what lay upriver. In truth, Sauwa figured it was largely a moot point. Whatever lay ahead, the disguises were simply to avert a second look from any enemy soldiers who might be lurking along the river. After last night's battle, they had to assume that concealment was no longer a consideration.

Most of the men were eating their breakfast of some canned food and dry goods that they ate cold. It had been a bit of a struggle persuading the guerrillas not to build a fire to cook their food and get warm. The notion that fire would give away their hiding spot did not seem to sway them. It took the more forceful approach of Oleg laying down an order with some growling commands for the men to comply. Even as Sauwa and he were preparing to head out on their patrol, the demeanor of the men was grim. She had no illusions that his order would be dismissed the minute they were gone.

With Bergen, tactical kit and a rifle, Sauwa waited for

Oleg to make the last-minute prep on his own gear while staving off a final plea from young Micha. Despite language barriers, it was obvious the young man wanted to come along with his adopted hero. Micha kept eyeing Sauwa as he leaned against Oleg, practically grasping his coat lapels. Oleg gently attempted to push the young man aside as he tried to leave. Eventually, Oleg broke free and joined his cohort.

"Is he going to be okay?" Sauwa asked as she looked back to see Micha watching her with the distraught look of a man losing the love of his life forever.

"He'll be fine," Oleg grumbled as he awkwardly climbed up to meet her. "He's young and full of the energy of a young man wanting to see the world. This is all about him wanting to be with you and not with a bunch of old farmers who will be boring him to death while we're gone."

The long night and the adrenaline rush were starting to take their toll. They were all tired and becoming despondent to the world around them. Some were already rolling out blankets and getting comfortable enough to doze off. She noticed that Smolesk had taken his weapon and was maintaining some form of a watch. He cradled his rifle in his arms as he peered out through the overhanging branches to see across the river. Some of the other men were sensible enough to keep weapons close as well. It wasn't the best security, but it would have to do.

With Sauwa taking the lead, the two moved out. Keeping to the tree line adjacent to the riverbank, the two carefully picked their way along the river. They had wanted to take the high ground but were deterred by a wide grassy field that offered no place for concealment. Using the high ground would leave them exposed to anyone around for a good distance. They opted to move along the riverbank despite it being far more cumbersome to negotiate. The sun was now directly overhead bringing a welcome degree of warmth. Sauwa's skin was still somewhat clammy from the cold and dampness.

She kept a constant eye out for any strange movement on the other side of the river. Thankfully, the river was a good 200 feet in width where they were. This provided a nice protective buffer if they should be discovered by someone on the other side. Still, she was quite aware how easily they could be noticed by an enemy patrol passing through. She wanted to use the camouflage field jacket she brought with her, but with Oleg not having his camouflage clothes with him, she figured camouflaging herself was futile.

Tramping along they kept to their usual procedure of stopping every 300 meters to listen for any alien sounds. The plan was to move out about 1,000 meters ahead, search the surrounding landscape to get a good idea of what was going on and then return. At the first pause, they listened. It was relatively quiet aside from identifiable animal noises. Confident they were alone, Sauwa and Oleg carefully crawled upward until they were at the edge of the bank looking out at the field ahead. Everywhere they looked was deserted for as far as they could see. They did not see any tracks that suggested anyone had been in the area recently.

Confident that all was good, the two slipped back down into the vegetation by the river bank and continued on. The soft dirt and the awkward position of walking along a hill made the journey difficult. As the long period without sleep started to take its toll, Sauwa felt herself fighting to remain alert. She didn't relish the equally arduous journey back. Observing Oleg, she assumed he was feeling the same way.

Dark circles had formed under his eyes looking like what Americans referred to as raccoon eyes. He was struggling to keep his head from sinking.

Sauwa took him by surprise when he felt her hand suddenly grab him. He froze and was about to voice a litany of abrasive words when he stopped at the sight of her index finger pressed tightly to her lips. She nodded over to the other side of the river and heard the sound of men speaking rather loudly. Both knelt down slowly and listened. The voices were coming from the tree line just above the embankment. Rustling bushes helped provide a more accurate sign of their location.

"Serbs!" Oleg blurted out in a shocked whisper. From the distance between them, it was impossible to tell who was there or what exactly they were saying. But Oleg's assumption was reasonable. The two remained motionless in the bushes as they listened and waited. The bushes on the other bank continued to rustle indicating the Serbs were moving in the direction where they had left the men and the boats.

"I hope our guys didn't disobey orders and start a fire," Sauwa whispered back to Oleg.

"Shit! What do we do?" he asked nervously. "We have to hurry back and warn them." He started to move, but Sauwa stopped him by taking his arm.

"Don't be stupid," she growled through her teeth. "We can't do anything. We would expose ourselves moving as fast as they are going. Besides, even if we could, we wouldn't get there quickly enough to do anything."

"So, then what?" Oleg was shaking with anticipation.

"They're on the wrong side of the river, and they don't seem to be looking for anything in particular. If our guys are quiet and in the bushes where we left them, they shouldn't be noticed. We press on as planned and finish the recce. Then we will double back and report to the others."

Oleg didn't like what he was being told, and his facial expression said as much. Begrudgingly, he nodded in agreement. The two held their ground as they waited for the mystery men to move on. In the meantime, they found protection behind a large feathery bush that concealed them like a shroud.

When they were sure the patrol was gone, they carefully stood up and continued their journey. Oleg was tense; he felt they had nearly been discovered and was looking around more carefully. He was certain a similar group was on their side of the river ready to spring at any time. Sauwa said nothing. She knew they escaped detection because the mystery men weren't really paying attention to anything. Their lack of tactical discipline and laziness telegraphed the message they would be heard well in advance. They also appeared inclined to stay in the field away from the challenging bushes along the rim.

She said nothing. It would have been pointless to explain anything to him in his current mental state. She understood that Oleg remained concerned about his men and the possibility of an enemy patrol catching them off guard. In truth, she shared his concerns and would like to give them a warning. However, she also knew that they would never have gotten to them in time. The amount of commotion they would make trying to race back would have alerted the Serbs anyway. But since he was convinced he was somehow betraying them, her explanation would come across as rationalizing.

At another three hundred meters, they were just short of a rock ledge that towered over the river closing with the other side enough to make a narrow funnel-like passage. "If we get ambushed in there, we'll be sitting ducks," Sauwa exclaimed as she observed the passageway. "We have to see how far this narrows out and if anyone is up above."

Oleg nodded as he gulped nervously. Sauwa led as the two began moving forward slowly. She kept her attention fixed on the cliffs above concerned that if someone were up there, they would easily be spotted. Traversing through the thickets they came to the base of a cliff. Circling around the base, they began working their way up the hill. Thankfully, the vegetation remained such that they were able to enjoy a fair amount of protection as they moved up.

Despite it being a small hill, it was steep — almost straight up. As tired as the two of them were, it was an arduous journey that slowly sucked away whatever energy remained. Halfway up the hill, the vegetation gave way to an open grassy field. Arriving at the bush line, they stopped. At Sauwa's direction, they removed their packs and kits. Leaving Oleg to keep watch, she crept forward on her hands and knees, armed with only a knife and her Tokarev pistol.

Her movements were slow and precise as each step and hand placement was taken with calculated consideration. She was like a predator from the jungle preparing for the kill. Her sharp instincts were tuned for the slightest sound, an unfamiliar odor, or the sight of any movement. Digging the side of one foot into the soft earth and stabilizing her hands, she pushed her body forward. Sauwa continued this exercise step by step until she was near the top.

As the land started to curve, she was finally able to see over the top. As expected, there were two men dressed in camouflage fatigues and tactical gear sitting lackadaisically near a cooking pot hung over a small fire. Both men were hunched over with their elbows on their thighs and hands holding their sunken heads. Sauwa identified them instantly as Serbians. She assumed they were an observation team meant to keep watch on the river and the surrounding low ground. By the look of their makeshift setup, bedding, and dug-in fire hole, she figured they had been there for a while and were going to be there a while longer.

Though the men were bored and oblivious, they would certainly notice boats full of Croatians progressing down the river. They could also pick them off going through the narrow water passage or, at the very least, alert their commanding unit and give them away. It was a dangerous proposition nonetheless. Killing them was starting to look like a necessity. On the other hand, if they were sending regular radio checks and suddenly missed a report time that would prove just as dangerous if they were dealing with one of those rare units in the Serb army that were organized and disciplined.

Noting their radio was under the tent canvass propped up by their bedding, she figured such orderly protocols did not exist. Deciding to go for it, Sauwa slowly reached for the Tokarev tucked in her belt at the small of her back. She had dried it off and changed out the ammunition after spending the night in wet clothes. But not having any oil to lubricate it with and no chance to test it beforehand, she worried the weapon might not fire when needed.

Just then one of the men rose to his feet and started toward the cliff grumbling something in his language that she couldn't understand. He stopped and began fumbling with his fly. The other man was still sitting with his back to her and only grunted in his response to whatever his comrade was mumbling about. Seeing her opportunity,

Sauwa released her hold on the pistol and instead went for the knife on her belt. It was a long double-edged bayonet made for stabbing.

The first man continued until he was at the edge of the cliff. At the same time, Sauwa seized the moment. Moving quickly she placed the knife between her teeth to free up both hands. Clearing the last few feet, she took the knife from her teeth into her hand. She was less than five feet from the sitting man and silently closed the distance when he started to turn toward her.

Before he could complete his turn, her free hand thrust up from behind grabbing his head and pulling it straight back. He barely had time to understand what was happening when the sharp steel blade tore into the soft flesh of his throat and down into his chest cavity silencing any sounds he would have made in the last brief seconds of his life.

Holding him steady, Sauwa dropped down behind the man's body. She kept him in a sitting position with her own body and, with her free hand, reached for her pistol. The man near the cliff's edge had finished urinating and started speaking while he admired the view. He glanced back briefly to see his comrade still sitting. He did not notice his friend was sitting awkwardly with his arms dangling, or that there was an arm over his shoulder wrapped around his neck clutching the knife in his throat.

The man returned to the view breathing in the fresh air. He turned around again when his mind had fully processed the image he had just seen. By then Sauwa had retrieved her weapon, reached over the dead man's shoulder took aim at the man on the cliff. She quietly prayed it would fire. She did not relish taking a larger man head-on in a fight, and she didn't have time to go for the rifle sitting several feet off to the side.

She fired a quick group of three shots. The first round missed by just an inch. The man continued his turn presenting a full silhouette; he was struck by the next two bullets. Both rounds landed in the softness of his lower stomach, and his hands dropped to investigate the sudden pain in his gut. Sauwa rose to her feet, taking the pistol in both hands aiming more carefully. She fired two more shots. This time both shots entered directly into his skull and tore through his brain. He fell back and dropped over the cliff.

Sauwa walked over to the edge to see the man's corpse float slowly down the river. She had just finished tucking the Tokarev back into her belt when she heard a rustling noise behind her. She turned to see Oleg racing up the hill with his rifle clutched tightly at the ready.

"Is everything okay?" He asked in between gasps of air. He looked around observing the scene. He took in the body of the knifed man who was laid out like a rag doll with arms splayed. "He's Serbian all right."

"Yes," Sauwa replied as she came back over to examine the dead soldier more closely. The few days of facial growth was nothing unusual. What caught her attention was the lack of any rank insignia on the man's uniform. Though wearing military fatigues were common in the Serb army, too many things suggested that these two were not regular soldiers. Examining the site further, she saw a flag draped along the far side of the tent. It was black with a white skull and crossbones tucked between Serbian lettering that she couldn't translate. "They're not regular Serbian army soldiers, they're Chetniks."

Chetniks was a general name given to Serbian nationalist

paramilitaries that had sprung up on their own at the start of the conflict. Called from the historic ashes of World War II, these groups had been partisans who had fought bravely against the Nazi invasion. In the current conflict, they were organizations of ultra-nationalists supporting the dream of a Serbian homeland free of Muslims, Croatians and any other *'undesirables'*. The Serbian government denied any connection to these groups, though it was common knowledge they gave them training and logistical support. In return, the paramilitaries gave cover to the Serbian government by performing the more criminal offenses of mass murder and ethnic cleansing. In the war with both Bosnia and Croatia, Chetniks were by far the most murderous and criminal. In the current conflict in Bosnia, it was estimated that there were some thirty-thousand Chetniks augmenting the Serbian army.

"Chetniks, you say!" Oleg exclaimed. His first nervous gasp was soon replaced by a look of sheer hatred. He marched over fired off a large wad of spit that landed with force upon the dead man's head. He began growling out something in Croatian as he looked down at the body with deep contempt. He was about to start kicking the corpse when stopped by Sauwa, who sharply interjected. "Get a grip. We have more pressing matters to attend to!"

It took a little time for the Croatian to calm down. Eventually, he turned back to Sauwa. "Well, now what?" He was much calmer and working to regain the bearing of a professional soldier.

"From this, we know that the Serbs are operating on this side of the river." She surveyed the landscape trying to determine if there were any enemy patrols close by and how exposed they were. "We can also assume these Serbs were who we encountered last night in that gunfight."

Oleg wiped his mouth with his sleeve as he began to pace. Sauwa looked down the hill to see how far the narrowing passage could possibly go. To her dismay, it appeared the passage went on for a considerable distance — possibly a kilometer or two. She also studied the hillside to assess the landscape. From her vantage point, she could see both sides of the river. The hills seemed to consist of bare, open grass fields with very little other vegetation. It was not a situation she liked.

The enemy would be shooting downward from an elevated position giving them a significant advantage. What concerned her was that in the absence of thick vegetation, the boats could not navigate quickly past any ambush. Her initial plan anticipated the attackers would have to negotiate cumbersome foliage to continue an attack. On open grass fields, pursuers would be far more mobile. In this tight setting with fast moving water coupled with pockets of jagged rocks guarding edges of the shoreline, they could only run the boats at a minimum speed.

"We need to get off this ridge," Sauwa commanded.

Oleg was still looking at the narrow water passage and how far it seemed to go. "This will be dangerous." He explained as if trying to inform Sauwa of this reality.

"We're hoping that no enemy will be up here lying in wait during the time we'll be moving through." Sauwa's tone and manner of speech hinted at uncertainty. She glanced at Oleg and saw his look of defeat. Apparently, he expected she would offer a plan or explanation that would make the situation less hopeless than it was. She looked around the campsite. "These aren't soldiers, they're militia fanatics. As a rule, they tend to be more trigger-happy psychopaths than disciplined soldiers."

Oleg perked up and started to study his cohort carefully. "What are you thinking?"

"I'm thinking that we are not dealing with a well-organized operation. I doubt that with all that's going on, no one is really concerned with doing regular radio checks. They probably just placed these guys up here with orders to report any suspicious activity and forgot about them. If that's the case, we have a good chance that these guys won't be missed for quite a while. That gives us a window of opportunity."

"Can't we try and move at night?" Oleg asked, throwing out the idea.

"We're in a bad place either way," Sauwa replied, shaking her head. "That was probably an enemy patrol we encountered back there. If they are operating on both sides of the river, then we can't take the chance they won't come upon us in a few hours. Besides, trying to navigate this passageway at night would be suicide even if we had the big flashlights and were moving at a reasonable speed. On the other hand, if we try to move out in broad daylight in the open water, we're sure to be spotted. As I see it, if we move at a good speed, we should be able to hit the passageway fairly rapidly. Since they don't have much of a guard up here, it will take them some time to figure out that their observation post has been taken out. This should create enough confusion to force them to take time to get organized. By then we should be through the passageway and, hopefully, in more open waters."

"That doesn't sound like much of a plan," Oleg replied skeptically.

Sauwa continued. "What's more, we don't know what awaits us once in open water. The Chetniks could be amassed on the other side of this ridge."

Oleg was becoming desperate. He was hearing one problem after another with no good end in sight. "So, then what? We simply chance it, and hope for the best?"

"No," Sauwa shook her head. "First, we get off this hill, where we're not out in the open. Then, we retrieve our gear. You'll return to the boats as planned and have them start moving downstream."

They began making their way down the hill for the safety of the trees. As they did, Oleg continued, "You will not be coming with me?"

"No," she replied. "For this not to be a complete gamble, I'll stick around and keep watch along the hill crest. When you start to approach, I'll keep watch along the hill moving ahead of you and provide cover in case you run into any unforeseeable threats. I'll try to stay ahead of you and keep the way clear. You can pick me up at the other end of the passageway."

The two made it into the tree line and picked up their gear. Oleg was still nervous, but the idea provided something more than the almost no-win situation he had been hearing minutes ago. "This plan sounds better. What happens if you see trouble at the end of the passageway?"

Checking her pockets and Bergen, Sauwa replied, "I have five grenades and several additional magazines of ammo. If I see trouble, I'll try and catch them by surprise. I'll let loose with what I've got and hope to dislodge the enemy as best I can. That should give you means to escape or at least fight your way out of it."

Strapping his pack onto his back Oleg nodded, his face

awash with sweat. It was obvious he didn't relish the idea of trekking the long distance back to the boats knowing the Serbian Chetniks were lurking everywhere. Sauwa had strapped on her Bergen and was fixing her hair neatly under a black knit watch cap. She unrolled her camouflage field jacket and cap and started to cover herself. She finished with a quick application of dark camo paint.

Oleg finished his cover, turned and started on his journey. Taking up her rifle and tucking it under her camouflage cover, she watched him make his way through the trees and thickets. Sliding deeper into the bushes, she looked for any signs of someone approaching. She was thankful when she saw no one else in the area and settled back somewhat to get more comfortable.

The long night and even longer morning were gradually creeping up on her, and she fought to keep her eyes open and not fall into a lull. She told herself over and over that once this little endeavor was concluded, she was going to crash out on the boat. She waited patiently with her eyes focused on the river and the surrounding landscape waiting for her people. Aside from the typical animal noises, birds chirping and squirrels darting about in the trees above, she heard nothing else, certainly nothing that would pose an ominous threat.

As she waited, Sauwa began to feel a cold shiver of concern. It was not the concern for any impending threat. Instead, it was the concern for what was to happen to her after they arrived in Mostar. They were only a few kilometers from that city. A few days after reaching Mostar, they would be on the coast. When that happened, she would have another very uncertain future ahead of her. She had virtually no money aside from a few British pounds and some Irish currency. There was only a slight hope that Marko or the people he trusted would keep to their word. She was not looking forward to her future.

A short time later she saw the boats traveling down the river. They were cruising at a rather more rapid pace than anticipated. Standing up abruptly, Sauwa began moving at a slight jog along the tree line up on the grass. She figured even though the boats would slow down to navigate the pass, they would still be traveling at a decent speed. Meanwhile, she was having to traverse the moist ground along the side of a somewhat steep hill and fight her way through the foliage.

It was a pace she estimated she would have to keep up for close to two kilometers. She ran along the tree line keeping her attention on the crest of the hill. As she had predicted, the crests were deserted allowing her to assume that the two men at the observation post had been the entire security. She couldn't speak for the other side of the river, but she didn't hear any explosions or gunfire and presumed they were deserted as well.

The hillside was moist and slippery. A few times she lost her footing and nearly went crashing to the ground. The canopy-like camouflage field jacket constantly tangled around her making movement even more difficult. The tired lull she had been feeling earlier had given away to a second wind as she felt her alertness return and was somehow able, despite fatigue, to keep up her pace.

On several occasions, she thought she heard something and dove quickly into the trees. A few seconds of observation was all she allowed herself before pressing on. At what she determined was the halfway point and offered a degree of foliage going all the way to the top, she sprinted several meters the rest of the way up the hill. Reaching the top she dove into the cover of a thick collection of leafy bushes. Her heart was racing and a cold sweat covered her body causing her T-shirt and undergarments to stick to her skin.

She looked down to see the Croatians guiding their boats through the thin strip of water between the high jagged walls of rock below. Though they were drifting at a slow lazy pace, they were only a short distance behind her. Satisfied that all was going well so far, she changed her focus to the crest across the river from her. She studied the landscape for a time until she was satisfied there was no concealed threat. Crawling out from under the bushes, she slid back down the hill a little way until she was once again flush with her protective cover. Needing to pick up the pace she started jogging.

Clouds were starting to gather overhead. By the dark grey coloring of the bigger ones coming in from the West, she figured there were only a few hours until a storm would hit. The weather was getting cooler and a chilly breeze was beginning to pick up adding to her discomfort. Still, she pressed on.

At the end of the line of hills, she slowed to a walk then to a creep. Sauwa slipped once again deep into the tree line as she prepared for her next move. She approached the end of the hill and heard voices. At first, it was little more than a low pitched murmur but, as she got closer, she could make out part of the discussions. It took her a moment to recognize they were speaking Serbian.

She worried that the boats would move past her and get taken by surprise by a possible hornet's nest of Chetniks. She also worried about attracting attention to herself. Maneuvering cautiously she wound through the woods carefully monitoring the landscape around the bend. Her eyes scanned the area as she analyzed and evaluated the terrain for tactical purposes.

As she rounded the bend, she caught sight of several men in various types of dress lounging along the river. From their relaxed behavior, she believed they were part of a patrol enjoying a break. Not surprisingly, their weapons were clumsily stacked off to the side, guarded by a single man only mildly attending to his duties. Thankfully, it appeared she had preceded Oleg and his men to the location. This oblivious group of Serbs hadn't yet noticed the boats coming toward them down the river.

Taking advantage of the situation, she knelt behind a thick berm concealed by wild grass and bushes. She watched a little longer. Setting her rifle against her knee, she reached into her coat pocket producing the green pineapple-like grenade she had been carrying. Pressing down on the spoon with a tight grip, she prepared to pull the pin when she caught sight of another group of men emerging from the woods across the way.

Stopping her action, she watched as this new group sallied out of the tree line. They were attired in combat fatigues, cradling rifles and carrying a few rocket-propelled grenade launchers. It was clear these men were not regular soldiers but Chetnik militia. Like the men along the river, this new group also seemed to lack any tactical discipline as they moved in a tight group as opposed to a well dispersed tactical formation. While a few held their weapons at the tactical ready, most kept them in a position that was simply comfortable. Though they weren't talking to each other as in a social gathering, they certainly weren't actively observing their surroundings either. All of these factors worked to Sauwa's advantage.

The problem was now that she was faced with enemies on both sides of her, she wasn't exactly sure how she was going to handle the challenge. To make the problem worse, the Croatians were due any time and were about to find themselves facing off against at least fifty armed men.

Thinking fast, she decided her primary threat was the group just coming back from patrol. Concentrating her attention on them, she pulled the grenade pin the rest of the way free and waited for them to get closer. Gripping the spoon tightly, she could feel the sweat dripping down her back. She hated working with Soviet-made explosives. They were cheaply produced, of extremely poor quality, and incredibly unpredictable. She had witnessed on more than a few occasions someone activating a grenade only to have it blow up instantly instead of the expected four-second delay. The thought of those poor souls worried her as she thought about what might happen the instant she released the spoon.

Preparing herself, she clutched her rifle with her free hand ready to move quickly to start firing on everyone after the grenade blast. The patrol came closer until there were less than ten meters between her and them. Concentrating on the part of the patrol where the most men were closest together, she took a breath. Flinging part of her camouflage cover over her shoulder so as not to be a hindrance she drew back her arm. As if a pitcher in a game of American baseball, she hurdled the destructive object and dropped to the ground seeking protection behind the dirt berm.

She barely had time to be thankful that it didn't blow up in her hand when a powerful blast exploded and delivered a force that she could feel vibrating on the ground at her feet.

Her ears were still ringing from the terrible rippling echo when she reached to pick up her rifle in both hands. Rising to a kneeling position behind the grassy berm, she lifted her Kolesnikov-47 until the wooden rifle butt was tucked tightly into the pocket of her shoulder, and she was holding it at eye level.

In front of her, men wildly ran about confused and scared. It was another sign that they were a far cry from a professional unit. Honing in on the one man who seemed to be in a position of leadership and trying to bring about some sort of order, she sighted down her rifle. Soviet military AK-47s were hardly precision weapons. Having had some time to gain familiarity with the weapon, she was able to compensate by estimating the windage and elevation. Sighting in on the suspected commander, a burly fellow, with a long shaggy beard who was gradually getting order restored, she fired a quick burst. The rounds tore into the man's chest cavity knocking him off balance. He stopped shouting and began walking about in a confused manner as if he had just been punched by some unseen adversary. This lasted a few seconds until he eventually dropped to the ground dead.

With the commander dead, chaos again took over as the remaining men took to wildly running around trying to escape from the mystery sniper. So inexperienced were the Chetniks, they never once took notice of her. At that time, she saw the boats with Oleg and his men arrive on the river. A few of the Chetniks caught sight of them and began firing sporadically in their direction. This was returned by a more coordinated blast of gunfire from Oleg and his men. They saturated the Serbs, who quickly dove for cover. A few tried to take to the tree line where they were picked off by Sauwa as she emerged from the berm and began moving sideways in the direction of the river but still making sure to stay clear of the barrage of fire being laid down by the Croatians.

Walking alongside the hill, she found herself once again in the open. Clearing the bend she took a chance and started for the boats. Trying to run, she found her camouflage clothing too restricting as it tangled about her. Tearing at the straps that tied it, she threw the cumbersome garment to the ground along with the cap. She bolted in a dead sprint heading for the boats.

Recognizing her instantly, the Croatians directed their fire away from her. Though it was only a few meters to the river, she felt like it was several kilometers the way her heart was pounding and her breath getting shallower. The larger boat had pulled out ahead of the smaller craft with the men on it laying down continuous fire on their hated enemies while the smaller boat, manned by Oleg and Smolesk, moved closer to the shoreline. Smolesk held fast at the motor while Oleg continued to fire.

Making it to the shoreline, Sauwa leaped onto the waiting craft. The wooden frame of the boat shuddered as she landed hard. She could feel the humming vibrations moving through the boat as Smolesk revved the motor to full speed. She felt a weight on top of her and realized it was Oleg covering her as they made their escape.

"Thank you for the warning," he whispered into her ear.

She said nothing as she felt her body start to relax and her eyelids grow heavy. Her last bit of energy was finally used. She dropped into a deep sleep.

20

Sauwa's first sensation as she started to recover was of rough cloth. The itchy annoyance turned out to be a blanket Smolesk had thrown on her the night before. Although scratchy, it gave her warmth and shielded her from the otherwise chilly air. The second feeling was a body pressed up against her, breath tickling her neck, and a hand resting firmly on her hip. The gnarled beard entangled in her hair told her Oleg had decided to join her.

The vibrations of the boat rumbled through the wooden boards inspiring the urge to pee. Using a little force, she managed to free herself from Oleg's grip. Little by little she peeled back the coarse blanket that surrounded her.

A chill accosted her as she threw off the last bit of covering. Her eyes gradually adjusted, and she looked up at the hazy, darkening sky above. Rising onto her tiptoes she looked further out to see the pinkish aura of the sunset gleaming over the skyline as the sun bidding its last farewell to the day.

"What is it?" The mood was altered by the groggy voice of Oleg gradually waking.

"How long have we been out?" Sauwa asked in an equally listless tone.

"I'm not sure of anything right now," Oleg slid his hand over the now unoccupied wooden boards in front of him. "Still warm," he signed.

Smolesk spoke, a slight chuckle accompanying his jovial tone.

Oleg interpreted without waiting for an invitation from Sauwa. "He said it was about time we decided to join the world of the living. He says we've been out all day."

"I have to pee," Sauwa announced. She was beyond caring about modesty having had to rough it for so long with men all around her. She went about her business lowering her garment and undergarment, her bare arse visible. Balancing carefully, she edged her bum over the side.

As she went about her business, Sauwa carried on her conversation. "What's our status?"

With a shrug, Oleg turned to look back at the following boat. "We've lost three men thus far. The first ones you already know about. Our last little engagement gained us one more casualty, but nothing dire or detrimental."

"What's happened since our little gunfight anyway?" She adjusted to stabilize herself on both arms. "Did they follow us? Have we seen any more signs of Chetniks or the Serbian army prowling about?"

After a quick discussion with Smolesk, Oleg replied. "No, they followed with some gunfire but made no attempt to pursue us. Since then it has been quiet."

"We must finally be in Croatian held territory," Sauwa

said. "After the damage we caused, they would be on us hard, if they had command of this area."

Oleg observed the darkened shoreline. "I imagine you are right. We're too tempting a target for trigger-happy Chetniks who had just been taken by surprise and blasted."

"How are we for fuel?" Sauwa finished her activity and was back in the boat doing up her trousers.

Smolesk had broken out some dried meat and dry bread. It wasn't a lot, but it was a decent evening meal for someone who had burned so many calories and had not eaten all day. It tasted like a king's feast for the starving mercenary.

Oleg spoke to Smolesk in Croatian. Smolesk waved his head from side to side as he replied. When Smolesk finished talking, Oleg turned back to Sauwa. "We've gone through half of our reserve fuel already. He says the others are in a similar position."

Rubbing her forehead, Sauwa raised her head toward the sky, as if expecting the answer to the dilemma to be somewhere amongst the stars. "We have to get more fuel soon. The question is where?" She reached for a map, unfolded it and in the remaining daylight and with the assistance of one of the flashlights followed the line depicting the Neretva River.

Smolesk reached out over the map pointing to a line. He said something guiding his finger a short way down to the dot representing the location of the city of Mostar.

"He says we are less than six kilometers from the city," Oleg interpreted.

"Do you think we can find fuel there?" Sauwa asked.

"I think the bigger concern is will we be able to get in?" Oleg tone was suspicious.

"We shouldn't have too much trouble. It's been under Croatian-Bosniak control for over a year." Sauwa looked up from the map. "My concern is finding assistance from our supposed friends when we get to town."

A strange expression flashed across Oleg's face. "Croatians and Bosnians share the city. We should tread lightly, tensions may still be strong."

Sauwa shook her head. "Since the signing of the Washington agreement in March, the standing militaries of both groups have reconciled quite a bit. I wouldn't say everyone's on friendly terms, but they're cooperating better. What we should be most concerned with is the possibility we'll be relieved of our goods. We're a militia dealing with a standing army. That has a tendency to cause issues when they decide their needs outweigh ours."

Oleg looked back at the second boat. "You think they'll pilfer our goods for themselves?"

"I don't see what's stopping them once we get near Mostar."

Oleg rapped his knuckles on his knee. He didn't know what to do.

Sauwa continued, "We should go into Mostar ourselves. Have the other boat turn out all lights and cruise past silently. We collect what we can and meet them farther downriver after we've all passed through. We have nothing in this boat that would be of interest, so we should be able to make a few pleas, get some assistance and hopefully be on our way."

"Do you think it will work?" Oleg was still rapping his knuckles.

"It's the only plan we have," Sauwa replied. "If we show

up with our boat full of equipment at their docks, we lose any ability to control the situation once they have us. This way we have a chance, a slight one but at least we have something."

Oleg ran his lower lip under his teeth several times as he contemplated the situation. He hated to think he and his men could be in danger from other Croatians. However, he was also aware of how standing military forces viewed guerrilla units. If resources were in short supply, HVO soldiers would not hesitate to confiscate anything they wanted. He looked back at Sauwa and studied her one more time. Then reaching for his walkie-talkie, he started relaying orders back to the second boat.

As this was going on, Sauwa's attention was diverted by a large hand on her shoulder. She looked over to see Smolesk staring back at her. His face was kind and warm. Taking his hand off her he reached down and grabbed some clothes that were on the floor near his feet and handed them to her. They were the clothes she had worn last evening and had left them out to dry.

Relieved at having something other than military attire to wear, she took the clothes from his hand nodded in appreciation and changed. Smolesk turned away to focus his attention on the darkened shoreline and the river ahead. In like fashion, Oleg tried to keep his attention on the boat behind them as he spoke over the walkie-talkie his eyes occasionally peeking in her direction.

Back in less suspicious civilian attire she leaned over the side and washed the remaining camo-paint from her face. Thankfully, she had only used a bare minimum, so it was not the usual tedious endeavor. Having had enough of the cold river water, she turned back and positioned herself in the boat. Even though the wood deck had left her aching, the deep sleep had invigorated her. Her energy was back. As she was taking in the fresh air and enjoyed the last morsels of her dinner, she felt a strange peace come over her. It wouldn't last long, but it felt good nonetheless.

To everyone's relief, the lights of the city were scant and intermittent, either from lack of energy access — due to the destruction from the conflict — or as a security precaution. The additional darkness worked in their favor. The night offered far better concealment than anticipated.

As they neared, they heard the voices of men talking to one another from the trees along the shore on the right. Sentries patrolling the city's outer perimeter crisscrossed the area with their flashlights.

The guerrillas remained silent on their boats. Sauwa, Oleg, and Smolesk slowed but kept their motor running to draw attention away from their comrades. The boat following them cut their motor and fell back. Their flashlights went dead. Then as planned, the second boat used the city lights to guide them past the lead boat heading farther along the river.

The low purr of the idling engine soon captured the attention of a security patrol. Lights flashed in their direction, and the gruff voice of a man speaking in Croatian called out in a way that could only have been a command. Without first conferring with Sauwa, Oleg replied to the dark figure in the wood line. He shouted back what was presumably a response intended to ingratiate them with the locals.

Sauwa's assumption changed when she saw Smolesk wince and become nervous as Oleg continued. She said nothing and allowed the conversation to go on uninterrupted. When he finished, Oleg turned back flustered. Smolesk spoke to him in a scolding tone, and Oleg nodded in response.

"What happened?" Sauwa interjected.

"They are suspicious of us," Oleg replied. "They wanted to know who we are and why we're out on the river at this hour. I tried to think fast to come up with something."

"And...?"

"I told them we were refugees escaping the violence up the river."

It was a believable story. The look on both men's faces suggested there was more to it.

"When they started getting quiet, I got nervous. I joked that we were smugglers. That's when they got more suspicious. They asked how we came to be out on the river, why there are so few of us, and why we weren't trying to get into the fight by joining one of the local guerrilla groups. I panicked. I gave them some story about how we had lost our farm and were stranded. I don't think they bought it. Oleg hung his head. Maybe that smuggler crack was a mistake."

Sauwa waved the explanation away. Now wasn't the time for guilt. "Did they make any reference to the other boat?"

Oleg shook his head. "No, they seemed focused entirely on us."

"Then we're doing exactly what we should be doing," Sauwa said. "If we can just get permission to land."

"Oh, that won't be difficult," Oleg quickly replied. "I think they're interested in getting a better look at us."

"No, they're interested in getting a better look at the boat," Sauwa explained. "They could give a shit about who we are. That they're so keen to see if we're smugglers is no more than wanting to examine what supplies they can take away from us. If we pull up, let them look at our craft and see we're just some miserable refugees with nothing but some odds and ends, and they'll forget about us."

Smolesk maintained the pained look of a fearful man. He gripped the rudder of the boat tightly as if contemplating to run for it. He was deterred by Sauwa's disapproving look.

The boat slowly approached the city. What few lights existed showed the outline of a place that still seemed rooted in the middle-ages with an abundance of venerable old stone structures lining the river. It felt as if they had gone back in time. Sauwa half-expected to have their boat met with a hail of arrows or threatened by men in armor.

Only a few isolated lights lined the river. They offered no real visibility for anyone watching from a rock cliff above which worked in their favor. She glanced back into the darkness behind them hoping the other boat would not be discovered. It helped that the river was much wider here offering better concealment. They could make out the dug-in fortifications that guarded the waterfront entryway, a defensive position designed to repel land assaults and survive artillery attacks, prime weapons of choice for the Serbian army.

Judging from what she could see, most of the city sat on the rock cliff that gave little in the way of useful docking locations. It explained why there seemed to be a lack of security. They came to a rock plateau a little way past the sparse fortifications. A man waving a flashlight to get their attention called out.

"He's ordering us to land," Oleg explained.

"The other boat?" she asked again.

"They haven't said anything," Oleg replied then turned to Smolesk and issued instructions. Their boat shifted toward land and the waving light.

As they docked, they were met by a small group of men armed with Kalashnikov rifles. The men closed in from all sides in a rough semi-circle.

Both Oleg and Smolesk tried to explain themselves to the shadowy figures.

Sauwa took the opportunity to look around. The river snaked as it went through the city. A few lights scattered along the top of the cliff didn't give much assistance to anyone braving the shallow, rock-lined waterway at night. The lights also inhibited anyone watching the river from above at night from seeing clearly. It was Sauwa's hope that between the lax security and the lack of illumination their comrades would have a fighting chance of sneaking through the city.

She turned her attention back to Oleg and Smolesk and the negotiations with the men surrounding them. Guns were not trained on them nor were they being pulled violently from the boat as they tied up. Sauwa took that as a good sign and kept quiet. Already dressed in civilian attire, she had discarded her rifle and kept her arms tightly folded across her chest, hoping to look vulnerable and terrified. If they were to sell the refugees act, she had to play the scared little farm girl.

Her ruse seemed to pay off. The guards gave her only a quick glance before deciding she was harmless. The flashlights moved passed her. They shined their lights over the entire boat, satisfying themselves that the recent arrivals had nothing of any value.

She had begun to think they were in the clear when the search was interrupted by the appearance of a figure who remained in the darkness behind the others but asserted a commanding presence acknowledged by the other men. She recognized his voice as the one who had originally called out to them.

The big man said something that had Oleg and Smolesk scrambling out of the boat. Sauwa started to follow suit but was stopped by the extended hand of one of the guards. Confused, Sauwa looked to her comrades.

"They said that they have more they wish to discuss with us," Oleg explained. "Important matters so they said to leave the woman here."

Sauwa took the situation as a moment of reprieve. Not speaking the language or looking the part of an ethnic Croatian, the less attention focused on her the better. She sat back down in the boat. The men lost interest in her. She directed her attention toward the river, the scared farm girl's eyes darting everywhere. In reality, she wanted to see if the other boat was through the city.

She couldn't see them but in the distance, she could make out the faint sound of oars dipping into the water. It sounded like the boat was staying well to the center of the wide river avoiding any light that could possibly give them away.

Feigning fatigue she turned her head back to the men on

the shore. They had walked a good distance away and crowded around Oleg and Smolesk.

Oleg's voice was easily decipherable as he took center stage. Whether it was a flair for the dramatic or seizing the opportunity to distract the security men's attention from the river, Oleg played a role that kept everyone's attention locked on him.

Pressing her arms tightly around her body Sauwa leaned against the rail of the boat and waited.

Several minutes passed before her comrades returned with a couple of the guards trailing close behind.

"Well, they seemed to have bought off on the idea we're just hapless drifters passing through," Oleg said, his voice was low and nervous.

"What is it?" Sauwa inquired. "You don't sound sure."

Leaning in inches from her ear Oleg whispered, "You were right, I think. These men are not to be trusted. The conversation they had with us centered a lot on the weapons we are carrying. They only half believe we simply acquired them in our travels. They keep probing for any knowledge of guerrilla groups operating upriver. In truth, I think they are looking to press us into service with their army."

"Then we continue to play ignorant and bolt the first chance we can," Sauwa replied. "What is their mood so far?"

"They seem unimpressed with us looking as ragged as we do. Most of the men seem inclined to let us go and be done with us. Their commander — the big one — on the other hand, remains suspicious and persists with questions. They want us to go get something to eat with them."

"Do it," Sauwa urged. "I'll wait here. Get some fuel if you can. I'll try to go up the river and meet you on the other side of town."

"What are you advising?" Oleg asked confused.

"We need the fuel. If they think I'm here with your craft, then they won't give it a second thought when you and Smolesk leave in the opposite direction. They wouldn't believe you would abandon me. None of these men think a helpless little girl is a threat or could fare well on the river alone. They should leave me alone and forget about me. We don't have any goods to offer, so the boat is worthless to them. And, as you say, they're looking for fighting men. The most they see in me is someone to cook or help out with the washing. Besides, if I go up there, they'll see I'm not Croatian, and it won't take long to figure out I'm a foreigner. When that happens, our story will fall apart."

Oleg nodded his head and keeping to his role snapped at her in Croatian. His tone was commanding. She could only assume he was giving her orders for the benefit of the guards observing from a short distance away.

She gave a helpless nod.

Oleg sauntered back to the group of men. As anticipated, they all headed back up the hill toward the city.

22

Sauwa waited, allowing time for the men to withdraw. Then she plotted her move.

The remaining guard had also waited until his comrades were out of sight before he ceased his casual patrol loops and drifted toward her, a shark scouting prey. He made an initial pass in a casual way. Then, feeling more emboldened, he came in close to the boat making a few gestures that indicated a more intimate interest in her.

Not wanting to put a soon to be rapist on the defensive Sauwa continued playing the role of a terrified, helpless girl, while she slipped her hand behind her to retrieve her Tokarev pistol. Removing it from her belt, she rotated it in her hand until she had the magazine butt upside down clutching it with her fingers firmly around the trigger weld and her palm pressed against the upper receiver.

Moving her hand to her side Sauwa waited for the inevitable attack. The guard was speaking to her, his tone sly, nefarious. Any doubts she had about the man's intentions evaporated. Playing to the man's feeling of superiority she trembled and whimpered and backed toward the edge of the boat.

He set one foot on board invading her space slowly to ensure she felt trapped with nowhere to go. Sauwa raised her free hand above her head in a mock-feeble attempt to defend herself.

This drew him closer. He lunged and grabbed her free hand. His other hand groped for her crotch, while she sat pinned to the rear of the boat.

She couldn't risk the noise of a gunshot, so she went for a more silent means to dispose of her attacker. She drove the muzzle of her pistol into his temple with a powerful stabbing-like blow. The blow dazed the man forcing him to release her other hand. She immediately wrapped it around his head pressing his face into her chest to silence any outcries. She repeated the stabbing blows, again and again, pounding the pistol's muzzle into his temple with all the force she could muster.

The guard's body went limp and his cries of distress stopped. From her sitting position, Sauwa was able to slide one leg off to the side. Pressing her foot against the boat, she used the momentum to lift the guard's lifeless body off her and put him over the side of the boat and onto the rocky shore.

Normally she would have punctured the target's lungs eliminating any remaining air before dropping the body into the river so it would simply sink to the bottom. But she didn't have the time nor did she want to risk alerting anyone if the body should drift the wrong way. It was better to leave the corpse where it was in the darkness to be discovered in the daytime after they were long gone.

Not wasting any time she released the ropes from the

rock they were tied to. With a thrust of her foot, she shoved the boat out into the water, retrieved the oars, set them into the locks, and quietly dipped them into the current. With light strokes, she headed down the river keeping well to the center.

Slowly she paddled past the city dipping the oars on each stroke with cat-like precision. She listened and watched overhead for any sign she was attracting attention. People, mostly men, shouted or conversed. A man lit a cigarette near the water's edge. Another appeared to be taking in the last of the view in the dim light. Otherwise, there was little activity going on close to the river. The only security was a few scattered sentries arbitrarily placed, who seemed more occupied with unruly pedestrians.

The lights above were erratic in the way they were positioned leaving several places on the river in pitch blackness. She peered out at the barely visible jagged rock formations guarding both river banks. The boat was surrounded by rubber tires to protect it against just such a threat, but there was a possibility of riding too close or too fast into the rocks making either too much noise when the boat crashed or getting the boat jammed up in the knife-like fragments. Trying to get a boat free in the dark with menacing individuals responding to the commotion was not an option she cared to ponder.

The current wasn't strong. It wasn't enough to gain speed, but it was enough to keep her boat moving when she was hesitant about rowing. Every so often she would stop rowing when she caught sight of someone standing over the cliff. When the individual left, she would wait a while before resuming her course. Every so often the boat came close enough to the edge to scrape up against the rocks. Thankfully, the scrape amounted to little more than a bump, the sound of the current was able to mask the noise.

She had made it to the center of the city when she came to a bridge. Like the rest of the structures, the bridge was made of stone with an ominous looking castle-like tower on one side and a smaller structure guarding the other side.

She ceased rowing. The boat rode on the current while she gazed over at the bridge, studying it. Silhouettes of people walked back and forth. Perhaps they were guards or simply people out enjoying the evening. In either case, they could sound the alert if they caught sight of her, a concern intensified by the floodlights pointed down from the far side of the bridge toward the water.

The floodlights were inadequate for the lighting task. There were just two, and they only covered small patches. They were stationary which implied no one was actively manning them, but they were enough to pose a threat.

A chill went up her spine as she got close. She reminded herself the other boat had already gone up this river presumably undiscovered. This gave her some small relief as she floated on.

Rather than risking people on the bridge hearing the sound of paddles, she decided it was wiser to let the current maintain her momentum. The slow pace of the craft, however, only built tension and anxiety. She remembered the words of her mentor, Devon Williams. *Patience was sometimes a virtue but lingering in a dangerous situation was always a great risk.* The longer she was near the floodlights, the better the chances someone would catch sight of her, and she would be a sitting duck.

She forced herself to remain calm. Above her, men were talking. Their tone suggested a leisurely conversation. One of them chuckled, easing her tension as she passed under the bridge.

Suddenly a sharp, burning pain seared the back of her neck. She almost jumped to her feet and screamed. Almost. She resisted the fierce urge to do both and gritted her teeth, remaining silent. Out of the corner of her eye, she saw bright red sparks floating in the air and her nostrils caught the odor of cigarette smoke. She touched her neck to investigate the pain which vanished as quickly as it had come. Her hand grasped some cylindrical object lodged in her collar. Someone above had flicked the remains of their lit cigarette — the bastards — and she had been the ashtray.

Angry but relieved, she dropped the irritant into the water. The boat was now under the bridge. The second beam of light lay ahead directly in her path. Lowering one of the oars in the water, she swerved just in the nick of time to avoid it. Now at an angle, she lowered the other oar softly swerving yet again to get back on course. She felt the boat brush against the rocks before she pulled it back out into the center.

A cold sweat covered her brow, and her heart was thumping wildly as she drifted out of the range of the lights. More idle conversations above told her she had sneaked through successfully. She started rowing again.

23

An hour later, Sauwa arrived at the far edge of the city. The security was virtually identical to what she had encountered when she first entered Mostar with emphasis placed on defending against ground threats. This left the waterways largely undefended and usable for an escape.

Finding a safe location along the shoreline, Sauwa guided her boat to land. She found a spot by a small plateau that led up to the city. She moored the boat at the far end well away from anywhere she could be discovered protected by trees and other vegetation.

It wasn't the best plan, Sauwa thought to herself as she waited. Neither Oleg nor Smolesk appeared to have ever been to the city. They'd had limited time to hash out an arrangement with the other boat, and she couldn't stop thinking about what could go wrong. There was no way to be sure her comrades would know to come to this particular spot. They had no pre-arranged time — nor definite place — to meet up with the others, if indeed they had successfully gotten through.

What lingered in her mind was the dead guard she had left behind. If he were discovered, her team would get blamed, and Oleg and Smolesk would be dead in an instant. She would have no way of knowing until security went on full alert, and by that time she would be trapped.

She realized it was no use fretting over things that were out of her control. All she could do was assess her current situation and work from there.

Studying the landscape, she established that the hill wound from the cliff line above down to the river line. If her comrades were to come her way, they would come from that direction. Pivoting, she observed the area she could make out with her limited visibility. She tried to predict any other directions Oleg and Smolesk might choose. Aside from her current location, no other point in the general vicinity could be used.

They knew to meet her at the edge of the city. She had landed on the same side of the river where they had initially landed. With limited ways to cross the river on foot, they would still be on the same side when they came looking for her.

Her next consideration was how she would contact them when they were trying to find her in the dark. A flashlight was too dangerous. She contemplated whistles or a loud whisper, all of which she dismissed as impractical given how close she was to a security point. Besides, she had no knowledge of what security elements or who else might be lurking in the darkness nearby. Eventually, she resolved to play it by ear when they arrived.

She was tired from rowing and leaned back in the boat to rest. Now motionless, the night chill bit at her. The sweat from her nervous energy had soaked her clothes, and the dampness was not helping. Hugging her shoulders, she tried to get warm resisting the urge to grab a blanket because she had to remain able to move promptly in the event her comrades arrived and they needed to flee.

It was a long half hour before she caught sight of two darkened figures — men searching for something — standing on the cliffs above her. Sauwa held fast, not quite sure they were her two friends. The figures stood at the edge of the cliff for a considerable time. Then they made their way down the winding trail toward the river carrying large objects which made their decent an awkward affair.

Progressing down to the plateau, they disappeared into the darkness. Sauwa could trace their movements only through the sounds they made. Eventually, they re-emerged into the scant light looking around nervously when they reached the river. Convinced they were Oleg and Smolesk, but needing to be sure, she grabbed a small rock and tossed it in their direction. It caught their attention with a sharp thump.

"Sauwa?" The smaller of the two called out in English using a heightened whisper as he turned in her direction.

"Oleg?"

The two men rushed to the boat. They dropped the containers they had been lugging into the stern and jumped in, practically landing on top of her.

Oleg pushed her to one side, and Smolesk took up his position at the motor. She had no time to ask questions before Oleg kicked the boat out into the water reaching for the oars. He was about to drop them into the water when Sauwa cautioned him by pointing out how close they were to the defense perimeter.

As Sauwa had done, Oleg rowed with gentle, quiet

strokes as they departed the land and headed for the perimeter barriers. No one said anything as they neared several shadowed figures manning the guard points.

Smolesk remained at the motor ready to fire it up at the first indication they were discovered and had to make a run for it. They watched the glow emanating from the flood-lights on the river. The lights remained stationary, but it was on everyone's mind how easily that could change. The boat only needed to be seen once, and a barrage of gunfire would follow.

They passed the perimeter, hearts pounding, eyes staring straight up. None of the silhouettes moved beyond their routine gestures, yet all three guerrillas held their breaths in anticipation as they got close to where the floodlights were aimed.

Sauwa had the same feeling she had felt so many times in her life when she was inches away from death. It was the cold sinking sensation of coming to grips with your own mortality. Their deaths would be instant.

Inch by inch, they passed the wide beams of light. Time stopped. Every stroke seemed to take hours rather than seconds. The lights did not budge from their positions. With every second gaining more distance, their sense of relief became stronger. Sauwa could hear Oleg start to chuckle. His strokes became stronger, and he rowed faster. Even from the other side of the boat, she could feel Smolesk begin to loosen his grip on the motor.

When they turned a bend and the city was far behind them, Sauwa flicked on the flashlight and Smolesk started the motor.

Oleg decided it was safe enough to start speaking. "We were worried we wouldn't find you. We weren't even sure you would be there, because it was taking us so long to find what we needed. Then we had to make our way through the city without looking suspicious. You must have been waiting for a long time."

"Not too long," Sauwa replied. "Trust me when I say my circumstances were not that much better when it came to getting to the other side."

"Difficult?" Oleg pressed expecting an answer.

Sauwa grimaced. She didn't want to give them an explanation but knew she was going to have to. "I killed one of the guards while trying to make my escape."

"What!" Oleg exclaimed, almost shouting.

Sauwa turned to look at him and was about to explain when Smolesk chimed in. He hadn't been able to follow the conversation between his two comrades since it was being carried on in English, but when Oleg had jumped with surprise, the older man demanded an explanation. Oleg obliged him. Once Oleg responded, Smolesk groaned and leaned back against the boat.

"We'll never be able to go through that way again," Oleg grumbled. "We still have to get back to our people when we sell these supplies and that means having to go through this all over again. Killing our own people is not something easily forgiven, especially if they discover that we had smuggled anything past them. You really couldn't have used any other method than to kill the guard to make your escape."

Sauwa could feel Oleg glaring at her even in the darkness.

He continued, "I should have expected this. What more could have been expected, when I leave such a situation in the hands of a psychopath. Murder is the way you deal with everything."

Sauwa's voice was calm and quiet. "I would have used less controversial means; however, I was left few options once the man attempted to rape me. He tried the minute you all left."

"A convenient situation for you, I'm sure," Oleg hissed angrily.

Sauwa didn't reply to his comment. Her dead silence created an uneasy atmosphere in the boat.

Oleg reconsidered. "I apologize. I understand you did what you had to do. Even if he had not tried to attack you, killing him might have still been necessary. Smolesk and I were under intense scrutiny from the commander. It was only when he was distracted by more important affairs that we had a chance to escape, find some fuel, and follow the river to the end. If you hadn't been here when you were, we would have been killed or pressed into their army. In truth, looking back on it, we barely escaped. I hate to say this about my own countrymen, but you were right. They would have seized our goods if they had known about the other boat."

"As long as we're all good then," Sauwa replied. "You are right. You won't be able to go through Mostar on the return trip." She had come to the same conclusion earlier.

Oleg nodded. "I was hoping you might have an idea for an alternate path going back since the river is becoming a less viable option."

"I'll have to think about it. Until I have better intelligence regarding the overall state of the region and the conflict, I couldn't give you anything of value."

Oleg nodded, though it was apparent he was annoyed not hearing a plan instantly. He turned and spoke to Smolesk translating their conversation.

Half a kilometer down the river, they saw a flickering light emanating from the river bank. A communication system had been established between the two boats using a series of flickering patterns with the flashlights in the event the two parties were separated in the dark and had to identify each other. Sauwa recognized the pattern and responded with a flickering of her light.

Smolesk didn't wait for an order. He steered the boat in the direction of the light. This alarmed the other two who wanted to approach with greater caution.

Soon they were by the river bank where a voice materializing from the darkness. Oleg cheerfully replied. Sauwa turned her beam in the direction of the voice and was excited to see their comrades moored along the bank looking in the best of health. There was a quick exchange of pleasantries and conversation and an exchange of adventure stories.

It took a little prodding from Sauwa to get the guerrillas back on their journey. She feared with all that had happened in the city, it was unwise to remain so close.

2 4

S auwa awoke to the usual icy chill, the chirping birds, the pinkish-orange crack of light emerging over the hilltops, and the now familiar scratchy blanket once more found thrown over her.

Smolesk observed her with a paternal look of affection. It felt strange to be seen by someone who wasn't viewing her as a mercenary or a potential plaything. Even stranger, she found she actually enjoyed the older man's doting concern.

Sitting upright she could see the flashlight placed at the head of the boat offered a well-lit view of the river ahead. She cursed herself for having fallen asleep during a dangerous operation. People were depending on her. She needed to be more attentive and not let such things happen.

As if reading her mind, Smolesk spoke to her. She was unable to interpret fully, but his words seemed kindly directed and meant to put her at ease.

"You have done a great deal for us," Oleg translated as he arose from his own slumber. "He's saying you shouldn't punish yourself for not always being the consummate professional soldier. The responsibilities you bear and the risks you undertake on our behalf are more than many people could handle. If you have lapses after all this, it should only be expected."

She turned back to Smolesk and nodded her thanks to him. His words did make her feel better. Yet, she was a soldier, this was a war, and moments of weakness were not acceptable when someone was counting on you.

She stretched and groaned, her joints and back protesting. Her body ached from both the wood deck and the awkward position she had been in while sleeping. Something as simple as a bed, not to mention a warm meal, seemed like a heavenly dream.

Oleg passed her more dried meat for breakfast.

As the sun came up, the land became more visible and soon the boats were heading to shore so the fuel tanks could be refilled and the motors topped off. Finding a patch of land that provided reasonable concealment, the guerrillas secured the boats along the river bank. No sooner had they landed, than a delegation from the other boat made their way toward Sauwa and her trio.

Oleg met them standing on the lead boat his arms extended with one of the fuel cans which they quickly grabbed. They took the second can with the same zeal and part of the delegation departed swiftly to tend to their motor. The remaining men carried on a conversation with Oleg for a time. The topic did not seem to require her assistance, nor did Oleg pause to translate.

Sauwa jumped off the boat and took up a comfortable spot next to a large tree to enjoy the remainder of her breakfast.

A short time later, the rest of the delegation returned to their boat. Oleg sat down next to her looking weary and a bit frustrated. Sauwa picked up her canteen and sipped some water. Smolesk finished pouring fuel into the motor and hunched over his own meal.

"They're concerned about the bodies," Oleg said. "There is some contention regarding what to do with them."

Not knowing if he was speaking to her or merely talking out loud Sauwa said nothing.

He shifted in her direction but kept his gaze directed out at the water which gleamed with the light of the sunrise. "Some of them want to dump the bodies because they take up space and will become a health hazard when they start to decompose. Others want to see them brought home to their families. I'm not sure what we should do." He looked at Sauwa with expectation.

"It will be hard enough getting to the end of this journey. Dead bodies are excess baggage we don't have the luxury to carry with us." Sauwa capped her canteen. Her own gaze was fixed on the river. "Even if you decide to stay with the rest of the men, as you have said, it won't be easy getting back, and the bodies will be even more of a burden. I don't like discarding fallen comrades either, but you have precious little to work with and a lot of obstacles ahead. Keeping the fallen really isn't an option."

Oleg ruminated uncomfortably for a time. It was clearly not the answer he had wanted. No leader wanted the burden of this kind of decision.

Sauwa stayed quiet. They both knew her volunteering to make the call herself would only make the situation worse. The men would be angry with one of their own giving such an order, but a woman — a foreigner —doing so would be an utter insult and a sure path to mutiny.

Sauwa sat back as Oleg hoisted himself up and went over to where the men were gathered. It wasn't long before tempers started to rise. Eventually, Oleg managed to reassert his authority. While a few retained their angry looks and stares, they all yielded to his control and backed down.

A couple of them diverted their eyes in her direction seeing her as the force behind having their comrades' remains dismissed so disrespectfully. She responded by casually lowering her rifle across her body, and placing her hand loosely near the trigger mechanism. She did this while delivering a cold stare back at them. The men who thought to exercise their anger on her quickly lowered their gazes.

The men went to the boat and carried the bodies onto land. They grimaced bitterly as Oleg and another man cut each stomach releasing air or body fat that would enable the corpses to float. Not having any shovels, or much time, they gave the dead a funeral then lowered the bodies into the river. It was yet another decision that did not sit well with some of the men. Afterward, the guerrillas watched in silence as the dead disappeared into the murky green darkness.

Sauwa respectfully stood at the correct time but opted to keep her distance during the funeral. She reminded herself she was still a mercenary, a soldier-for-hire who happened to be in their employ, not a loyal patriot fighting a passionate crusade like they were. This was a personal time for the guerrillas, a private ceremony to honor their dead. Her presence demeaned that in the minds of several of the men.

After the sendoff, the men went about their activities in a daze going through the motions. They finished servicing the motors and ate their breakfast. Given it had been another long and harrowing night, Oleg — with Sauwa's advice — decided to give the men a few hours of rest before they set off again. Since she had already enjoyed a brief respite, Sauwa offered to stand guard while others got some shut-eye.

As the men pulled out blankets and found places on the soft dirt to sprawl out, Sauwa picked up her rifle and walked the area circling their location. She ascended a small hill overlooking the bank and cut through the bushes.

Carrying her rifle at the ready, she tramped through the trees scanning the distance for movement. Further on, she lowered herself to a knee, closed her eyes and listened. Nothing.

Rising to her feet, she set out again moving along the perimeter. The surrounding area was relatively spartan with trees and bushes well separated from one another. It reminded her of places she saw in the English countryside when she had been there. It was beautiful but hardly strategic. She enjoyed a clear view of the area but had little protection from anyone who was lurking. Devoid of any camouflage, she would stick out in her jeans and flannel clothing.

Still, recce complete, she decided they were reasonably safe. She slid back down the hill along the river bank. There the trees and bushes were much thicker giving her better protection from anyone who might be observing her from across the river. She stopped a couple of times to look across the way, scanning for any suspicious movements. After a while, she was satisfied they were alone.

Making her way back to where the guerrillas were resting, she climbed up the hill once more until she could just see over the crest. The men were all fast asleep; even Oleg, who was sprawled out on the ground just a few meters from where she was.

In the quiet, she nestled into some bushes to remain out of sight, keeping guard.

A t noon, the boats were back out on the water with the motors buzzing at a steady pace.

Sauwa took the opportunity to catch a nap. Given the icy attitude toward her by some of the guerrillas in the other boat over the dispatching of their dead comrades, she felt for the time being it would be safer to sleep in the company of Oleg and Smolesk in the isolation of the lead boat.

The journey continued calmly enough.

Now, well inside Croatian controlled territory, they found the landscape more civil and orderly. Armed patrols and soldiers had given way to civilians trying to re-establish their lives and communities. The guerrillas relaxed and smiled more and enjoyed short exchanges of pleasantries with their countrymen. Villages they passed were peaceful, and a few times the locals even invited them to join in an afternoon meal or offered some other form of hospitality. The hot, well-cooked food came as a godsend for the guerrillas who had been subsisting on a diet of dried meats and some edible plants since embarking on their river escapade.

The friendly faces were a welcome change from the adventures and narrow escapes that had started their journey.

In a few villages, local women befriended Sauwa, taking pity on her — a poor girl roughing it with smelly men. In one case, they even arranged for a hot bath. It was a luxury she was not about to pass up.

Also during this time, the mood of the guerrillas lightened toward her. Those who had been bitter about the treatment of their dead warmed up, accepting her back as one of the group. This made life easier, but she still remained on guard and kept her distance.

Though they encountered rough waters or the occasional small waterfall that required a workaround, they crossed into Croatia in a few days. It was a milestone that met with much rejoicing by all. Surprisingly, they found virtually no security at the border. The few security officials they came across waved them on the second they heard their native language. The guards assumed the boatmen were Croatian fisherman or peasants going about their daily business. To avoid any trouble, the guerrillas hid their weapons, burying them under blankets or other articles.

Along the way, they bartered for more fuel and supplies. When they broke into materials meant for trade on the black market, Oleg protested. "Those would have brought a good price."

"Which will count for nothing if you never reach your destination," Sauwa pointed out.

"You may as well take food out of the mouths of our children," Oleg whined, then whined again to Smolesk in Croatian.

Smolesk snorted and turned away. With no audience to listen, Oleg was left to mourn his loss of profit in silence.

When they reached the city of Ploce, a town of about ten thousand people, that sat on the Adriatic Sea, it felt as if they had once again gone back in time. The city lay just a few kilometers north of where the river fed into the sea. In the distance, the city presented a spectacular view. It was well preserved having seen little damage from the war that had been waged only two years before. Far from being the pinnacle of their journey, it represented the culture and heritage of Croatian society that the guerrillas took so much pride in.

"I have a cousin who lives here," Oleg beamed, his bad mood discarded. "I want to track him down and see if he can arrange a better means of travel into Montenegro."

"If you can, that would be great," Sauwa replied. "I really wasn't looking forward to attempting to move flat bottom boats down the coastline." She had initially assumed the worst case would be to take the river boats out to sea but stay close to the shoreline. Even then, it would be a long shot for the boats to make it without confronting some other serious difficulty.

At the mouth of the river, they moored the boats.

"Stay here and guard the equipment," Oleg ordered his men — the Croatian vocabulary familiar enough for Sauwa to understand.

He and Sauwa left for the city. To avoid scaring the locals or draw attention to themselves, they left their rifles behind. They tucked their pistols into their waistbands hidden under their over-sized shirts to distort any outlines the guns might have created.

Confident they looked nothing out of the ordinary, they trekked the short distance across an open field and around a couple of small rolling hills. Initially, Sauwa was apprehensive about coming with him; she couldn't understand the language very well at all and looked nothing like a Croatian. She capitulated only after Oleg persisted stating she would be a benefit.

The journey through the town was a pleasant one. The villagers went about their daily affairs and paid no attention to them. It was as if they had no idea a genocidal war was raging just over the border. The town was small and compact, the buildings nuzzled tightly together. It was divided by the river fed by the sea that the guerrillas had used. On the other side were the residential homes and buildings with smatterings of small businesses. A marina full of boats lined the seaside. On the other side lay the large shipping port that accommodated the cargo ships entering their harbor every day.

The two strolled the narrow roadways viewing shops and stores full of merchandise and produce. It had been a long time since either of them had seen such a display, which was a stark change from the hard world they had just come from. Oleg addressed anyone who engaged them with a warm smile and friendly greeting which made it easy for Sauwa to be overlooked and dismissed.

They made their way through town, then strolled down a row of apartment buildings a block from the marina with spectacular views of the sea.

"This is it," Oleg said in front of the fourth building along the tidy lane.

The entrance opened to a long, dark hallway running the length of the building with doors lining both sides. Two steps into the hall, a figure emerged and slowly walked into the light. Oleg's eyes widened as he recognized the figure and suddenly leaped toward the man throwing his arms around him in a friendly embrace. When Oleg released him, the tall, lanky man leaned against the wall as they traded greetings. This must be the cousin. The stringy man was in a pair of grey sweat bottoms and a flimsy, white buttoned shirt covering his malnourished frame.

Sauwa looked down the hall confirming the cousin was alone.

"Sauwa, meet Victor," Oleg switched to English, his cheeks flushed from the exuberant exchange.

Victor, maintaining his grin, waved the two guerrillas further inside the building. Oleg followed behind without hesitation, while Sauwa fell in last, pulse raised, guarded. She fingered her pistol and darted her eyes from side to side ready for any signs of a trap.

They walked a short distance down a small, dimly lit hallway then up a narrow flight of stairs. The two men spoke continuously. Trying to get a feel for what was happening, Sauwa listened. All around her were the sounds of other tenants echoing from behind the doors.

It wasn't just her survival instincts that made her uneasy about this meeting. She didn't like the setup. It was strange that, with no prior warning, this cousin should be so conveniently there to meet them, especially given he lived on the top floor.

Along the way, other tenants appeared in doorways and in the stairwell. They cringed and backed away at the sight of Victor.

She had seen this condition many times in her past dealings with the black market. The countries may be different but the setup was usually the same. And, like those other times, everything about the situation told Sauwa to be leery.

Oleg paid no attention as he happily carried on with his cousin.

Reaching the top floor, Victor led them to the far end of the hallway, dove his hand into his pocket, produced a key, and unlocked the door. Sauwa followed the men inside, remaining alert and cautious, and keeping her distance.

Neither man seemed to notice her behavior.

The room looked like a prison cell with drab, grey concrete walls and a poorly carpeted floor. It was decorated with mismatched western furnishings that looked both expensive and gaudy against the dreary eastern bloc, communist construction.

Sauwa strolled to one corner of the living room, a position where she had a full view of all entry points and windows. She leaned casually against a solid wall so no one could sneak up behind her.

The men plopped down on the plush, Italian sofa and continued conversing, oblivious to everything else.

Neither man noticed her reaching under her shirt to slip her pistol into her hand and proceed to move it behind her back. The room was small enough she would have little time to react should a threat present itself. She wanted to limit the number of obstructions between her and her weapon should it be needed.

Changing positions, she found a more advantageous spot in another corner near the windows. From there, she was able to view the area outside.

The room, the furnishings, the reactions of the tenants — as she took in details, a picture came together, and Sauwa's hand on her pistol began to relax.

Victor was a smuggler, possibly more, but a breed of man with whom she was familiar. She had crossed paths with many criminal types of all shapes and sizes — an image of the charming Banker, from her job in Dublin, sprang to mind — and she knew what motivated them, knew how to deal with them.

While Banker had mixed a bit of style into his nefarious dealings, Victor oozed. More importantly, from everything she saw in the room, discretion was not something he practiced. He would be someone known to the authorities. If that were the case, she worried their arrival at this place would have piqued the interest of the local gendarmes.

She peered outside again—careful to stay out of view—and scoped out the surroundings below. If the police were keeping an eye on Victor and had an interest in his associations, they would likely have some sort of visual surveillance.

The small plaza across the street, wedged between two grey concrete buildings, offered no good places for a long-term surveillance mission. Sauwa's next concern was the pedestrians walking below. She directed her focus on anyone who stopped for any period of time, or who took up a position where, if they looked up at Victor's apartment windows, might be able to see anything. No one looked to be taking an interest in Victor.

The conversation concluded with the cousins embracing each other warmly. Victor led his cousin and Sauwa to the door. They said their goodbyes one more time before Oleg nodded his head toward the hallway, beckoning Sauwa to follow him. She did so, sliding her pistol under her flannel shirt to conceal it. She turned to Victor, smiled and kept walking backward keeping her eyes on him until she was out in the hall and the door had shut leaving her alone with Oleg.

Oleg jaunted down the stairs, exuberant. Sauwa managed to keep pace as she stuffed her weapon back into her belt and pulled her shirt back over it.

Outside, Oleg was all smiles. "I knew my cousin could help us," he stated triumphantly. "He has a boat that can accommodate our load and carry all of us. He is familiar with the place we need to go and has the means of reaching out to the people Marko wants us to get in touch with. This will make it easier for us since we won't have to be alone in a foreign place trying to deal with all this business."

From what she had seen, Victor had the ability to make grand promises. The man was clearly an operator. Whether he cared for any cause not involving a profit was doubtful.

She had not been privy to the discussion and was not in the mood to place her trust in a sleazy stranger based solely on a blood tie. On the other hand, in light of their limited options, she had to admit they wouldn't be much better off if they chose to undertake the mission alone. With boats ill-suited for coastal waters, going to a place none of them knew, and dealing in a world they were not versed in, Victor presented a possible solution, for better or worse.

Sauwa and Oleg made their way back to the boats, circumnavigating the village, zig-zagging their line of travel over the hills and fields and setting in among shrubbery in a modified hasty ambush to see if they were being followed.

When they arrived back at the boats, they found the rest of team lazing about oblivious to the world. No one had even noticed their approach until Sauwa and Oleg were upon them.

Oleg — arms waving, chest puffed out — recounted the results of the expedition to the group amidst whoops and cheers.

Sauwa took a seat on the grass and watched the small celebration. For them, it was an achievement: medical supplies and much-needed material for their people back home. For her, it was nearing the end of one life and once again entering a world of uncertainty.

2 6

E vening was approaching when the boats once more
were launched into the last leg of the river and made
their way out to sea. As if he were a general leading his men
in battle, Oleg was at the front of the boat propped up on
one knee peering at the water ahead. In the distance to the
north, the lights from Ploce harbor winked over the
guarding hills. The waves of the sea belted the sides of the
boats spraying the hapless occupants.

Flashlights guided their way. Though the water was not
rough, it was choppy, causing the boats to separate from one
another. Using the oars, the guerrillas worked to stay
together, so the boats would not get lost or go unspotted by
Oleg's contact.

She had asked Oleg what he knew of the Croatian coastal
security in this area. Given they were emerging from the
mouth of a river that ran through most of Bosnia and lower
Croatia, she assumed this area would receive some degree of
attention from the authorities.

Oleg brushed her off. Victor had assured him local law

enforcement was an inconsequential threat. She didn't think Victor was the best intelligence source, but she had learned — while with the CCB — you often had to work with the resources available to you. For the guerrillas, Victor's connections were it.

That didn't stop her from scanning for security patrols.

They had been out in open water less than a half hour when they saw a circle of lights from a boat some distance away. Oleg picked up one of the larger flashlights and flicked it on and off in the direction of the vessel. At first, it looked as if the boat had missed them or was not inclined to acknowledge them. Then a larger light flashed brightly in their direction. Soon the vessel was moving their way.

Sauwa clutched her rifle. It was too soon to be sure who they had just contacted, and she prepared for a possible gun battle. Within a few meters, the boat became more visible. It was a fair sized, ocean-going commercial fishing boat.

She could hear Smolesk heave a sigh of relief. Apparently, Sauwa was not the only one fearful of this unknown engagement.

The fishing boat pulled up closer. A man stood against the railing of the bow holding an electrical bullhorn, his voice booming. The excited looks of her two comrades suggested there was no longer any doubt who they were dealing with.

Oleg cupped his hands around his mouth and shouted back a reply over the noise of the fishing boat's engine and the lapping waves. It must have been adequate because it garnered a response from the man with the bullhorn. The larger fishing boat moved up tight against them and cut the engine.

With Oleg playing diplomat, Victor skillfully directed the

operation of shifting both people and equipment from the humble flat-bottoms to the more formidable sea craft. The two smaller boats were tied to the railing. Given the efficiency, this was not Victor's first expedition of this sort. Once all the equipment was loaded and the guerrillas on the fishing boat accounted for, Victor gave an order to the crewman steering. The engine of the large craft roared to life, and they were moving again.

The fishing boat crew cracked open ice boxes and offered the guerrillas bottles of beer. The guerrillas grabbed the bottles and drank gratefully. Sauwa remained back taking a spot in the corner. For her, it was far too early to begin celebrating.

The various men comprising the crew appeared to be no different than their employer. Rough and sordid. She fingered the outline of her pistol through the fabric of her shirt as she scanned the rest of the ship. The pistol would be easier to get to than her AK-47 rifle strapped behind her back.

They might be professional pirates, but their skills as combat operators were amateurish. The men in Victor's employ revealed assorted tell-tale signs about their lack of tactical prowess. One of the men who passed by her had a revolver tucked in a side pocket in his coat. It was visible even in the limited light. As deep as it was buried in the twisty cloth, it would have been impossible to pull out quickly in a critical situation. Likewise, the knife he carried in his belt was a long, serrated model that would have proven equally cumbersome to pull quickly. It was a K-Bar tactical knife that looked more impressive as a combat instrument than it actually was. The man was obviously more show than practical knowledge judging from his arsenal and the way he chose to position it on his body.

Other men mulling around carried themselves in a similar fashion. They were probably criminals, but men with any sort of viable military background they were not. Hopefully, if things did go badly, she could exploit this weakness.

AN HOUR later the door leading to the hull cracked open. Victor emerged, followed by Oleg, who looked haggard. Oleg was breathing hard and appeared to be in a cold sweat.

Sauwa was about to confront him when she saw Victor take his cousin by the shoulders and speak sharply. Oleg nodded at first. Eventually, he took Victor by the forearm, looked at him with a penetrating glare and spoke firmly in return. Victor responded with an abrupt nod before patting his cousin on the shoulder and walking away.

Seizing the moment, Sauwa walked over to her comrade. "Everything okay?"

Oleg looked out onto the water with a thousand-yard stare. "Victor just informed me that he received news that NATO has begun landing their forces in Bosnia. According to him, they have begun seizing the border to control crossings. It looks like we just barely made it out." He accepted a beer from a passing crew member and took a long pull.

Sauwa felt a cold chill shoot down her spine. If what Oleg said was true, she had just barely escaped capture.

For a time, he stayed quiet, focused on the waves. When he spoke again, his voice contained a tremor. "My cousin says it's just more death in a life built for death, and I should not let things affect me so much."

Another drink. He slumped over the railing, his breath wheezing out of him. "War takes everything, doesn't it? What it doesn't destroy, it corrupts. And, now it has taken my country with foreign invaders."

He smiled bitterly and finished the bottle. He reached over and took her by the arm. In the inadequate light, Sauwa thought she saw the glisten of a tear in the corner of one eye. "You're a good friend," he said, "and a valuable ally." He released her arm and walked off, disappearing down the man-way.

Sauwa returned to the corner to watch and think, but not too much. Oleg's words threatened to call up her own demons, but she couldn't think about that now. Oleg had told her NATO had landed and was moving to assert control. It wouldn't be long until they were sending intelligence missions over the border to stem arms trafficking and search for those identified as war criminals. The longer she stayed in the region the more dangerous it became.

A crew member ambled over and dangled a beer in her face. He yammered away in Croatian striking a macho pose to impress her. Sauwa blinked, unresponsive. When the crewman got no encouragement, he wandered off.

Smolesk came and sat beside her. He smiled at her through his bushy mustache and shooed away the next drunk male trying his luck. Thankful, she allowed her head to lean against Smolesk's burly shoulder. They sat together, saying nothing, long into the night.

THE NEXT MORNING Sauwa awoke with a slightly groggy head. It was punishment for not getting a full night's sleep.

Sliding from the thin mattress on the metal framed bed, she nearly fell over trying to balance in the lurching boat. She collected her Bergen and slipped her flannel shirt over her cold shoulders. She patted her waist to feel her pistol, then walked by the long row of double-decked beds. Everyone was fast asleep.

The night's activities had taken its toll on them all. She didn't like the idea of sleeping in such a place, having concerns about how easily they could be trapped down below. But there was nowhere else she thought would have been any safer. Given Victor's crew was crashed out in the same lodgings, she felt it was probably her safest spot.

She slid out the door with minimal noise and started down the narrow hall which was lit by a succession of small lights. Finding the shower room, she seized the chance for a quick shower. The warm water and privacy was something she savored in the brief time she had. Feeling clean, she dressed and made her way to the galley.

To her surprise, she found Oleg alone at one of the tables picking at a plate of food and sipping what she took to be a cup of coffee. Moving over to the table, she took a seat directly across from him. He barely noticed her for the first few seconds.

"We'll be making port later this evening." He opened the conversation in a curt, businesslike manner. "We're going to Herceg Novi," Oleg stated curtly.

"Herceg Novi?" Sauwa asked.

"Yes, it is a small coastal town near the border. It has several thousand people and a sizable boat launch. According to Victor, it's a good place to conduct business one doesn't want the authorities to be involved with."

Sauwa furrowed her brow then asked, "Is that the place Marko arranged?"

"Marko is not here!" Oleg seemed angry. "His knowledge was old. I'm the one in charge of this mission, and my cousin is the one who knows this place, this world, and the people who do business in it.

"Peacekeeping soldiers are beginning to pour into the region and assume positions in locations known as staging points for running weapons on the black market. We have to be careful where we go to sell our weapons. We don't want to be picked up by western authorities. An issue I'm sure you are concerned with given your dire situation."

Oleg let his fork drop to the plate. It clanked against the tray getting her attention. "Since Victor has made our job easier, I'm trusting him and his experience. Don't worry, I've spoken to him about you. He will connect you with people who will get you to a bigger port and to where you need to go. He says there is a great demand for a person with your skills and abilities. If you don't have a place to go, he will find you suitable employment in your area of expertise."

She looked at him suspiciously, not entirely satisfied with his answer.

Oleg grimaced. "Look, I know you don't trust my cousin. But, he knows this market, and Marko doesn't. Neither do we. As I see it, we have few options to work with, wouldn't you say?"

He was right, she didn't trust Victor. Begrudgingly, she admitted they had few options available.

A part of her felt the need to press the matter. A last minute change in plans with so little information would normally have peaked her instincts for survival forcing her to be more alert. However, the continued stress from the arduous journey and lack of sleep had left her exhausted. She was still very preoccupied with her own concern for the uncertain future she would be facing in the next few hours. At some level, she had accepted that the Croatians were concerned with their own problems, and she was no longer part of it.

She supposed Oleg's sudden attitude change was due to his own nerves. He was frazzled from the long, arduous journey and trying to assert himself as a strong leader to his tired troops. Then, just maybe, after the last few years of being hunted and having only strangers pushed into her life, she was just desperate for some kind of meaningful friendship. Or, desperation had blinded her to the reality that her supposed friend and the others still saw her primarily as a hired mercenary. She didn't want to think about it anymore. In the next few hours, it wouldn't matter.

Oleg returned his attention to his food.

Better to give him a few minutes. Sauwa rose and went over to get a plate of breakfast.

The galley cook, a gross, obese man who made no attempt to hide his lusty interest in her, served her a meal of sausage, eggs, and a few vegetables. As she walked away, he grunted something that she couldn't make out but understood it was intended for her.

Oleg glared at the man with a near murderous rage.

"Something tells me the comment was less than complimentary." She sat back down with her food.

"He noticed you had come from the shower. He was saying how if he knew you were in there, he would have made a point to catch a peak."

Sauwa didn't bother to turn around. "That's original."

Oleg was still glaring.

"Are we at all worried about coastal patrols?" Sauwa asked as she tried to change the subject.

"Not at the moment," Oleg replied. "Croatia is still recovering from the war. They have limited resources and whatever police exist out here are few in number. They will likely overlook a simple fishing vessel. If they do not, we are close enough to the border that we could evade them easily."

"Won't they simply catch your cousin when he comes back over?"

"Oleg shook his head." I asked that. "According to my cousin, the police patrolling the waters have limited communication capabilities and horrible methods for maintaining reports and collecting intelligence. All they need to do is wait in Montenegro for a day. When they come back over, they will be dealing with a different patrol, one who will have no record of the activities incurred by the previous unit before them. They will be dealt with as if it's their first time crossing. NATO will make changes, of course, but it will take days or maybe weeks. Victor will be long gone by then."

Sauwa thought it sounded like a well-considered plan. Slowly, she ate her meal. "What about the authorities in Montenegro? I know you said we should be all right in Herceg Novi, but what about the time before we get there. We still have to deal with the coastal authorities in Montenegro, don't we?"

"They're in just as bad a shape as Croatia. Between the devastated state coming out of communism and the difficulty the country has had attracting foreign investments because they are so close to three countries engaged in a genocidal war, they have few resources and a police system that is primitive, to say the least. All the coastal cities here are little towns and villages that are incapable of hosting shipping traffic of any consequence, or a large and wealthy enough populace to make a black-market worthwhile. They prefer to focus their energies in the south where smuggling affords more lucrative seizures. It's also the reason so many black marketers prefer to do more complicated dealings around here."

"Sounds like we're in the clear." Sauwa was impressed. "That's why we're selling or trading wares here as opposed to in the south?"

"We're trafficking military weapons. It's not the same commodity as drugs or luxury items. Trafficking weapons tends to garner more trouble from the authorities given it attracts the attention of governments who don't want to see them in the hands of terrorist or exacerbating other hostile conflicts in the world."

As the conversation dwindled, Oleg's bad mood seemed to soften. He cleared his plate and left her to finish her meal alone.

Sauwa scraped up the last morsels of her breakfast. Begrudgingly, she had to admit that the pig of a cook made a delicious meal. Grabbing her kit, she was making her exit when she was confronted by Smolesk's bedraggled figure leading the guerrillas into the galley. His hair, long and unkempt, flared wildly about his head. He looked like an extremely tall and gnarled version of Albert Einstein. He smiled through his puffy mustache and patted her on her head then went to eat. An entourage of guerrillas and crewman followed behind him.

Outside, the clean brisk ocean air smelled fresh and gave her a sense of freedom. The sun was just rising in a grayish-blue sky revealing the landline. A cool breeze wafted through the atmosphere catching her by surprise as it swept over her body.

Aside from the crewman manning the helm, the above decks were deserted. The only other person topside was Oleg, who leaned over the bow appearing to admire the view. He motioned her to come and join him.

She stepped up alongside him and leaned against the railing.

He smiled at her for the first time since the night before.

"I should warn you," he began. "Micha has not given up his dream of accompanying you when you leave."

"I didn't think he would," Sauwa sighed, gazing out at the scenery.

Oleg continued. "He pleaded with me last night to speak to you on his behalf and see if I couldn't get you to change your mind."

Shaking her head Sauwa kept her attention on the sea. "I'm not sure what my future holds after this. Contrary to what you may want to believe, this is not my chosen occupation. I'm out of this life the second I can be."

Oleg looked directly at her, his smile gone. "I promised him I would make the pitch to you again. I want to know, if he asked to come with you, what would your answer be?"

Sauwa tilted her head to face him. The expression on his face was serious; one that told her he demanded an answer.

"I would tell him no, of course," she replied.

Oleg turned away to look back at the sea, somehow disappointed with her answer.

27

They had reached the waters off Montenegro several hours before. Not wanting to risk attention by entering the harbor in broad daylight, Victor had driven the craft around in arbitrary circles to eat up time. Once night began to fall, he navigated his boat toward the Herceg Novi harbor.

It was dark when the fishing vessel docked. Aside from a few lights coming from houses in the hills and a few more greenish blue ones posted along the small harbor, there was no sign the town was even occupied.

Having stayed close to the steering room all day, Sauwa knew neither Victor nor any of his crew had used the radio at all. They were either winging this last minute change like a bunch of idiots, or had prearranged their plan well in advance. Based on how experienced Victor and his men had proven to be so far, she decided it was the latter, a fact which raised her confidence in his abilities and her concern over his intentions in equal measure.

Victor had taken control of the helm for the movement

toward land. By the way he skillfully navigated with limited visibility, it was obvious he had made this trip several times in the past.

Unconsciously, she fingered her pistol and mourned the lack of access to her rifle, which was locked deep in the hull of the boat along with the guerrilla's other weapons. This was to avoid unwanted attention should they happen to be stopped.

There were few other boats tied along the wooden dock, which made it easy for such a large craft to slide in. The boat landed with a curt thump, and all the guerrillas were out on deck waiting attentively in hushed silence, preparing for the next step. As a bunch of village farmers turned fighting guerrillas, they put on hardened faces and tried to look as if they weren't novices conducting their first black-market deal.

Victor convened a hasty meeting with his cousin in the steering room. The door was shut leaving the two of them alone. Sauwa waited just outside her back pressed against the bulkhead adjacent to the door. The meeting came to an end with the cousins marching through the door. Victor looking triumphant, while Oleg looked defeated.

"Everything alright?" Sauwa asked as her comrade passed her.

At first, Oleg seemed dejected, then he looked at her. "Everything's fine. Victor was just telling me we aren't going to get the bargain I had hoped for, that's all."

The small amount of respect Sauwa had begun to feel for Victor and his operational skills vanished. The weasel would not think twice about stealing from his own cousin, changing the deal at the last minute, taking advantage of a group of desperate guerrillas in need. She felt her face flush hot and started to take issue with Oleg's willingness to accept whatever deal Victor saw fit to make for him.

She followed both men down the ladder well onto the main deck where everyone was waiting. Oleg moved to the center of the group and began addressing them. He had shifted to a happy confident demeanor. As he spoke, the rest of the guerrillas nodded excitedly. Taking the crates containing the merchandise, they began unloading them onto the docks.

Concerned that Oleg was putting the guerrillas further at Victor's mercy, Sauwa approached him. "Shouldn't we keep the stuff on the boat? If things should go badly, we can make a quick getaway and not risk the possibility of losing it."

Oleg shot a cold glare in her direction. "Woman! I know what I'm doing. So does Victor. This doesn't concern you anymore."

She backed off, distracted by a subtle engine rumble somewhere in the dark. The Croatians finished unloading the crates. When they were done, they filed off the boat onto the wooden scaffolding.

Victor had broken away from the crew. Now he motioned to Oleg who took Sauwa by her arm. "I need you to come with me," Oleg said quietly.

"Where?" She asked still clocking the vehicle.

Oleg followed her glance. "Victor says we're meeting his contacts in a nearby boathouse." Oleg explained. "The three of us are going to go check it out. If there's any trouble, I want you close. There may be NATO security in the area so we must be careful."

She didn't like it. There were too many unknown variables. And the reminder of NATO sent shivers down her spine. Oleg seemed to read her mind. He barked orders to his men, presumably to move the goods back on the boat. Then he tugged at her arm. "We need to hurry."

They walked several blocks before arriving at a house, which sat away from the docks. Aside from the greenish blue lights strung over the doorway, the place looked deserted. Sauwa reached under her shirt and gripped her pistol while the Victor and Oleg moved slowly toward the door.

Victor knocked.

They had not seen a soul on their way from the docks, including any sign of security or a police presence. Sauwa positioned her feet in a firm stance ready to jump into action at the first sign of trouble.

Further away, she heard the truck engine shift, growing louder.

The boathouse door creaked open, and a voice from the shadows spoke. It was a deep male voice. He traded words with Victor briefly, then opened the door the rest of the way. With a wave of his hand signaling them to follow, Victor headed inside. Obediently, Oleg trailed Victor, nodding his head for Sauwa to follow.

Sauwa's instincts screamed at her to run. To go into the small confines of a dark room with men she didn't know went against all of her training and her own common sense. Except this was not about her. It was about the guerrillas, waiting on the dock for the payout that could support their families to the end of the war.

She peered past Oleg into the boathouse where a yellowish light from a small lamp hung from the ceiling. Oleg entered and left the door open. Sauwa stepped into the doorway and stopped.

Men were gathered around a table directly under the

light. Victor and Oleg were seated beside a grizzled looking man with a frazzled salt and pepper beard. He was wearing a camouflage field jacket, the same pattern worn by the Serbian army.

Oleg remained silent as Victor and the grizzled man talked like old friends. Eventually, Oleg rose from his seat and came to the door.

"Everything is alright," he said curtly. "Please, come inside. Someone might see you out there."

She kept her hand on her pistol and stepped inside. The house was an old relic that appeared not to have any particular use. Aside from the table, the place was empty. Shutting the door behind her, Sauwa made a quick scan of the premises. There were no other doors and only one window on the far side.

Moving around the table, she positioned herself in a corner where she had direct sight of the door, but out of the way, so she was not in the immediate line if someone should come bursting in with a gun. She shifted her gaze from the window to the door and then to the grizzled man, who was looking her over with deep interest.

Victor and the grizzled man resumed their talks, interrupted by a chirp resonating from the grizzled man's foot. Bending over, he retrieved the small handset from what appeared to be a ham radio and spoke into it. He received a response from a crackling voice on the other end. As the conversation went on, Oleg rose from his seat and moved over to where Sauwa was standing.

"Those are his people contacting him," Oleg whispered into her ear. "They're telling him they are coming into port with their merchandise to trade. He's telling them where to go right now." Oleg looked down at this hands. "The docks

are clear. We'll be heading out to meet the contact shortly,"
Oleg paused. "You'll be getting on the boat with them."

There was no way she would trap herself on a boat with
these men without a solid understanding of who they were
and their plan of action. "Does he have anyone who speaks
English so I can communicate with them?"

Victor and the grizzled man reached a break in the
conversation. They shook hands and the tone of the room
changed.

Oleg shrugged. "At this point, it doesn't matter."

Sauwa felt the change, but was unsure what it meant.
Her mouth went dry. "What are you saying?"

Pointing to the grizzled man, whose eyes had not left her,
Oleg said, "He wants to know if you are indeed Sauwa
Catcher, the former South African assassin."

Sauwa's eyes lit up. She had never divulged to the guerrillas who or what she was. Shaking her head, she looked
back at Oleg. "Tell him he's got the wrong person?"

Oleg was about to turn back and interpret when the grizzled man stood. "I already know you are Miss Catcher, the
notorious assassin." The man's English was heavily accented
but polished and showed signs of someone who had spoken
it for many years. "In fact, when Victor told me about you, I
had to come to see you for myself."

Oleg's eyes were wider than hers. She couldn't tell if it
was the shock of the man speaking English or that Oleg had
just realized he'd been working with a "notorious assassin".

Sauwa had two seconds to consider how much Oleg
knew of Victor's deal before the piercing sound of multiple
guns went off from the direction of the fishing boat. Shortly
after, blood-curdling screams joined in with the gun fire, a
sound she was all too familiar with.

Drawing her pistol, she moved for the door when she felt something hard smack her across the side of the face. She dropped to the ground dazed. The next feeling was an equally powerful blow knocking her pistol out of her hand. She rolled over. Oleg stood over, desperate. She turned retrieve her weapon. Victor snatch it up. The grizzled man, Victor, and Oleg pinned her to the dirt-caked floor boards.

The gunfire and screams continued.

"Oleg, the others!" She cried as she attempted to get up and was quickly forced down by Victor's strong hands gripping her arms. Her Bergen prevented him from getting her all the way onto her back.

"The others are dead," Oleg knelt down on her lower body, pressing on her legs that were kicking like scissors. "They always were dead."

"That's bullshit. That's the line of a two-bit smuggler."

"I'm done with this fucking war," Oleg growled. "I'm taking my payday, and I'm going my own way."

"The camp, your people; they are depending on what you bring back. You can't just abandon them."

Oleg's face went from cold to dismal. "There's no one to abandon."

She processed his words, trying to piece together what he was telling her.

"A few days after we left, the Bosnians began a purging campaign. It has been well reported and received a great deal of attention. We were in too remote of an area to find out about it until we got to Ploce. When we got on the boat, Victor showed me the newspapers. The Bosnians found our camp." Oleg stared at her, his eyes accusing. "You taking out the Iranian, all our training and preparation. None of it mattered. They killed everyone."

He choked on the last words. A high pitched laugh escaped him, then he pulled himself together. "So you see there is nothing to go back to. And the others? I'm sparing them the pain of having to find out all their loved ones are dead."

Sauwa felt sick to her stomach. She began to breathe hard.

For all his emotion, Oleg kept a tight hold of her legs. "After Victor told me what had happened, I decided I was done. I'm taking these guns and enjoying my split."

"How far do you think you're going?" Sauwa growled through her teeth. "That's not a large amount of hardware, hardly enough to live well."

"Oh, you're right," the grizzled man chimed in casually. "Market value, I would offer maybe seventy thousand U.S. for the lot. On the other hand, I found you. The infamous Sauwa Catcher, the Apartheid's most lethal assassin, and covert operator and one of the Croatian army's most gifted mercenaries. You are in high demand, young lady. There are certain interested parties that would like to have your services at their disposal and are willing to pay handsomely to have you delivered. For that, I'm paying well over half a million in U.S. dollars to these two fine gentlemen."

Sauwa's mind was awash with fear and outrage. The men had her pinned. They had her pistol. Her rifle was on the boat, a boat now loaded with bodies of the men she had been hired to protect. She had never felt so helpless.

Together, Oleg and Victor rolled her over onto her stomach and tore off her Bergen. Her face scraped against the floor. She managed to ram a heel into someone's thigh. She wrestled, and made it as hard as possible for them, but it was useless.

"Check her sleeves," the grizzled man ordered. A quick check showed she had no knife or other sharp objects. Satisfied she was clean of weapons, Victor held her hands as Oleg bound her wrists. Once restrained, she was hoisted to her feet.

The grizzled man led the way holding her Bergen. The two cousins escorted her out the door.

The screaming had ceased with it the gunfire. The night was deadly silent. Heartsick and defeated, she walked without resisting in the direction of the boat where the guerrillas had been.

Another vessel, one slightly larger than Victor's fishing boat, had pulled up alongside it. On the docks, several figures were managing the corpses of the dead guerrillas. One by one, they dropped the bodies into the water as casually as throwing out the daily trash. Smolesk, left until last, looked like a stitched doll sprawled out near the water, his wild hair matted to his face. His mustache dripped red.

Behind her, she heard Oleg heaving about to vomit. A few curt words from Victor put a stop to that.

"You going to be able to live with this, Oleg?" she asked through gritted teeth.

"Half a million dollars, I'm sure, will ease his conscience," the grizzled man said indifferently. He accepted a large canvas bag from one of his men posted on the vessel. He handed the bag to Victor, who bowed with gratitude as he took the bag and walked away.

"You should know you have their blood on you as well," Oleg whispered into her ear. "If you had considered taking Micha with you, I would have spared him and had him come with us tonight. Think about that."

"You keep telling yourself that, asshole." Sauwa responded with a disgusted look.

Two of the men who had been disposing of the bodies marched over to the grizzled man. On his orders, they grabbed Sauwa and forcefully escorted her up the walkway onto the mysterious ship. The grizzled man followed closely behind.

Sauwa took one last look at the men who betrayed those he had called his friends. The cousins reached their own boat. Oleg never once looked back. With Victor's arm wrapped around him, they vanished into the night.

S hoved through a door that led inside the grizzled man's boat, Sauwa was steered down a narrow walkway. The boat wasn't lavish, but it was well lit, clean, and more accommodating than the fishing cruiser.

Brought to a thick oak door secured with a reinforced lock, she was made to stand there while the grizzled man fumbled with some keys. The door opened, and she was ushered inside.

It was a relatively nice, warm, and well-appointed cabin, not the makeshift accommodations she had become accustomed to. Her two escorts rotated her until she was face-to-face with a large, gruff-looking woman in her fifties with the same salt and pepper hair as the grizzled man, who was standing right behind her.

"This is Katia," the grizzled man began. "You need to be watched, and since I have only men working for me, I asked Katia to accompany me on this voyage. There are times a woman is needed to negotiate the complicated matters that you present."

"I will make sure the men don't see you in compromising situations and make sure you cannot play such situations to your advantage," Katia said sternly. She towered over Sauwa and, by her athletic frame and stance, it was an easy guess that she was not simply a housekeeper, a governess, or a babysitter. More than likely, she had been an operative of some kind. And one who was more than able to deal with another skilled female assassin if it came to one on one.

The grizzled man had planned well and chosen his people wisely.

"We're going to untie you, little one," Katia said in a commanding tone. "When we do, you will undress. When you are down to your underwear, they will take your clothes, and I will finish your search myself."

"Search?" Sauwa did not like what she was hearing.

"Or, if you wish to be difficult, I can conduct a search of your body cavities in front of all these men. I'm sure they would enjoy the show very much." Katia was making it clear she was in no mood for any nonsense or protests.

Sauwa nodded.

Katia waved her hand, and one of the men came around behind Sauwa with a knife. The cold steel against her wrists sent a shiver up her spine. When the rope snapped, and her hands were free, she let them fall to her sides. With the older woman's approval, she raised her hands and began to undress. In seconds, her clothes were in pile on the floor, and she was standing in nothing but her bra and panties.

At the grizzled man's direction, the two men gathered up her clothes and exited the room followed by the grizzled man. He shut the door behind him leaving the two ladies alone. Katia performed a thorough search of her bottom, vaginal area and finally her mouth — unpleasant, to say the least. Naked, Sauwa was marched off to a bathroom and shower area.

"I want you looking like a young lady when you get done," Katia quipped and pointed to a collection of female hygienic and grooming paraphernalia.

The older woman stood by watching as Sauwa entered the shower. She remained present, directing the ritual of Sauwa's grooming: shaving her legs, under her arms, and applying creams and lotions. When she finished and met Katia's approval, she was escorted back into the main room where a simple t-shirt and silk shorts awaited her on the bed.

"This is it?" Sauwa asked, shocked at the skimpy garments.

"You're a prisoner who is worth a great deal of money," Katia said. "Injuring you would destroy your worth and cost us our investment. This way, you can't hide weapons, and you have limited places you can go. Now get dressed. Dinner will be here shortly. If you don't fight us, we will try to make this trip painless. Fight us, and I won't injure you, but I can make this trip very unpleasant. Do something that costs us our investment, and I'll drown you."

Dinner was a meal of bland vegetables, fruits, and a small portion of meat. Starved, Sauwa devoured the meal. When she was finished, she was escorted back into the washroom where she brushed her teeth and gargled with mouthwash. Then it was back into the bedroom.

"What now?" Sauwa asked, unsure what the tightly controlled regimen entailed next. She received no answer. Her eyes grew heavy and her knees grew weak.

The last thing she felt was the strong hands of her

watchdog directing her onto the bed. The soft wool blanket felt pleasant as she lost consciousness.

SHE AWOKE to the strange sound of a man singing over an intercom from a good distance away. Raising her head, she felt as if a cinder block had crushed her skull. Slowly she stirred from her bed, the singing rang quickly realized it was an Islamic prayer. Where was she? This question went through her pounding head, rattling her teeth.

It was an Islamic prayer. Where was she?

"Get dressed," a woman's curt voice took her by surprise. Swinging around, Sauwa saw Katia sitting next to her bed. "I trust you slept well."

When Sauwa didn't say anything, Katia cleared her throat. "Your dinner was drugged. I decided you would be easier to handle if you slept the whole way.

Feeling violated, Sauwa swallowed her protest. It would be futile and waste her limited energy.

Katia threw a pile of folded clothes onto the bed. "Wash up, then get dressed." Like last time, Sauwa went about the choreographed ritual demanded by her tender. Then, dressed in a pair of tan cargo pants, grey T-shirt, a blue jacket, and a pair of tan tactical boots, she tied her hair up in a loose pile behind her head leaving a few strands to dangle about the side of her face. Once finished, Katia escorted her out the door.

"Where are we?"

On the deck of the boat. They were met by a warm breeze. Sauwa looked around and gaped at the massive city.

The architecture, the smells, the earlier singing: she figured was somewhere in the Middle-East.

"Welcome to Izmir," the grizzled man said, appearing from out of nowhere. "We're on the coast of Turkey — your new home."

"Turkey?" her aching mind raced.

"Come, shall we." The grizzled man waved his hand toward the gangplank. She noticed he was holding her Bergen and wondered if he had gone through it. He seemed to be enjoying every minute of holding such power over her.

As instructed, she walked down the gangplank and came over the bow where a sleek, black limousine parked next to the boat. She touched the asphalt, and the grizzled man's hand pushed her firmly toward the car.

The back door of the limousine opened and out stepped a well-dressed man in a black tailored suit. It was difficult to determine his age with all the salon work, but she guessed he was in his late forties to mid-fifties. His features were soft yet, despite his manicured hands and expensive haircut, he bore signs of a man who had seen some hard living, a man with considerable military experience, a man who would be dangerous to underestimate in a fight.

This prince walked up to her and, through his shiny black sunglasses, looked her over. Sauwa felt like a farm animal at an auction. He then acknowledged the grizzled man who greeted him as if he really were royalty.

Grizzled man handed Sauwa's Bergen over while speaking in a language Sauwa recognized as Russian. Taking the Bergen the prince rummaged through it, paying no attention to the displeased look on her face. Giving a satisfied nod to the grizzled man, he handed her Bergen to another underling who had emerged from the front seat of the limo. The attendant took the Bergen and returned to the vehicle leaving his employer alone with Sauwa.

Minutes later the attendant appeared again carrying a leather satchel. He handed the satchel to the prince, and the prince handed it to the grizzled man, who snatched it up eagerly and opened it. With a quick look inside, the grizzled man nodded several times in appreciation as he spoke again in Russian. Then, with a sharp turn on his heels, the grizzled man raced back to his boat.

"Ms. Catcher," the princely man now spoke English. "I imagine this is all very overwhelming for you."

"Who, are you?" That was all she could manage to say.

"I'm Andre Valikov," the prince said. "I'm a former officer of the defunct Soviet army. Now I'm an entrepreneur…and your new employer."

29

P retoria South Africa:
It was a strange moment for David O'knomo when
he received a sudden invitation to join Charles Goodings for
lunch at the British embassy. Goodings' official title in the
country was Deputy Cultural Director for the British diplomatic mission in South Africa. It was well known that he
was the liaison to the South African intelligence community.

That Goodings had knowledge of O'knomo and his team
was not surprising. The mission of pursuing the infamous
Apartheid assassin, Sauwa Catcher and the other members
of the so-called Dark Chamber, had become of great interest
to the British government after they had learned the extent
of the unit's activities in their country.

The British took particular interest in Miss Catcher
because she had been a highly productive assassin on their
shores. Her status as a target was heightened a year before
when she was on the run in Ireland and left a trail of a dozen
bodies within a two day period before disappearing. This
was a huge embarrassment for both the British and Irish

governments. Afterward, the high ranking leadership in those intelligence communities determined that bringing the young femme fatale to justice was a priority if not a matter of honor.

When O'knomo entered the offices of the British High Commission on Hill Street, he was accompanied by Jamie Nawati, his right-hand man. He was not surprised to find a young woman waiting for him. O'knomo wasn't sure why he was being summoned by someone who normally engaged with the director level of leadership for his organization. He had assumed the lunch was a means to informally inquire about what information the South Africans had regarding the Sauwa Catcher pursuit. Based on her recent disappearance from Bosnia, they had suspected she had gone back to her old hunting grounds in Africa.

The young woman made quick introductions before leading the two men through the lobby, past security, and up a flight of stairs. They entered a large office lined with old turn of the century polished wood furniture. In the far corner sitting behind a large oak desk, sat Charles Goodings. His neatly trimmed silver hair and slightly lined face gave him the appearance of a man who enjoyed a mixture of adventure and good living.

Rising from his elegant leather chair, the old spy smiled as he moved around from behind his desk to where the two younger men stood. He gave them both a firm handshake and politely dismissed the young woman. "Gentlemen," he began, a thin smile on his face. "Thank you for coming. Would you please sit down?" He led them to a small meeting table that stood in the center of the room.

As asked, the two Africans took seats on one side of the

table. Goodings grabbed a briefcase from his desk then slid into a chair directly across from his guests.

"I take it this will not be an eating lunch," O'knomo quipped. He watched the Englishman open his briefcase and produce a thin manila folder that he promptly placed on the table in front of them.

"No, Mr. O'knomo, this is not," Goodings replied dryly. "This is cutting through the red tape in furtherance of a mutual goal. And, that goal is the eventual capture of Sauwa Catcher, the little psychopath your country created."

"I don't understand?" O'knomo said looking first at the Englishman and then at his colleague, Nawati. He thought perhaps he had missed something in the conversation.

Goodings shook his head. "Your government talks about open dialogue when it comes to information sharing. Yet, we find that you're still an operation as steeped in the toils of gradual change as the old government bureaucracy mixing with the intelligence elements of the former rebel groups. As a result, we find the higher echelons of your intelligence community is in utter chaos. So, after some discussion with my own superiors, we decided to come directly to you."

"What exactly are you coming to us for?" Nawati finally spoke up.

"Yes, what? If this is because you believe Sauwa Catcher is in Africa, and we aren't telling you…" O'knomo protested but was cut off.

"We know she was in Bosnia a few weeks ago," Goodings cut in. "We know that because the imagery of the location had caught pictures of her that we forwarded to you. She was in central Bosnia working for a French mercenary, one Maurice Augin. Then she suddenly dropped out of sight."

"This we already know," O'knomo stated still unsure about where this conversation was going.

Goodings seemed to ignore the African as he continued. "One of our planes conducting a routine aerial recce over Bosnia captured this." He slipped a large black and white photograph from the folder and handed it to O'knomo. The African carefully examined the blown up picture. It revealed a couple of boats along the river. What made it unusual was what looked to be a serious gunfight being carried out with another group along the shore.

When the African finished studying the picture, he handed it to Nawati as he returned his attention to the Englishman. Goodings continued. "Once we saw this, we decided it was necessary to continue monitoring these craft that at first looked to be just fisherman. It was during this time that we noticed one of them was female. "He produced another enlarged photograph that he handed over to the African. It showed a woman with long black hair wielding a Kalashnikov rifle. O'knomo showed it to Nawati who, after a serious study of the picture, nodded in agreement. It had to be Sauwa.

Confident the two men were in agreement, Goodings continued. "We tracked her boat down the river all the way to a coastal village in Croatia. We lost her again. We assumed they were in the village to do a business deal of a criminal nature. So, we did a little research and found out a man named Viktor Heisvic, known to deal heavily in the black market, lives in the village, We had our signal intelligence boys at the General Communication Headquarters monitor his phone conversations in his apartment and radio connections on his boat. We also found several references to a woman, a female mercenary, who was apparently quite sought after by someone who has been interested in paying nearly a hundred thousand pounds for her. To narrow down the playing field, even more, Mr. Heisvic referred to the young woman as the South African killer."

"Do you know who bought her?" Nawati again chimed in.

"We know these messages were intercepted just before the deal went into effect. The man with whom he was having these talks was a small-time arms broker named Mikael Gurov, a Ukrainian who deals mainly in small arms for local gangs around the Mediterranean. Not long after this, we received a report about some dead Croatians floating in the water near Montenegro. We assume the switch occurred there."

"I trust you're keeping tabs on Mr. Gurov in the hopes he will lead us to Miss Catcher's whereabouts, assuming she's still alive," O'knomo asked.

"You think someone else purchased her for the purpose of killing her?" Goodings exclaimed.

"In her area of expertise, you can't help but make many powerful enemies," Nawati explained as if speaking from experience.

"I don't think so," Goodings continued. "From what we've ascertained, Gurov deals in weapons. And from his conversation with Heisvic, it seems she was being spoken of as a weapon more than in the context of a reprisal."

"The path is clear." O'knomo's deep voice captured everyone's attention. "We investigate Mr. Gurov and find out who wanted Sauwa Catcher and why."

"And then?" Nawati asked.

O'knomo eyed both men before answering. "Then we bring her home by any means possible."

SO WHAT DID YOU THINK?

Thanks for reading!

Would you please take a minute to leave a review on Amazon?

Honest reviews help other readers make informed decisions about which books might appeal to them.

They also help me to better understand my audience, what I'm doing right, and where I might improve the reader experience in the future.

I greatly appreciate your feedback and your time.

—J.E. Higgins

ALSO BY J. E. HIGGINS

Want more Sauwa?

The Dublin Hit: Book 1 of the Sauwa Catcher Series

ACKNOWLEDGMENTS

To my family, Suzi Lamb, Bob Liepold and Arne Woodard, as well as the many others who contributed to the making of this book, I would like to give thanks.

ABOUT THE AUTHOR

J.E Higgins is a former soldier who spent 12 years in the US military, first as infantryman in the Marine Corps and then in the military police with the Army. He holds a B.A. in Government and a Masters in Intelligence; Intelligence Operations.

The Bosnian Experience is his second book.

You can reach J.E. Higgins at his website: www.thehigginsreport.com where he publishes monthly papers on international political trends.

Made in the USA
Lexington, KY
06 September 2018